Mary O'Donnell has been publishing novels, short stories and poetry since 1990 and her work is regarded as key in expanding the horizons of Ireland's traditionally male-dominated literary world. 'The Light Makers', Mary's debut best-selling novel, received the Sunday Tribune's Best New Irish Novel 1992 Award and her other published novels include 'The Elysium Testament' and 'Where They Lie'. Her most recent and highly praised collection of short stories, 'Walking Ghosts' was published in 2025.

Mary has taught Creative Writing at the universities of Galway, Maynooth, University College Dublin and University College Cork, as well as for the University of São Paulo. She has also held several prominent international writing residencies including at the Princess Grace Irish Library Monaco, the Irish College in Paris, and the Irish College in Leuven and she is a member of Ireland's affiliation of artists, Aosdána.

'*Sweep the Cobwebs Off the Sky* is a subtle, intricate and thoughtful study of life, of the painful process of ageing, of sibling rivalry and the vicissitudes of family. I have no doubt it will be a success with reviewers and readers alike.'
John Banville: author of Booker Prize winning, *The Sea.*

'This is a profound novel about the life of a dutiful daughter, caring for her once beautiful, charming mother – now suffering from dementia in her old age. The complex relationships of mother and daughter, and of sisters, are explored with compassion and sharp psychological insight. Perfectly drawn characters,lyrical but lucid writing, and above all an understanding of the love and hate, patience and intolerance, which can bind or destroy families, render this Mary O'Donnell's finest novel. Seldom has the role of the daughter as carer for the aged parent been so subtly and honestly portrayed. It's a masterpiece.'
Éilís Ní Dhuibhne: Laureate of Irish Fiction.

'A piercing exploration of the immemorial themes: family, memory and the desire to investigate the mystery of what holds us together.'
Colum McCann: author of *Let the Great World Spin.*

'Absorbing, meditative, and deeply attentive to the power of place – and to the long shadows that memory casts across our lives.'
Neil Hegarty: author of *Inch Levels* and *The Jewel.*

'*Sweep the Cobwebs Off the Sky* is a brilliant study of the blighted relationships within a family. In scenes that are deeply moving, and in moments that can veer from the tender to the tempestuous, it evokes the extreme feelings, vulnerabilities and contradictions of love that exist in all families. More than anything, O'Donnell captures, with vim and verve, the sometimes brutal love between a mother and daughter.'
Mary Costello: author of The Irish Times Bestseller, *Barcelona.*

'An intimate and searingly honest book that surely will stand amongst the very best of Irish novels.'
Christine Dwyer Hickey: author of *The Narrow Land.*

'An extraordinary, bewitching novel. Eccentric, irreverent and constantly, wonderfully, surprising. In Frankie, I was reminded of the fearlessness and self-possession of Nuala O'Faolain's *I Dream Of You*, and also of the style, the delicious wisdom of the protagonists of Elizabeth Jane Howard. But in truth – and can there be a kind of truth, as Frankie asks? – it is unlike anything I've read before. It gripped and nourished me.'
Belinda McKeon: author of *Solace* and *Tender.*

Sweep the Cobwebs Off the Sky

Mary O'Donnell

époque press

Published by époque press in 2026

Typeset in EB Garamond Regular, Regular Italic, Semi-Bold, Semi-Bold Italic & Retros Light.
Typesetting & cover design by Ten Storeys®

Printed and bound in Great Britain by
Clays Ltd, Elcograf S.p.A.

British Library Cataloguing-in-Publication Data.

A catalogue record for this book is available from the British Library.

ISBN: 978-1-0687162-5-6 (paperback edition)
ISBN: 978-1-0687162-6-3 (electronic edition)

Martin. Anna.

Always and ever

'Like sexual desire, memory never stops. It pairs the dead with the living, real with imaginary beings, dreams with history.'

Annie Ernaux: The Years.

'With the years, time has become my ally, as it does for every woman — I've become invisible, see-through. I am able to move around like a ghost, look over people's shoulders, listen in on their arguments. . .'

Olga Tokarczuk: Flights.

Sweep the Cobwebs Off the Sky

1

Kilnavarn House is something I carry with me forever. Kilnavarn continues. Kilnavarn resists. Kilnavarn, the family stronghold, lives on into its dreaming self as if it had the power to stop change. There were once three of us in the house. Before Tess. We arrived one autumn afternoon in a Morris Minor, several lorries lurching and tilting on the stony, tree-shaded, long avenue that rose ahead of us, our furniture stacked and strapped, two men holding it in place, flickers of golden sunshine catching their strong arms. I remember the doors on one wardrobe swinging open, and how I cried out in fear that it would tumble back on the car and kill us. Before Tess. A threesome with a playful, handsome father, who would throw snowballs at the window in winter to make me laugh, and a joking, funny mother. Strict, yes, but also funny, and with father there it didn't matter so much. Mother's dresses were a fanfare of unending summers. Gay skirts and blouses with red and yellow umbrellas and a blue sea, or green, silky ferns, shining buttons and a slim belt. Patent high heels I could play grownups in when cousins visited. Before Tess.

*

Even after Tess's arrival there remains something that sits brightly in my mind, which can never be erased. My mother and father, Elma and Paddy, at their best, throwing a winter party. Infant Tess upstairs in her pink cot and a baby-sitter brought in so that my parents can get on with the party, celebrating her arrival. I am allowed to stay up later than usual, but I race upstairs once and into the new baby's bedroom. The baby-sitter is playing with her, bobbing a soft stuffed rabbit up and down the cot, much to Tess's amusement. This is laid down in the bunker of memory as an occasion in which everything seemed colourful, happy. I race downstairs again and elbow my way through the big room with the long windows, past the little groups wrestling with their mushroom canapés, their skewered bits of pineapple and cheese, as they chat and laugh. It seems to me that adults laugh a lot when they come together. Some people lean down and ask me questions, or pass remarks about how tall I am. The kind of questions they ask are for the most part unanswerable. Isn't my new little sister a dote? Isn't she marvellous? Your Mammy and Daddy must be delighted that you have a little sister. Who do you like best, your Mammy or your Daddy? Do you like school? I field these questions as Elma floats around the room, in her element, making people welcome, dressed in a navy short-sleeved dress with a large polka-dot bow at her cleavage. She has done one of the things she excels at, having prepared a huge buffet. I eye the dressed salmon, jellied tongue, clove-pricked hams, the Russian salad, potato salad and garlic and vinaigrette dressed tomato and rice salad. The grownups pile their plates, pick up the napkin-wrapped silver cutlery, and move out into the room again. On a smaller table various desserts lie in a shimmer of glory, the raspberry mousse, lemon mousse, two apple tarts, a mountain of cream-filled profiteroles over which soft, warm chocolate falls, lava-like, pooling along the bottom of the platter.

What also stands out is that it is the first time I feel perhaps I have a brain. The Department Schools Inspector and his writer wife are also guests. Only the week before he has visited our classroom in the convent and asked if anyone could name a famous Greek monument. Silence. No comers. I had raised my timid hand and mumbled 'Pa-Pa-Parthenon'. That night I overhear him tell my mother that I am an intelligent child. I retreat back to the dessert table, stretch out and help myself to a lemon mousse with its little florets of piped cream. I am happy. My parents are happy. I am also smart and now my mother knows this and will stop calling me obtuse. As I scoop spoonful's of mousse into my mouth, I watch Paddy, who has just pushed open the long windows as the room is over-heated due to the blaze of coal and logs in the high stone hearth. He is puffing a pipe, nodding gently, smiling with some of his medical companions from the hospital. It is the early years of our time at Kilnavarn, a time which will, one day, pour us over into a new century, way beyond the moon landings, beyond 9/11, right into a present that is uncertain for everyone.

*

Now it is springtime twenty years into the new century and I'm more than grownup. I sing *Happy Birthday* to myself at the kitchen sink as I scrub my fingers. Repeat, I instruct, to prolong the finger-scrub for twenty seconds, stretched vowels and all.

I'm in bare feet. When the ditty finishes, I twist the tap hard to stop it dripping. The washer needs replacing. Behind the taps, two tiles are hanging loose, revealing mould. I dry my hands, then turn to the tiny bottle of hand sanitiser salvaged from the bottom of a handbag, and squeeze a few drops onto my palms, even dabbing it around the base of my nostrils.

It's not my birthday and these are extraordinary times. Hands, to be washed as many times as possible every day, preferably to a distracting tune that will last two minutes. *Happy birthday* sung twice is just less than a minute unless sung slowly. *Eleanor Rigby* might be better. Or *Soap your Arse and Slide Backwards up a Rainbow,* 1970s Dublin music-hall theatre, when times were also tough, albeit for different reasons.

The boredom of constant hand-washing will ensure that the virus continues to spread, as people grow lazy or forgetful. For all I know, I may contribute to this. Despite the Health Minister's scolding, I haven't the patience to prolong every single bit of washing and self-arming recommended daily — no, hourly — on radio and television. My actual birthday is mid-June, still months away. Overnight, I will become a pensioner, just like my mother. Elma could be at risk, but at her age she is at risk of many things. Am I concerned? Not in the slightest! Falling. Heart attack. Stroke. Cancer. Parkinson's. The sickness shelf is full of possibilities, yet none, apart from many falls, have struck my mother. When found after her falls, Elma always explains them away by saying she has been doing floor exercises.

I occasionally convey to others my views on the question of medicalising people of very advanced years who have a touch of dementia. The fact is, my own soon-to-be pensioner attitude reveals a pre-existing antipathy to both sentimentality and cruelty, both common companions where care of the old is concerned.

On one level, I have achieved something by default of age. That is, relative invisibility, occasionally annoying, but in general liberating. Not the kind of liberation I'd have sought in the past, but liberation has layers. For example, my views are no longer top-layer, can be half listened to by younger women, without being taken seriously enough to intrude on their unshakeable belief that they are the first to know anything.

All things being equal and relatively sane, I take pride in my ability to state a case, even on the sensitive subject of what is called *elder care*, which such women, often absorbed by the care of younger children, know nothing about. Nobody has yet frowned when I shake my head and murmur what a shame it is, this prolongation of elderly cardiac systems far beyond the time when the person whose cardiac system it is, can either think, remember, walk, or wipe their own backsides.

One of the tests of true adulthood is the ability to wipe a parent's buttocks without giving it a second thought. My first concern, though, is always this: *will Elma allow me to do it? Will she allow me to change her incontinence pants?* This is by no means something to be taken for granted. In old age my mother has polished her obstinacy so that it radiates, its emotional neutrons, beta particles and gamma rays sometimes striking others like a jolting current.

My bare feet are not yet chilled on the tiled kitchen floor. Still toasting from a night beneath the winter duvet, I enjoy the relief of coolness climbing through my lower limbs as I turn now to the day's first task.

It's time to feed the dog. In my mother's house, particular rules and strategies have long applied. Lottie is a traumatised rescue dog. Like any creature that has been beaten when young, she is easily cowed, terrified of men, and must be approached gently with a bowl of dog-nuts. I could say the same thing of myself, minus the dog-nuts, although I was never beaten. This bowl of food, to be laid on the floor beside Lottie's water-dish. No sudden movements. The slightest jerk or noise will send her skittering back into the second, inner kitchen to her basket beside the stove. This morning though, impatient me flings nuts to bowl with a grating clatter, and the dog freezes. Then I drop it roughly enough on the floor. The dog waits. She will not approach until I've moved away.

How many years now is it? How many years since Paddy's death from cancer, have I driven the three hours to spend a weekend with Elma? Eighteen years too many, I've calculated. No sooner did Paddy's death seem inevitable than Tess and I both realised that a future shared to some extent with Elma seemed daunting.

'How are we going to manage?' I remember whispering in the kitchen the day after the burial.

'Manage her, you mean?' my sister responded, the cheeks on her pale face drawing inwards as she smoked, blowing out in a fierce stream, 'She's fucking unmanageable.'

One year after Paddy's death Tess went to America, which infuriated me because it left me alone with Elma. At the time, we were naive enough to consider her seventy years to be quite ancient. I was optimistic, believing Elma would survive perhaps ten years, that she might reach eighty and then stroke out on one of the usual things that used to eventually whisk the elderly into the arms of Charon.

Twenty-two years now. I'm sixty-six, Tess sixty, and Elma ninety-two. There has been no stroke. Mostly, Elma cannot stand unaided, forgets the present and gobbles a saucerful of pills each day that ensure no strokes, heart-attacks or haemorrhages.

The dog has finished eating. I unbolt the back door and the animal charges out in a flare of claws across tiles, doorstep, old patio slabs, down to the deep lawn below the house. The buds on the lime trees have sprung open at last despite a niggardly, cold spring, with no loosening in its airs.

My stomach rumbles. What I would really like is to prepare some crisp, buttered toast, with the bitter marmalade Elma enjoys, and piping hot coffee, to carry these along the long hall that traverses the front of the house, and up the red and blue carpeted stairs, past the black oak grandfather clock at the top, around the corner where Tess and I used to hide or read as children, to Elma's bedroom. On the way, I would pass the unusually wide and draughty attic stairway which rises just to the left of her bedroom, and turn in to my mother's room. I try to imagine such a scene. It is, ironically, one of the best rooms in the house, the least cluttered with tokens to do with Paddy. Downstairs in the hallway on a time-shabby oak table with barley-twist legs, photographs crowd beside silver awards and trophies on which his name is cut, Waterford glass ashtrays and shitcunt crystal on which his name is also inscribed. Everything about Elma's adoration of Great God Paddy makes me mouth obscenities. Paddy's face smiles pleasantly and sometimes shyly in different photographs all along the mantle in the downstairs sitting-room. He was a good man, a gentleman according to everyone, but the endless memorialising is tiresome.

Continuing this dream in the Conditional Tense, I imagine how I would arrive in the bedroom and Elma would stir, then smile in a surprised way. I further imagine my mother probably in her mid-sixties, around the age I am now. I would lay the tray carefully on the bed, then draw open the drapes which Elma likes to have sealed completely at night. No chinks for moonlight or dawn light. Then she would sit up in bed and pull the tray towards her — civil, pleasantly surprised — as if this was something delightful and welcome. We would sit together on the bed, me perched on the edge as I sometimes did thirty years ago, on what was once Paddy's side, chatting and catching up. We could talk about the ordinary human events, many of them unimportant but still pleasant to share. People met, shopping done, who said what and what expression was on their face — Elma always enjoyed that kind of account — and the latest on my writing career. Elma understood my career mainly in terms of awards and recognitions, rather than the slow act of writing that underpinned it. And Elma could once again cough up the script of injuries and hurts done to her in her youth, which I once used to tolerate, before demanding more views from me on this or that person and, again, who said what. Elma had always demanded opinions and views of others; in fact she challenges and goads until she gets them.

It isn't like that anymore. I stand in the kitchen, kettle on the boil, deliberating in a patch of watery sunlight that spills onto my head from the high field above the house. The tap is dripping into the stainless-steel sink. I note how clean it is now, compared to a time some four years ago when everything my mother touched or handled became either broken, filthy or discarded. The question of domestic normality now seems as philosophical and remote as Hamlet deliberating on whether to be or not to be, or whether, in my case, to suffer Elma's sodden night nappy, which must be changed. Should I insist on changing it before I bring Elma her breakfast? This dilemma connects each day of the week, and is characterised by my mother's first mood-struggle. All she wishes is to be left alone to doze. And this morning, I'm really not ready for a wrangle. I'll leave her as she is and bring breakfast upstairs regardless. No matter what her state, Elma always insists that her nappy is dry. So let her have it her way. It could be worse. My mother is not violent now. But Elma's carer, Hilda, a lone woman caring for three children, has locked herself down, and I haven't yet found a replacement. I'll get through it. One day, I'll reach a point when I can, figuratively, weave Elma into a willow basket by the strands of her soft white hair, placing a single purple orchid in her hands instead of a Rosary. She'd prefer that, I'm certain.

2

I mostly miss Christoph, dearly loved German husband of over forty years. He has been up here twice over the weeks, sorting out plumbing problems, trimming shrubs, occasionally mowing the front lawn if Alex the gardener isn't around, then replacing the old mower when it finally packed in for good. God knows, the mower was almost as old as the marriage, but the marriage is in working order, I mostly think. When he leaves I feel I should be with him, should soon return with him to Tipperary. But somehow, it has not worked out that way. I feel obliged to see Elma along her way, especially now that we have been deserted by Hilda.

As I climb the stairs with the tray, I put thoughts of Christoph on a little shelf at the back of my mind labelled *To be dealt with later*. There is toast, coffee, half a peeled orange, the segments separated so that Elma can grasp them. Now the first whiff of the bedroom reaches me. Night breath. Urine. The cat, Jimmy. The black grandfather clock ticks heavily, all brass patience and gazing Roman numerals. You again, they stare archly, wobbling with trays up and down the staircase after all these years, trying not to unbalance. To the right of the clock, a four-foot statue of St Joseph, inherited from Elma's late sister Elizabeth. Although Elma is not religious, she has kept it as a memento of the peak years when the two vied and competed over everything, from clothes bought in Dublin or London, to domestic refurbishments. They were attached, just not in an ordinary sisterly way. St Joseph is wearing Elma's ash blond wig. Elma still misses Elizabeth, and her brothers, the salt and pepper of contrarian discourse which she always needed. There is no one to argue with now but me, and I have never quite understood my mother's rules of combat.

Crossing the landing, I glance up at the small triangular corner window that flickers the daylight in a strange uneven architectural blip considered a good idea by some early Victorian builder. Light from the east streams down. The boughs on the oak-tree are trembling. The wind is dancing up the hills. I can hear the soft *shoosh!* of it rising. There's comfort in these drumlin hills, although there have been times when I wanted them to fuck off for themselves, and me to drive as far away as possible from them.

The house itself always felt benign. The carry-on in my bedroom didn't even affect that. At the moment the room isn't quite behaving itself, but I can live with it. Sounds disturb me at night as I lie in the dark. Despite this, the house itself always carried interior goodness in soft drifts, the layers of each generation that had lived there seeping into the hand-made bricks. Those bricks have now been painted over five times during Elma's life, from 1959 to the present, having moved from cream to yellow to pink to orange and finally, for the past twenty years, to pure white, its whiteness touched up each spring by Lithuanian Alex. There have been climbing shrubs and roses, cut down with brutal pruning year on year, then thickening again until only in recent years have they begun to establish themselves freely. Already in this warming spring the leaves of the roses are itching around corners towards the southwestern aspect of the house, will bloom reliably before the end of May. This year above all, everything appears in better bloom because of the silence and rest enforced by the new sickness, that keeps most people at home. The sky is darker and deeper at night, the stars fierce and easily identified, the dawns more vigorous with clamorous birds. It is magnificent.

As I cross the landing I glance briefly to the left and up the attic stairway. I wonder about going up there sometime soon, if only to do the one thing I always enjoyed: standing to peer up and through the oculus window installed in the 1860s by the house's most adventurous owner, Roddy Boyd. Ah, Roddy, I think, pushing the door open to enter Mother's bedroom. As he made his way home from travels further afield, Roddy saw the Pantheon in Rome and, inspired by Marcus Agrippa's commission during the reign of Augustus, decided to erect the first oculus window in his own home county.

Elma is lying on her left side as usual, loosely curled, eyes closed. She wears a blue protective mask, the kind worn by mostly careful and informed people to the supermarkets around the town. It is upside down and the loop dangles off one ear. Automatically, I move to open a window. The cat lies curled at Elma's feet. He doesn't so much as raise his head but opens one eye and stares impudently at me.

'Don't,' Elma groans.

'The room could do with some air.'

'Just leave it,' she repeats. Then, 'You'll disturb Jimmy. He might get out on the roof.'

'He's a cat. He'll survive,' I mutter, approaching bed with tray. The teacup rattles on its saucer and some tea sloshes down, but I've brought a sheet of kitchen paper in anticipation of slops and spills. Jimmy stretches, arches his back, unsheathes his claws. Mother cannot push herself up high enough to balance the tray on her knee, and I'm not strong enough to elevate her, so I place it on top of the commode. The old woman slowly turns in the bed, pale blue eyes focusing on my face. I instruct myself. *I must roll the duvet back to help her.* Elma raises her knees then and attempts to turn to the right and to pull herself up. Her night-dress is tangled around her waist, but the night nappy has not leaked. I hold out both hands and Elma grasps them.

'Hold on now,' I encourage, 'let me do the pulling.'

'Careful,' a whisper.

'You won't fall. I won't let you fall.' My better nature rises to reassure her that she will not tumble off the bed, that I will hold her steady against the buffets of a lost sense of balance. Gradually, I manage to draw her forward until she can turn. I take her legs and lift them gently out over the side of the bed so that she can sit, then prop her with four pillows. The commode serves as a tray-stand and is rarely used for its proper purpose. Recently the Health Board released a range of such treasures needed as much as five years before: safety rails and shower chairs, a wheelchair and the brown commode. Christoph had already put up handrails and had ordered a stair-lift. Finally, after a tumble down the stairs from top to bottom, during which Elma broke nothing but looked like a bruised aubergine while recuperating in hospital, the Health Board got the message. The fall tipped Elma into moments of mild dotage. But mostly, she is lucid.

A string of words with unpleasant connotations dangles in the air around her, around all of us really. Dementia. Early onset

Dementia. Alzheimer Syndrome. Going gaga. Losing it. I prefer to say that my mother has memory loss. I bristle defensively when people speak of the diseases of cognitive decline as if it could never happen to them, as if they too know best about everything, and about how to handle the old. They speak of 'they' and 'them', as in 'Sure they love the céili music in those nursing homes,' but never think of the Stones, Sex Pistols or Dire Straits although those homes from home are full of old rockers, the blades and chicks of decades ago, now imprisoned till the end.

Elma loathes the word 'old'. I consider it a valuable word that deserves a fair situating in the chain of life, that should have equal respect, at least as much as what the middle-aged claim for themselves. They who know everything, I reflect, considering some of the still itching-with-hormones-career-and-partner-changing forty and fifty-year-olds of my acquaintance.

'And maybe remove the mask?' Gently, I unwind the elastic from Elma's other ear and place the mask on the far pillow. Her white hair is trailing in coils on her shoulders.

'I'll want that later,' Elma says. 'You can't be too careful.'

'You don't need it here in the house, Mum. We're all safe here.'

'Are you sure about that?'

'Yes. But put it on again if you want. Better still, I'll bring a fresh one. They're supposed to be changed.' Despite myself I am smiling.

'Good girl,' Elma replies. 'It was always a safe house, wasn't it?'

I don't reply to this. She sits on the edge of the mattress, gasping slightly. I remind myself, *I must bend now to slip on her sandals.*

'You shouldn't be doing that. Stop now,' Elma tuts.

'You need to put on your sandals. You could slip without them.'

'You still shouldn't be bending like that,' she replies. The strange thing about my mother. She finds the sight of a daughter, kneeling with head bent and fiddling with sandal straps, somehow undignified. As if this simple act of service offends her because she considers it beneath anyone in the family to be serving someone else.

My inventory of tasks includes shopping, cleaning the kitchen, bringing the dog or cat to the vet, adjusting the central heating yet again because home-carer Hilda keeps switching it to a constant setting and oil is being wasted. The house feels sub-tropical. I also unblock the drain, fix the lock on the front door, change bulbs, change the fire-alarm batteries when they begin to pip, and clean up dog-shit as needed. The cat's litter tray must also be emptied and refilled. Then more shopping. Fixing. Changing bulbs. Paying Alex, phoning electricians, repeatedly calling plumbers. It is an ailing, crumbling house, never damp thanks to the heating, but in the morning, I sometimes smell lake-water and mist, as if they breathed through the crevices. The scent of decaying leaves, slippery fronds of vegetation, reeds and bulrushes.

I leave Elma to her breakfast, telling her I'll be up to make her more comfortable afterwards. A euphemism for whipping off the night nappy, wiping my mother down quickly, and fastening on the daytime incontinence wear but not before asking if she would care to use the commode. The reply is always in the negative, the expression disdainful, as if this foolish daughter is clueless.

The public health nurse has spoken to me on the phone about a client's right to choose. As in, whether to be changed, showered, clothed, or fed. Apparently the local carers have encountered people who have refused to wash for two years. Bet they'll wash them now whether or not they choose.

Instinctively I glance out the bedroom window, check below the house, watch the lake. Within a matter of minutes, the wind has died down so suddenly, the surface is like glass, specked with moorhens, a few ducks, a single swan. I'm looking forward to a strong, hot Java and toast.

'See you in a while, Mum,' I say, leaving Elma on the side of the bed.

'Alright, sweetheart,' Elma replies.

I check the fridge and discover a bowl of tinned pineapple right at the back of the bottom shelf, where it must have lurked for weeks. Mould has gathered in a beautiful blue-green map across the surface of the juice. It lies there, like the whole of Indonesia, I realise. Mould islands, Java, Sumatra and all. I wonder why Hilda is so careless as to not remove the bowl and its contents. I'll have to have a word if ever I see her again. If she comes back. The silence from the road below the house chills me. Nobody is out and about. Nobody leaves home.

*

'Do you realise how much of my time is taken up with you and with keeping this place in order for you?' I guldered once at Elma.

'What do you mean? What do you do when you come? We watch television, don't we?'

I stopped myself and remained silent about what I normally had to do. Washing or even showering Elma (when she permits it), wiping, changing, and the intimate exposure from which I avert my eyes where possible, as if during the exposition of the Blessed Sacrament in the heydays of Catholicism. Then the slow dressing of tremulous flesh with its incessant and querulous stream of *No*s. No to washing. No to changing. No to teeth-washing and finger-nail trimming. No to getting dressed. No to the lavatory. No to the commode. No to going to bed at night. On nights when Hilda has stayed over in the past, Elma has refused to go to bed until three o'clock in the morning. Not with me though. She's slightly afraid of me.

Elma's selective vagueness is perennial, as in the past. She no longer understands, nor remembers, the passage of days and the endurance of her long life, the patterns of business and banking to be managed by me and Christoph, a large garden and many acres to tend.

That is what I do. Stuff. What Christoph and I do. He is recently retired from university life as professor of German. He sees to the maintenance of the land on both sides of the road and stays in touch with Alex. Alex enjoys talking with Christoph about history in both their countries, though he is not an instinctive German-lover. But Christoph understands divisions of land and culture, and Alex is happy that Christoph completely shares his own antipathy to villainous Russia.

Christoph and I would rather travel to Japan as we once did in the past. We'd planned a repeat visit but cancelled for fear of something happening to Elma. We'd also like to revisit the new and radically altered Germany with its huge immigrant population transforming some cities while others retain their high roofed, cutesy-folk style. Brutalist Wuppertal, where we both know the university, the streets milling with migrants, so different from Tübingen, which draws crowds to its chocolate festival in early December, before the first snowfalls. The poet Hölderlin lived there, the town in which he eventually killed himself.

I have overseen the cutting down and selling of a forest planted by Paddy some thirty-five years beforehand. I secured an interested buyer who did not mess me around. He came, felled, sawed and stacked and bore the lot away. To Christoph, though, fell the task of replanting the fields. Oak. Ash. Elm. Cherry. Birch. Some future owner will have fields filled with beautiful native trees. At home now in Tipperary, Christoph is digging a three-foot deep hole in our garden and making a large pond during quarantining. We don't regard ourselves as cocooners, being too young. What a stupid, childish word, intended to appease the aged and make them feel special for once, but really to prevent their gadding about on mountain hikes, attending bridge classes, art-classes, men's sheds, yoga, taking seafront walks, and all the other activities they practice to distract themselves from decreasing hours on earth. From the photographs he's already sent, I'd gauge he's gone too deep, but even so, a pond is a pond and who am I to complain? Our own place is spacious but flat. It looks across sheer green plains towards the Galtee Mountains, and many years on from the time I first left home, I still miss the hills around Kilnavarn.

I consider how much I have loved a place and a house. Tropes on transience and change still apply, now as much as in Chaucer's time, now as much as in Wordsworth's day. Now I'm not enjoying breakfast after all. The toast got slightly burnt, and the coffee is too weak because I levelled the scoop instead of rounding it. But that's not the real reason why my enjoyment is lessened. I drop another slice into the toaster and reduce the temperature. Re-boil the kettle, prepare stronger coffee.

Sometimes, a creature — it feels like a creature, with claws and hurtful fangs — is catapulted from the past, strikes me, and suddenly I find myself plummeted into a murky ditch. It's like an entity around my throat, sucking my blood. There are honest things I no longer wish to say to my mother, partly because she has long ago asked for and been granted a half-forgiveness from Tess. Elma has done her sorrys, the way Australia says sorry to the Aboriginal people for pain, suffering and hurt on May 2nd every year. For many years, apology for Australia lay in a Conditional

Tense, imagined as a vision of change before they actually implemented it. But often, conditionalising isn't helpful, any more than those primary school essays did anything other than impart a grammar, and impossible longings. *If I had ten pounds I would buy big bags of cinnamon drops. I would give them to my friends. I would not give them to my sister because she prefers gob-stoppers and would not like cinnamon drops.*

Honesty. Not always a good thing. Something the very frank forget as they share everything from their view on someone's recent loss (financial or otherwise), to the state of their latest verruca, to conversational nicks on your failures as a feminist, a mother, or work colleague. The very frank are often the only ones who feel marginally better after such a virtue-reveal, because they inhabit morally high ground. Perhaps I can avoid saying the things that fizz at the root of my tongue, and hope that Elma goes before —

Vaguely I plan the day. I add brown sugar to a cup of fresh coffee, then full milk and a tincture of double-cream from the creamery down the road. The toast is slathered with bitter orange marmalade spooned from a new jar, mould-free and pristine. Lottie is on the floor beside the table, brown eyes registering each crunch of toast. I hand the beast a crust. Then Jimmy arrives, hopping onto the table, settling himself beside my plate. He stretches a paw towards the toast.

'Naughty Jimmy,' I scold softly. The paw is withdrawn and Jimmy settles, blinking slowly with yellow eyes, feigning lack of interest. I observe him as daylight shines through his yellow stripes, and deepens the gloss on the darker ones. Jimmy doesn't give a shit. But some nights, I hear him outside my bedroom, his claws working on the door, as if he wants in. If I open the door, he sometimes freezes, refusing to enter, releasing a series of low growls and hisses. I tell him it's alright, there's nothing to worry about. It's all under control, I whisper. Yet off he springs in the opposite direction, towards Elma's room, his fur electric and huge with fear.

Christoph dislikes cats. Christoph, coming from a restrained background, would not have a cat sitting on the table. Yet it was his sense of order that deepened my need for him when I was young, especially after growing up at Kilnavarn. He brought calmness and possibility when I — too thin and too shy — arrived in Germany at his university. I was fortunate to be a student of his during his first teaching semester, in a module on antisemitic German literature. Of which there was a lot. And from which I absorbed a template for half-understanding cultural exclusion, stereotyping, and rage. I still see the ancient forms of Kurds, Jews, Palestinians, tremulously balanced on my imagined scales of justice.

It was a long way from our later debates on whether or not to get a domestic animal. Under no circumstance would Christoph's family ever have tolerated cats on tables, regarding it as filthy. His mother once announced with some conviction one Christmas Eve that there were no fleas in Germany. She didn't understand why I laughed outright at this as we helped ourselves to her delicious roast goose. The first time Christoph visited Kilnavarn to meet Paddy and Elma, he made a good show of being dog and cat tolerant, and ignored the drooling hound whose head was fixed to his thigh as he ate. However, he was unable to bring himself to stroke the large ginger cat that strutted around the place. But somehow, none of that mattered. He was so fine — tall, dark-haired, with a barrel of a chest in which I could hear his heart thud slowly when he held me close, at the end of that first semester. Nowadays, he'd be sacked. I have to smile. The good old days.

3

Christoph is an only child. Like me, he has lots of cousins. They are scattered throughout Bavaria as mine are scattered throughout Ireland, but mostly Monaghan. I have wondered how it would have been in his childhood home had his parents decided to adopt a baby boy or girl when Christoph himself was very young. Frau Bachmann was over-pragmatic, but kind. She was Lutheran, a teacher in a remedial school and she took all responsibilities quite seriously. So, I imagine that had a child been adopted in Christoph's home, it would have worked out well enough. Above all, Frau Bachmann had self-control. So much so that one could not always imagine her deeper feelings and moods. This was not such a bad thing in my view, raised in a home where unpredictable feelings and moods were often to the fore.

*

The Catholic Protection and Rescue Society of Ireland offices nestle upstairs in an old South Anne Street building. We travel on Friday, November 11, 1960. I sit with Elma's mother, Nana, in the back of the silver-blue Vauxhall Victor. Nana is dressed in one of the Queen Mother outfits she favours, a moss-green wool coat with an Astrakhan collar, and a toning shell-shaped apple-green hat tilted to the side of her head. There is an air of happy expectation as Paddy drives from the town and the car buzzes along the undulating road through Castleblaney, on to Dundalk, Dunleer, Drogheda, Balbriggan and, eventually, nosing into Finglas. I envy the Finglas children who live right next to one another's gardens. Because Kilnavarn is in the country, there's only our garden, which I love but which is quiet. I imagine a permanent, unsupervised playtime in Finglas, with children running from house to house, in the front door and out the back, and two parents, a father with rolled-up sleeves, a mother with a floral crossover apron and probably a frying pan, both smiling and maybe drinking tea together, ignoring the chaos and high spirits.

Paddy and Elma chat about the new baby. We are all excited, although I don't know what to expect. I imagine that finally having a baby sister to talk about to other girls at school will make me feel just like them, no longer different as an 'only child'. Finally, I can join in the patter about babies, be like one of the girls who comes from squads of anything up to ten brothers and sisters. There are plenty of babies going for adoption, plentiful as batch loaves, and no shortage of young women who want their babies to go to good Catholic homes.

We make our way towards the building from where the baby will be collected. On the way, the soft brown fragrance of coffee from Bewley's café, its windows displaying cakes and meringues, then the inviting clatter of delph, cutlery, drifts of cigarette smoke and chatter emerging onto the street. I wish we could go in and have tea and cakes. Dressed in old-fashioned clothes and a shawl, an old woman playing a big classical harp catches my attention, but we have to keep moving, there is an appointment, even if I stop to stare at a Butterfly Nun with a stiff cornette crossing the street, a Daughter of Charity.

Then, the wait in a tiny room, while a narrow, steel-haired woman goes away to fetch the baby, whose name on her birth certificate is Goretti Therese. She is already six months old. I watch as the bundled infant arrives to be passed into Elma's arms. She, Nana and Paddy confer agreeably before lowering the baby so that I can have a squint at my new sister. She lies in Elma's arms, pink, white, unperturbed. Elma has already renamed her Tess. 'Tess of the D'Urbervilles!' she laughs later in the back of the car, jiggling the baby in her arms.

I observe the newcomer closely in the long evening light as the car tilts around curves and tight bends on the way northwards. I really want to cuddle that baby as I would cuddle my dollies but am not allowed. 'You might drop her,' Elma murmurs, 'Sit back and go to sleep.'

Impossible. The twisting road and the new baby keep me looking and watching, either out the window at the deepening sunset or at the baby herself, who, already, seems to have her own mind. Her eyes are very blue, like bluebells, I decide. She wears a pink hat, which she repeatedly pulls off her head. Elma pulls it back on again. Then Tess slumbers and all is well. The adults chat about their things — local news from *The Northern Standard*, Paddy's private views on the bossy matron at the hospital where he is county surgeon, a recent photograph of the newly appointed furniture factory manager, who is a tall woman, not married, and, according to Elma, will be well able to handle the men.

The following morning, Saturday, I wake to tremendous screaming from the kitchen, which lies directly below my bedroom. Downstairs quickly at the sound of crisis, I push the door open. My mother struggles with soap, water, and the baby in the big Butler sink. Paddy looks on, benign above his teacup. I have never heard anything like this, even in cousins' houses, where there are always babies. It's not what I expected.

'The baby is making strange,' Elma explains. 'It'll take a few weeks, then she'll be right as rain.'

Paddy agrees, handing Elma a towel in which to wrap the child. 'Oh, it'll take a while for our little Dubliner to settle in.'

'She's not from Dublin,' Elma amends. 'She's from an orphanage in Cork.'

'How did she get to Dublin? Did they send her on the train?' I enquire, puzzled.

'What a question. How would I know how she got to Dublin?' Elma, frowning, struggles to dry the still-screaming, wriggling infant. 'Paddy I'm out of practice,' she gasps with a nervous laugh. 'She won't stop moving!'

'A kind nurse probably went on the train with her to Dublin,' Paddy says, winking at me. 'In a little basket. Like Moses, except not on the Nile, on the train.' He winks again.

The following Monday in school I give Sister Apollinaris a full account of my new sister. An earnest telling of the baby's name.

'It's Goretti Therese, but Mammy says we're calling her Tess.'

The nun's eyebrows tilt questioningly upwards. 'So Mammy isn't using saint's names?'

'I don't know, Sister.'

'Anyway, they're lovely names,' the nun concedes.

'Mammy says Tess is after a woman in an English book.'

'Does she now?'

'Yes Sister. She's called after Tess. . .Tess of the. . .'

Sister Apollinaris gets the picture and congratulates us on little Tess and for half remembering the name of a famous English novel which she happens to have read herself before she entered convent life.

'Mammy has good taste, hasn't she? And sure she's a very pretty lady. The Sisters and I sometimes see her when we're out walking in the town. And sure names don't really matter, do they darling?'

'No Sister.'

*

By eleven o'clock, I've changed Elma's night wear and cleared up after breakfast. I remove the kitchen curtains from the window over the sink and place them on a hot wash in the washing-machine. I sort the waste from two bins, then drag a heavy black sack filled with urine-soaked nappies down the stairs across the kitchen and out the back door into the boot of the car. I drive to the bottom of the avenue and lift and drop them into their different bins. Then I drive out to pick up groceries from the supermarket. I drive cautiously. There's no rush. The road has changed a lot since Tess and I were children. Instead of twisty and rural it's now straight and sign-posted on the far side of our lake, bypassing an austere and monolithic boys' school and, since the last recession, the almost closed down creamery. But the river Blackwater still flows on, north towards the Bann and from there into Lough Neagh. Sometimes I still stop at the river bridge, a place of shy herons and trout. This is a secret part of the world and I've always loved the fact that it never became interesting enough to attract tourists. No beaches or sea-fronts, no mountains, no theme parks. Instead, there's the spread of the drumlins, like green snails sloping north-westwards, laden with heavy hedges. In between the hills, a scatter of lakes with attendant folk tales and a steady trawl of quiet menace behind the beauty, good for fishermen. There's also a wonderment of narrow networked roads leading around the townlands, connecting local people but which confuses visitors. Now, there might as well be no border separating the North from the Republic. Nobody cares about borders and religions at this moment. All most people care about is economy and survival.

I wonder about survival, about myself, with a cancer scare averted in the recent past, and an unpredictable condition that has struck intermittently since my teenage years. *Stills Disease,* admittedly more or less under control, my immune system pulled into order by a weekly injection. A physiotherapist on the radio is telling the presenter about pelvic floor exercises, about supporting the core, about the perineum and how important it is to do the exercises after childbirth and then to increase them during menopause. There's always some part of the female biological self to attend to. I switch her off. In the supermarket carpark, I don two masks and fine disposable gloves. I am afraid of this virus. I still need to be careful. But it's possible to shop without making physical contact with anybody, although background fear is ever present. My pharmacist in Tipperary sent me a video shown on Spanish television purporting to show in a cartoonish way, how the virus spreads, how it is in the air, everywhere, dancing lushly, sailing up our noses and into our mouths.

I queue outside the supermarket at the prescribed two metres between me and other waiting customers. My eye scans the mothers, fathers and children who move carefully and at distance from other groups. They look satisfactory. Normal. But you can't really tell. One of the children is crying, ignored by its parents, the other customers glancing in their direction but none willing to intervene. Perhaps there is no reason to intervene.

*

There was plenty of what I call 'life literature' in the house, including a copy of The Catholic Marriage, which later gave way to a guide to Tantric Sex, bought on one of Paddy and Elma's trips abroad. In their wardrobe also lay a copy of Mary McCarthy's *The Group.*

And then came Dr Benjamin Spock. By the time Tess arrived, our mother had absorbed some of the central tenets of the American paediatrician whose ideas once poured like grim weather on parents world-wide.

Spock's thoughts on sleep, for one thing, were pounced on by the more informed coteries of our small island, from city to parishes in the back end of nowhere, wherever women aspired to modernity. Leaving a baby to cry itself to sleep became the thing, introducing to the inarticulate being its nascent discovery of human aloneness. The theory of the day was that all babies and infants will self-soothe, even if they are adopted at six months and have unmet attachment needs. Bonding with a parent. A few basics, I reflect. At seven o'clock Tess would be removed promptly from her wooden highchair, changed, and brought to her cot, where Elma would place her, then leave, closing the door.

I recall something of those nights. They are spikes still hooked into my heart. Some part of me is crushed by the recollection of a young creature alone and crying, then screaming in outrage, finally then weakening to sobs of. . .what? Gradually quietening despair, more than likely. Exhaustion. No one is coming. No one will come. No one might ever come. That is the message, surely. The great I-am-alone descending on an infant's consciousness. What part of Dr Spock's brain failed to function back in 1947 when he published the book that would screw up a couple of generations of kids? One of his favourite phrases was *chronic resistance to sleep.* Well, leave it to old Benjamin and he'd sort it out, ladies of the Western world. Your baby's yelling and crying? Leave it to cry! Leave it, get on with your evening in the knowledge that you are progressive!

Once, I go up to Tess's bedroom when she is screaming. Paddy is at the hospital due to an emergency and Elma is listening to Renata Tebaldi on the new record player he bought her. But Tess's cries cut through the music again and again. I cross the room and peer into the cot. The moment she sees me her crying fades, then stops. Her eyes are wet, her pillow moist with tears and drool. I lean in and offer her my finger, which she grips. She stares steadily into my face, then smiles and coos as she yanks at the finger, moving it back and forth. A few small stubby teeth have already broken through her gums and her cheeks are fiery. I don't remember how long I remained there. But I still feel her firm little clutch at my forefinger and how she jiggled it. When I leave the room, she begins to wail again, but I continue on downstairs since Mum says babies always settle if you leave them.

I know now why Tess was adopted. Elma hadn't actually wanted another baby. She wanted to adopt a four-year-old girl, a companion sibling for me, she tells me only this morning quite spontaneously, as if the thought of Tess's origins in the niche of our family had suddenly popped into her head. This, while I was changing her, she staring at the ceiling, muttering about a letter. 'Your father kept letters, you know. I'm sure the letter is somewhere in the house if you care to look.'

I don't care to look but I do believe her when she tells me they hadn't wanted another baby. 'One baby was enough for me, I'm afraid,' she sighs and smiles sadly.

'But didn't you feel the pressure to have loads of children?' I probe, sprinkling talcum powder lightly across her belly and smoothing it. Elma regards me then and pulls her nightdress down as best she can with her stronger hand. 'Not really, darling,' she shakes her head.

'You were always so independent-minded,' I say, almost admiringly. Elma is very lucid today, and not querulous. She shakes her head again. 'It wasn't that, so much as I was sick of having people, my dear departed brothers mainly, in my hair when I was a child, God bless them I wish they were around now! But there was always someone shoving me around, uncles, my mother, your Nana, and then the seven brothers. No, I never wanted a crowded house again and it's not that I was unhappy. I don't think I was unhappy, your Nana was a good mother. If any of us got sick she couldn't do enough for us, she was the best of mothers. Mind you, she didn't spare the rod either but that was because there were too many of us. That's what I think now. No, having a big family wouldn't have suited me even if your father, God bless him, would have been the best of fathers. But he let me have my way, which was what I always liked.'

'But did it never strike you to simply leave things alone? To just have one child?'

'In this town?' She laughs at the top of her voice at the idea. 'Don't be ridiculous! I couldn't turn without someone feeling sorry for me having only one child. Oh, they were all so busy breeding, your aunt Elizabeth, our sisters in law and everyone I knew, and they were all hooked into the Irish Countrywomen's

Association too, none of which interested me in the slightest, and while I'm at it, I thought giving birth to you was one of the worst things that ever happened me. I probably shouldn't say that to you Frankie. The twilight gas made me see rats! I thought there were rats crawling over me while I was having you! And then I picked up some fucking infection in the nursing home and that blocked my tubes. You and Christoph did the right thing in never having children.'

*

I'm now so distracted as I replay this conversation that I accidentally brush against a woman at the ham and cheese shelves. She turns sharply. *Sorry, I wasn't thinking,* I murmur, taking a step back while the woman rummages, hands in blue plastic gloves, through the cheeses. It was the first time Elma had openly commented on the fact Christoph and I have no children by choice. But she'll never know how badly I couldn't face such a prospect, how any desire to have a baby and make my own future was wrecked by her and Paddy. That insight makes me angry. It could have been different, so different, if I'd had the courage, or had Christoph insisted on becoming a father. But I was too afraid.

My turn at the ham and cheese counter now. A wheel of ripe Brie. A wedge of Stilton. I have no idea of how *I* was handled as an infant, although I suspect myself, from the few photographs I've seen, of being smothered in many blankets. Everything was new and optimism-filled at that time for my parents. It's possible I got away more lightly, although Elma always said that once I opened my mouth to cry I didn't know when to shut it again. I imagine that to have been true. In the wrong mood as an adult,

I take things too seriously, more than my friends do, more even than Christoph. On the other hand, I believe myself to be wildly happier than any of them when my mood spikes.

To this day I can hold tears back with unusual determination. No crying or weeping in public, or at funerals, an unwritten code I legislated for myself by the age of twelve or so. Be the one who comforts, find solace in reaching out. Be strong. Heal others. The only time I've cried in recent years was when Tess's daughter Allegra was born, and in that primitive moment of seeing the first emailed photo, I was too stunned by the sight of the baby to remember to *not* cry. Stunned too, because now Tess, although she never established a backwards family connection, had a forwards one, a link to a future.

What did Paddy do in the middle of it all, I wonder. What agency, if any, had he? I cannot remember, I was too young to absorb everything. Yet he adored Tess. In the morning before leaving for the hospital, he checked on her in her cot, in her gay, sheep-and-pony wallpapered bedroom. He often described Tess's hands, 'ah, the little hands,' he'd say, 'hard with the cold. A little pair of farmer's hands,' sympathetically, after covering her up again. And he remarked wonderingly on her hair, morning-tangled, and how she was 'like a wee wild woman in her nest.'

Tess's hair. Not curling and blonde like mine, but straight, brown and to be permed every few months. Exasperated and just out of bed late on the mornings she was to drive us to school, Elma would tug too hard to untangle the morning tats. More tears, followed by a belt on the arm, or possibly a scratch from one of Elma's diamond rings if things took an angrier twist. It still shocks me. Tess sometimes went to school still sniffling, me beside her, ignoring it for the most part. I didn't know how to ask the right questions. I didn't know how to console her. Inside and already I possess a growing sense that Tess must be told on, must be monitored. Above all, Elma to be kept calm, happy. Smiling Mammy, who was a wonderful cook and could sing in Italian. A future was shaping up, a feeling I could not speak about had drifted in, infecting me with powerlessness. The fate of being a good girl. Good girls became better girls, who grow into successful ladies, whether they like it or not.

*

Shoppers are moving slowly, picking their way along the aisles. Into the trolley tumble a few of my mother's favourite items: coffee-cake (2 boxes), baked beans, ham, tinned pineapple and a bag of jellies. And into the trolley what I find essential: eggs, moistened skin wipes that will not irritate fragile skin, paper wipes, the last remaining 4-pack of toilet-paper on the shelf, and from the health section some cannabis oil, which I find useful. Nor do I forget a few rolls of large black plastic bags and sacks. I think about how residential homes for the elderly are single-handedly responsible for the mountains of non-recyclable plastics, given the amount of soiled disposable garments to be disposed of. I pause near the stacks of scented cleaning agents — lavender, rose, citrus — surrounded by rolls of plastic bags, disinfectants, dishwasher tablets and toilet cleansers.

Two Russian families are out with blonde-haired children, a keenness and even urgency to their stocking up. They all wear masks and have used the latex gloves supplied at the supermarket entrance. I adjust my masks and hook them behind my ears, trying to keep the strings free of my earrings. My ears stick out. They are like faun's ears, a man who used to flirt with me once said.

My mind returns to the question of soothing an infant. A truism floats into my head as I pause at the chocolate section to lift a few bars of fruit and nut: an orangutan cares better for its infant than my mother did for Tess. Likewise, a gorilla. What is it about primate cousins that equips them better for nurturing the very young and helpless while humans sometimes fail badly? First answer is the available wilderness, life in a natural environment. While in captivity in a zoo, it is not uncommon in the least for a gorilla or an orangutan to reject, or even eat, its young. This is a result of either the stress of captivity or early separation from their own mothers. I recently watched an online video of primates mothering in the wild. The tender care poured on the very young moved me indescribably in a dry-eyed way. Why the world's educating types consider zoos a good idea in an age of, until now, unlimited travel, and unlimited nature programmes on television, is beyond me. But then, so much is beyond my comprehension.

I do recall food being shovelled into Tess's ever-open gob. Tess the insatiable, when it came to food. Weaned by nuns in the orphanage, drinking milk from a cup at six months, then passed on like a bread loaf to market to the Catholic Protection and Rescue Society of Ireland, she has neither attachment nor sucking to rely on when the airs in the household are brittle. So she eats. Porridge from an adult-sized bowl. Sausages in sixes. Fish-fingers on Friday. She eats so much yet never becomes obese, instead remaining athletic-looking all her life.

Still shopping, pausing too long before the cabbage and carrot mountain in one aisle, then hovering even longer in front of the wine, I attempt to concentrate, then my thoughts return to maternal orangutans. I move to another shopping aisle, instinctively drawn to the screaming of a toddler. Screaming upsets me. I cannot bear it, yet am irresistibly drawn to it in public spaces, in case there is something I can do to arrest a situation. I have a tendency to jump in and try to rescue, instead of walking away.

The toddler sounds as if it is being skinned alive. The tension in my belly rears up as I push the trolley, but to my relief this is nothing to be concerned about. The child is merely in meltdown due to over-stimulation or sheer tiredness, I'm guessing, judging by the smear of red-jelly drool around its sticky mouth. The parents don't pull it to its feet, or scold. They simply wait, chatting casually together, pretending to look at the baking produce while the child kicks and screams. They are there, within its sight. Every so often, the mother calls over to the still-kicking infant, *yes, I'm here honey, I hear you. When you're ready, we can go to the park.* They have not gone away. They are trying to be parents. We are here for you, is the message. It doesn't matter. We will stay near you until you no longer need us.

Thinking of orangutans in unnatural settings reminds me of the women of the 1960s, especially the middle-class ones, housed often beautifully, elegantly, all aspiration for themselves and their offspring, harbouring a muted kind of social ambition. Yet often constrained by the need to assimilate, to fit in. Although there were some who wanted to be different. A woman Elma once knew shaved her head on a whim because she was tired of her hair-style. I dated her eldest son a few times, no shortage of hair there, dark fuzz tickling my face every time we tried to get close. He understood his mother, he told me. *My mother needs to sound off, y'know? We're cool about it, Dad too. She doesn't believe in bottling up feelings. That's very healthy, don't you think?*

Some years later, I wonder how he felt when his mother drank weed-killer and died. Now, there is therapy. Everybody has a chance to talk to someone else, who might throw light on a bad situation. Immediately, I hear Paddy's voice bordering on sternness when I once suggested it after Tess's suicide attempt, when I was twenty-five and Tess nineteen. The hospital wasn't that sympathetic when she was rushed in, Elma apparently speeding into town and up the hill to skid to a halt at the entrance of the white building with its concreted carpark. What I find so astounding to this day is a sense that Paddy was quietly embarrassed. Imagine. Matron told him not to worry, she'd keep a lid on any gossip. They'd pumped Tess's stomach and, according to Matron, this was only a first attempt, an attention-seeking, bedroom effort at suicide, in other words. Tess knew she'd be found.

I was on a writer's residency in Germany. I was told about it a week later. What part of my parents minds didn't grasp the significance of an overdose? What prevented them from phoning me immediately with this news? Photographs taken in the days after the event show Tess and Elma hugging closely, Tess on the arm of the sofa, and our mother dressed in a turquoise kaftan reaching up, arms around Tess's small waist. It amuses me when people say nobody is to blame when a family member commits suicide. The old school psychiatrists of the 1960s would have something to say about that, RD Laing would say that mental disturbance was a sane response to an insane world. But our parents refused responsibility. Paddy should have known about these things.

'Therapy? Absolutely not,' I still hear his response to my timid suggestion.

'Why not, Daddy?' I press on, 'Therapy is healthy. Especially family therapy. It helps people think things out.'

'Some of these people who set themselves up as psychologists aren't reliable resources. I know from my work, pet. They don't always know what's best.'

Neither do you, I want to say but don't. 'Talking is good. It might be helpful.'

There I go, intervening, moderating, trying to work some measure of diplomacy within the household, even from the distance of my own new, young marriage, and swamped as Christoph and I are by an apartment rental barely within our means in the arse-end of Roscrea town.

'No therapy.' Paddy's final word. 'We resolve our problems in private. It's nobody else's business.'

I flew home from Düsseldorf the day after I heard, left Christoph starting lectures in Wuppertal. He wanted to accompany me, but I insisted on travelling alone. Somehow, this had to be a solo journey. Tess was in happy form when I arrived home, helping Elma with some domestic chores, going shopping with her in the town. A car trip to Armagh and the planetarium, where the astronomer Patrick Moore was director. I accompanied them on another trip, up the M1 to Belfast, even though the IRA had just carried out an attack on Eglinton Airfield, destroying four planes. At least it wasn't people, and Elma was always blithe about crossing and re-crossing the border. 'Sure those English soldiers, they're just lads, they could be my sons, they don't even want to be over here,' she'd remark after being waved through the barricade and accelerating into the North with ease. She was still toasting in a glow of what I can only think of as love — from Tess especially. They were both so full of good intentions, looked forward to new beginnings. This was a new beginning. Except it wasn't, really. It was the first time I realised they had a bond, dark like a dark rose, emitting a not-quite-sweet perfume, but perfumed all the same.

Why did Paddy not intervene? What kind of a wimp was he

that he never stood up to his wife? While Elma stood with a bottle of Milk of Magnesia for constipation, roaring at me to swallow it while I stood mutely, lips sealed until, finally, I had no choice and opened my mouth. Big metal spoon shoved in and yanked up against the roof of my mouth to ensure teeth catch every morsel of the sickening liquid. Upstairs Tess screaming. Nobody went to her. I am embroiled in new confusion, in which both parents appear to know what they were doing but everything has gone wrong and they don't quite see this. Yet I trust them and believe that this strange feeling of wrongness that mangles my innards is in some way my fault.

I comply. I ignore. I fall silent. I am six years old.

The kitchen walls are yellow, the warm stove full of dry crackling hardwood, there is a ticking clock and a Belfast sink. Elma installs a fashionable formica table with tubular metal legs and six matching chairs, in bitter lemon with black squiggles. All visiting children adore it. They also adore and then bicker over the very modern, colourful tea-set, an unbreakable set, in yellow, green, red, brown, blue and orange. Every child who comes in likes to choose their own colour. They find Elma hilarious. At birthday parties Elma joins in, once placing a box of Dairy Milk on the centre of the sitting-room floor and then shouting, 'Okay children, go for it!'. She watches and laughs as the children rush forward to grab every last chocolate from the double-layered two-pound box. Elma tells me not to get myself into a tizzy, to relax, that I am too shy and need to come *out* of myself. I don't know how to do this, not realising that I am *in* myself and that this is not a bad thing. If I could speak up I would tell Elma to stop joining in my birthday party as if she was a child too, to stop telling funny stories from her own childhood in which she, Elma, plays the ever-bold child during the 1930s and early

1940s. Elma recounts many adventures, from robbing orchards and loading the apples into her elasticated knickers, to getting her elder brother to prise open a can of peaches, which they all eat, and then allowing the baby of the family to lick the juice off the floor. She recounts how she threw a bowl of cold water over the top of the lavatory door onto one of her brothers, and how he ran after her, an enraged bull of a boy, up and down the street, until finally she outran him and escaped to the Cathedral grounds and the safety of the bell tower.

At my tenth birthday party, things tilt even further out of control. The children stand around the long kitchen table. They are still at the sandwich stage, served with orange juice. Everybody wants to get to the iced cakes and buns. One cousin decides to lob her unfinished sandwich into another cousin's mug. The other cousin lobs back. Soon, the whole table is splattered with spilt juice and soggy sandwiches. Elma looks on, laughing her head off, as the young black-haired girl who helps out looks on in disbelief.

Sometimes, Elma takes week-long courses at a cookery school in another county, returning with fresh cooking and baking plans, and with books by the latest Irish cooks, among them Maura Laverty. The birthday parties come to be shared parties, which means they are really mine, with my friends and cousins, and perhaps two of Tess's, who the elder children always hide from anyway, or tease to make them cry. Elma sings for the children, making the duck-sounds from *There Once was an Ugly Duckling*. They laugh. I laugh too because my mother is funny, and my friends adore her and the way she lets them run wild throughout the house and garden. A few of them ferry home the stuffed oranges she makes, with clown faces piped on in white icing and a pile of jelly and tinned fruit cocktail inside.

*

I wheel the shopping trolley along the tarmac to the car, it's a light enough load of shopping. The bags plop on the back seat and I lay the two bottles of my favourite red wine more carefully beside them. Portuguese, from the Douro Valley, a place where Christoph and I have felt the rich soil between our toes during hot summers of drifting travel. We would select a town at random on the map of Portugal or Spain and set off driving across the burnt-earth countryside, past fields of tawny sunflowers, and hilly outposts with herds of goats.

Now it's a cool spring afternoon. All around, hills rise darkened here and there by thicketed, wooded patches. Some of this land is owned by local grandees whose houses are sheltered and hidden behind a screen of high-spread trees. The old town, once founded beside a Franciscan monastery, is stone quiet, with a few parked cars and my own making its way across the square past the sharp-spired Church of Ireland limestone church. It's like looking at the light of history — golden, undisturbed by human interaction, the stonework warmed and lit by the season, even little trails of moss visible in the pointing. I don't really miss life before quarantine all that much. The meetings, seminars, the hectic discussions with friends — too loud, over-energetic, not as funny as we imagined — over cups of coffee and glasses of wine in an evening bar in Limerick or Galway. Here, pubs known as The Cut Spud, The Dipped Chip, The Steak Shack, and Frontier Chophouse, are shuttered, the bistro cafe chairs on their outside terraces are tilted desolately against metal tables. The high-end women's fashion shops are also shut. The town, deserted by its people, is incredibly beautiful — curve-cornered, deep-roofed. A secret and unpretentious weave of old stone, brick, worn plaster and a now silent shopping centre. In this translucence of early spring, of chiff-chaff and squeaky wheelbarrow sounding sparrows, everything seems gentle.

Sometimes I feel sheer relief and think the world is so much better without so many people charging around. I'm not gregarious at the best of times, believing Sartre's line that *hell is others*, although I can put on a good performance and sometimes enjoy myself with them, mostly for Christoph's sake. But essentially I am a little misanthropic. I sent Christoph a long, long WhatsApp message to this effect recently when we were joking about 'others', 'les autres' and the question of what hell is. 'Outside Europe', I wrote, 'famines, wars, imprisonments, everything from Before, continue uninterrupted, with no break in the day's disasters, but in Europe we're acting as if the crisis is the worst thing that has ever occurred on the planet. It isn't. The worst will continue long after it has passed and we're all back on the streets. The worst will continue elsewhere, just as it has always done. The worst may lie behind us in history as you know, dear, but also in the Now, and will trail us into the future because the spatial and the temporal are not really as people imagine them to be.' His reply was brief. I needed to put my ideas into an essay, he texted.

I feel I ought to return to Christoph, but something prevents me, a loss of nerve perhaps. I could arrive late at night, and find him perhaps at his desk, with a glass of wine to hand. I've tried to be a good companion and wife. I've played my Sudden Appearance card, my Seduction card when I get drunk and we have a hilarious time and terribly bad, but funny, sex. I've done all that. He would be surprised to see me. I've stayed here too long already, but so far, he hasn't complained beyond saying that he misses me. I can't fully explain this need to stay with Elma. No,

I can't explain it at all. A current of sympathy for her perhaps, cutting through all the rage.

Not ready to face my mother, not ready to try to lure her out of bed while she is still able and not quite fully bed-ridden, I drive slowly three miles outside the town to Rossmore Park, where a castle once stood on a high hill and where Elma's grandfather was a beef and pork butcher who sold prime cuts to the Rossmores.

*

As the car noses into the park I wonder if I'm dressed properly for the weather in my ten-year old navy hoodie. It could rain. Slowly then along a wide avenue and a row of forty-year-old poplars unlike the native trees on the old estate. A few other cars, and inexplicably, given the cool breeze, a family of four perched at a picnic table on the knoll beside the car-park. I lock the car. They look up from their chatter and go silent. I call out a hello, but they ignore me and return to their careful feasting, a bottle of hand sanitiser beside a pile of chips on greaseproof paper. I smell the vinegar and fried fish, which means they're Irish and not one of the healthier kind of park user, the Lithuanians or Polish. The latter catch fish on the lakes.

I walk with hands plunged in jacket pockets. I'm hoping Tess will call soon to let me know where she is and what time to expect her. I stop and open my Twitter feed. Emergency legislation freezing people within their own regions. Some numbkin claims the army may be called in. Everyone to stay put. Social media a fizz with paranoid claims of possible detention for individuals who refuse to self-isolate, that last one from a man who doesn't believe in Covid. I slide the phone back into my pocket.

I take the Castle View walk up a sandy path overhung with

ash and beech-trees. Then around the lake. The wind is shirring along the surface on the near side, while out in the centre the clouds are reflected, large and lush. Inexplicably, words learned over fifty years ago in a school production of *Murder in the Cathedral* come to mind. Me, in the chorus, happy there. *We wait, and the time is short, but waiting is long.* This is how it will be. Short time on the physical earth. Long wait for release. Not awaiting release from the trials that surrounded Thomas à Becket, this release from a chain of elegant, stubbed microscopic balls of virus that courts spongy, wet, lungs, then makes room for itself within and eventually destroys them for many.

People in medieval times got through it after a fashion. The wealthy pulled up the drawbridge and locked themselves in the castle, defending themselves against pox-ridden and pitted-skinned village wenches and swains. Noblesse oblige out the door, and a return to the fear of God.

I mount the hill on which Rossmore Castle used to stand, and stare across the county, spread grey-mauve-green, then more hills and small forests, a single straight plume of smoke rising in the air from the direction of the Bragan mountains. The enfolding silence. I do love that. My phone rings. Not wanting to be disturbed, I don't check to see who it is. It stops. A moment later, it resumes. I reach into my jacket. It's Tess.

'Hey you,' I begin.

'Woohoo, I'm here!'

'At the house?'

'No, in Killaloe.'

'Killaloe?'

'Yep.'

'Are you on your way?'

'Not yet.'

I can hear Tess's smoking breath, hoarse, deep. Then a change of subject, as if it was any ordinary conversation and she was home for Christmas and we were approaching normality, whatever that is or ever was.

'I've brought loads of stuff for everyone. Didn't know what to get Mammy though.'

Stuff. Presents. Mammy. Tess has always adored gift buying and giving.

'I'm sure you did, but she has everything and she doesn't expect anything from us.'

'Yeah, but you know me.'

'So what did you get her?' I train my eyes on the distant horizon in an attempt to remain calm and not irritated.

'I found this adorable wrap... a poncho really... close by in the Village...Mexican themed, her colours really, quite autumnal —'

'She'll love that.' I doubt our mother will ever don a Mexican shawl and become a last minute *campesino* sitting up in bed.

'The thing is...'

I hate qualifiers. 'What?'

'Don't be annoyed.'

'Tell me.'

Deep breath from Tess. 'I can't come today. It's a long trip.'

'I didn't think you would, to be honest.'

I keep my voice light and non-accusatory, though I suppose that statement is a bit accusatory anyway. There's always a hitch.

'I'm with Stella,' she continues breezily. 'Remember her? Amazing girl I was at school with?'

Of course I remember Stella. One of the girls that attended the Limerick boarding school Tess was shoved off to at the age of fourteen when our parents believed that a distant boarding school would put a bit of discipline on her, to quote Paddy.

Discipline was the thing that set a girl or boy up. Character-building regimes, resistance to soft comforts. Early morning rises, daily Mass, hockey, javelin throwing, music and supervised study at nights.

'Stella,' I turn the name over in my mouth. Stella once stayed over at Kilnavarn, her long hair sun-bleached around her face. She was pleasant and agreeable to Elma and Paddy, she fitted in, dissolving the tensions between us for a few days. We'd played Monopoly and Scrabble. Tess won everything. And we'd taken turns racing Tess's pony along the flat part of the low field. Elma had happily ferried us from one gymkhana to the next and when we returned home got us to set up a trestle table on the lawn where we gobbled sandwiches and slugged at tumblers of Elma's home-made lemonade. It was like something out of Enid Blyton. Briefly, that made me so happy. Our mother was at her best, enjoying entertaining, luxuriating in a *plein air* out-of-the-kitchen moment.

So that's where Tess has been hiding since landing at Shannon airport? With Stella, in Killaloe of all places! I'm descending the hill, making my way down the stony avenue past the Rossmore family mausoleum.

'It was so weird,' Tess starts to explain. 'Before I left the hospital I texted to let her know I was coming to Ireland, and to arrange meeting her. . .and she said why not drop by and stay till I got over my jet-lag? She's not far from the airport. She's working remotely like everybody, but really wanted to see me. She's marvellous Frankie, and you have to see her house. It's my dream house, a view of the Shannon and all that. So I said. . .'

'You said yes. Of course you said yes.' Stella is charismatic.

Tess ignores my clipped tone. 'So you won't be mad if I don't arrive over to you guys for a few days? I know it's been ages, but

I promised I'd help with cleaning out the stables and a few things like that. And she's got a new gardening project, she's creating an actual box-hedge maze, like a labyrinth!'

I almost burst out laughing but don't. It's hard for me to visualise Tess working in this way.

'Um, romantic.' I'm thinking of the classical labyrinths of Italy, then, more sourly, of the underground labyrinth in a Lawrence Durrell novel I once read, in which a group of English tourists gets lost and each receives the death they richly deserve when they encounter the legendary Minotaur.

Tess is blithe and happy. 'It's like a little vacation after NYC to be honest. I have this grey cob I've been riding out, great view down to the river shallows too. It's so mythic.'

'It's actually megalithic,' I reply.

Then I concede that the area *is* mythic, as well as dripping in megalithic dolmens, a ring fort or three, and the occasional underground burial chamber, and we talk about how great that is, that they're still so accessible, with lots more to be discovered.

'It's so cool,' she muses. 'I've missed these things. Not that I'd be thinking of them all the time, or hardly ever, but when they're suddenly there, you realise what you've left behind.'

'Home,' I say.

'What?' she is momentarily baffled.

'You've left home behind,' I repeat.

Then she tells me how busy the clinic is at the hospital. Her case load is packed but under-funded. Sometimes, I really appreciate the miracle of Tess's recovery, how hard she worked once she got to New York, a job in Starbucks five mornings a week, and night cleaning at the weekends to fund her degree as a Speech and Language Pathologist. After she left Ireland, Elma was certainly not going to crack open the coffers and release some of the trust fund. Now she talks about placements in rehab units, about working in public schools, often funding from her own pocket the materials such schools need.

'I guess you need something completely different for a while,' I grudgingly remark. Then, trying to sound less uptight, 'Before orbital re-entry, I mean.'

She laughs at this. 'Thanks sis. I won't even say when I'm arriving. I'll just arrive. Surprise you all. Don't prepare anything, right?'

'I won't.'

'Elma okay?' This, in a more muted voice.

'Fine, really. She could still be around when we've both had our first hip replacements.' We titter at this.

'We have to talk about that,' I say then.

'About what?'

'The future.'

'Sounds heavy. Let's wait and see.'

It is heavy, I want to add. Tess knows I'm pissed off with her. She knows the shape of my soul just as I know hers. It's a question of love and anger residing as twin spirits in both of us. And it's a reminder that Tess isn't always to be pitied, that I'm hauling decades of the shittiest and most useless guilt, which I should rid myself of. Sometimes, I think I take after Paddy, that I've been weak. Knowing so much, unable to act, to give voice.

4

I park at the back of the house and yank the handbrake. I unload the groceries, flinging bags of fruit into a wooden bowl, and coffee cakes into a cupboard. My movements are jerky and I realise I'm sweating to the roots of my hair. My body sometimes releases what I no longer have any capacity to admit. I read somewhere recently that these things dwell in the anterior insula and the anterior cingulate cortex of the brain, somewhere beneath the wrinkly grey cortex. They have dwelt here all my life, largely ignored or worked around like a massive boulder that impeded movement.

What I haven't yet told Elma is that Tess arrived in the country weeks ago. By some hair's breadth miracle, right before all flights into Ireland and the UK were closed, Tess had landed at Shannon and after a night's rest at an airport hotel, the plan was to make her way northwards to join me for a few days. The plan was also that we would both care for Elma while Hilda was herself off cocooning. Gloves, masks, hand sanitiser ad nauseam. It was a plan. Together. Tess was to remain for an extended period, while I would escape back to Christoph. A few days together would give us time to catch up.

Now I'm registering an internal short-waveband of babbling rage that never quite goes silent, while Tess remains calmly elsewhere. Tess fled Ireland and Elma twenty-two years ago. We have long since fought and reconciled. Emailed insults were screamed in block capitals across the Atlantic. WELL FUCK YOU, you always were so FUCKING selfish, and then a swift reply, FUCK YOU TOO and furthermore DON'T TRY TO TELL ME HOW TO LEAD MY LIFE! You haven't a clue what I went through ALL MY LIFE, have you?!

A day's silence perhaps. Then I'd initiate contact again (mostly in lower case): Well you haven't a clue what I've gone through either! Being stuck in the middle, listening to the pair of them! It was all you, you, YOU! Always you!!!! Exclamation marks proliferated, followed by long silences. Eventually one or other of us would break the embargo on communication and the relationship would resume again tentatively, before building back to a semi-comfortable level. Almost as if nothing whatsoever had happened between us. It is one thing I admire about our family. Many insults and hurts — though not quite all — were recovered from, moved on from, forgiven even if never quite forgotten. I have long acknowledged that Tess brings a freshness to everything, that she is charm and pleasantness itself for the days she stays. She flies in as a tourist, rather than as a fully-fledged family member, trailing a chaos of luggage, gifts and initially high spirits. If it's Easter, she brings a bag of chocolate eggs for everyone, and if she arrives for Christmas, one suitcase is stuffed with presents. But something more also. Fun, possibly. Laughter too, if she can be pinned down long enough in her butterfly flutter of a visit. She reconnects with old friends, who adore her. But she does nothing around the place, and gradually the feeling builds that she is judging me — us — tolerating us at best.

Did we ever reconcile? The word suggests a clear-cut making up, a resolution of some kind. I'm not so sure. I glance at my phone. A text from Tess. She's looking forward to being with me again, under the old, slated roof and the oculus window, she says. It's a guilty text, I conclude. Admittedly, Tess is as attached to the house as I am, what was once an estate manager's generous dwelling. High-ceilinged, respectable for its day. A larder and a china pantry, an inner kitchen, old brass taps that Elma ripped out in her modernising frenzy, and a scullery with stone floor-tiles, also removed and replaced by Amtico tiles, and *God* why can't I stop everything leading back to Elma's barbaric domesticity? I've broken out in a panic and instantly it feels like menopause again, except it's not.

I struggle to moderate the immoderate. As a result, I'm concentrating mentally on my mother's collection of maps, long stored in the old china pantry after she tired of the tiered tea-sets and dinner services gifted to her and Paddy as wedding gifts. Then, the pantry became the place in which pheasants and turkeys hung before Christmas, threads of thin blood hanging from beaks as these gifts arrived from Paddy's grateful patients, along with bottles of whiskey, boxes of cigarettes, and Tullamore Dew. Paddy was generous. He never turned anyone away from his consultation room if money was a problem, and sometimes paid hospital fees on the patient's behalf. He believed in mercy, and that God was merciful to all sinners, which is ironic when I look back. Eventually, Elma's maps began to fill those shelves, though not entirely. It would take a lifetime's travel to fill them, deep and wooden, rising high up white, distempered walls.

I enter the pantry now, pushing open the heavy panelled door with its layers of old, cream-coloured paint. My fingers begin to explore. First European destinations, I note, bought decades before the internet and Google, in a time when the traveller might go to a good bookshop in the city and pick up a map. Torremolinos, Benalmadena, then Granada, Seville and Cordoba. Paddy and Elma became inveterate, three-times-a-year holiday-makers once they got Spain, France and Italy out of their systems. The maps would arrive home in Elma's luggage, every journey inscribed in biro along roads, railways and city tramlines. She was keeping an account, she who did not travel anywhere much before 1975. There was, apparently a lot to account for, judging by the different shades of biro ink. Some roads are inscribed in red, others in green, and yet others in black. I have no doubt that a map was a precious thing for my mother, as paper maps remain for me, me who often feels map-less and disoriented.

I know that figuratively there were no internal maps in the 1960s. The absence of a space in which to spread an idea, a plan, a project was not consciously felt, but its consequences were like a spade digging into people's lives. Some people, finding the project, the plan, could not be fitted to their map-less lives, returned the project to its origin. They were able to reject the thing that could not be slotted into their family, their home, their village. Not Elma. Not Paddy.

As my fingers explore, I withdraw a couple of very battered maps. Syria, Jordan, and the Empty Quarter. Elma was mesmerised by extravagant vastness, the Arab deserts along the Tropic of Cancer. On the other hand, they once took a holiday on a small Greek island, where, according to a scribbled note in the margin of that map, they 'had the time of our lives in bed this afternoon, never better, though no air-con!' Elma was always free with her diary entries.

I lug the maps upstairs to her room. My mother is awake, staring at the ceiling, one arm flung dramatically across her forehead like a heroine in a 1940s movie.

'I'm just admiring that lamp fixture,' she remarks idly. 'Bought it in Capel Street back in the days when Capel Street had class.'

I nod. 'It's an antique,' Elma goes on.

'I've brought you a few maps,' I announce, placing them on the bed.

Elma stirs slowly, the space between her fine eyebrows furrowing slightly. 'Maps? What maps are those?' Her earlier lucidity, the information about having wanted to adopt a four-year old girl rather than a baby, has vanished.

'Your maps, Mum. The ones you collected?'

There is a longueur. My mother's eyes close momentarily, then open again. She starts whirling her right hand agitatedly, as if trying to remember.

'Did I collect maps?'

'You did. They're stacked in the pantry.'

'What are they doing there?'

'You must have put them there.'

'But it's a china pantry.'

'Not anymore, it's mostly a map room,' I shrug.

Another delay as Elma absorbs this information.

'Well I suppose that was clever of me, wasn't it? To collect all those maps?'

'I suppose it was,' I reply. 'They're decades old now.'

'Like me. Many *many* decades.' Elma shuts her eyes again. Suddenly, they shoot wide open and her good eye is in focus. 'I loved maps! I always wanted to remember the places. When I was a child there was nowhere to go. A week near the sea occasionally with your Nana and the other eight of us. In a rented house in Blackrock, outside Dundalk. The tide went out so far I used to think we could walk to Wales. But the places we visited, your Daddy and I, they're a bit of a jumble in my head now. We went everywhere after he retired, holidays three times a year. I enjoyed keeping our plans secret from your aunt Elizabeth. You know how she liked to impose herself. But it never worked out well, and when she did accompany us, she treated your father like an errand boy, carrying her heavy shopping, and all the kelims, wall hangings and copper urns that could be carted back to Ireland.'

I spread a few different maps on the bedspread in an effort to stimulate and amuse her. Slowly, Elma props herself up and I slip in a third pillow behind her shoulders. She is interested in this display.

'Organising wasn't my style, I suppose...' she chuckles. 'Elizabeth would have had all those put into dinky files and locked away, not flung on the shelves of a pantry.'

'She was a businesswoman,' I remark mildly.

'Businesswoman my hat. She ran the health shop and collected the rent on the apartments they built near the ring fort. With no planning permission, I might add. There was a right royal row about that from the heritage crowd, but she got away with it.'

'I guess to aunt Elizabeth ring forts were ten a penny throughout the country,' I say, 'she wasn't going to worry about fairies and the Tuatha de Danann!'

At this, we both giggle and all tension dissolves between us. Then we both stare at a map which shows the archaeological site of Petra. Elma has marked in blue biro the short routes she and Paddy walked to get around on some heat-seared day, she has marked their approach to the high monastery of Ad-Deir. I can see them, Paddy walking slightly ahead as they approach northwest of the city centre, Elma lagging behind but willing to carry on.

'We had some good times together. Only for him I'd never have seen such lovely places. It was him, you know, he made the difference to everything.' She settles back and makes herself more comfortable on her pillows. 'Once we sat on a plane, everything else was forgotten. We were together. Just the two of us. I never gave a thought to home once we went away and that's the truth.'

This is no news to me. Tess's appendix burst while she was in the Donegal Gaeltacht and they were in Egypt. She was rushed by ambulance from the mountainy isolation of Irish college to Letterkenny Hospital. A year later, when I was fifteen, I fell and fractured my skull while on a school hike in the Sperrins. More hospital, but neither of them cut short a holiday in Abu Dhabi. I sometimes think that being a doctor had desensitised Paddy to pain and physical distress, focused as he was most of the time on major operations, removing lengthy strips of diverticular bowel, or checking the indenture below the right lobe of the liver when removing an unhealthy gallbladder and its biliary tree. A phone-call confirmed that my fractured skull was a mere hairline affair, but that I was concussed and would remain under observation for a further 24 hours before being discharged. Yet when I became really sick, a year later, Elma's focus on me escalated. Her watchfulness was oppressive.

At least nowadays Elma does not become maudlin when she recalls Paddy. She has long passed through the kind of grief that involved torrents of tears.

'But you never went to Australia,' I say. 'And I think you missed something there.'

'No.' Her right hand chops the air. 'Australia is too gruff, and too into its family circles and barbecues to have any real culture.

Don't make me laugh. Never had the slightest desire to go when our own country was becoming so modern. I preferred to read Dame Freya Stark and then do the Middle East. Did you know she lived to be a hundred? Very inspirational.' Elma smirks at the idea of Australia, reminding me of a distant cousin who returned from there in the 1970s and was very surprised to see how well she and Paddy were doing, how modern Ireland was becoming.

'Ireland wasn't really modern, Mum. I remember. It was a repressed shithole for young people like me. For women.'

'But things were changing.'

'You had no rights as a woman. Not when you got married. You'd have to give up your job if you got married.'

'Oh don't start that feminist guff. I was married to your father. I had all the rights I wanted or needed.'

*

Downstairs again, I traipse around the kitchen, straighten a few plates on the dresser, check the fridge for milk. I forgot to get milk at the supermarket. Lottie follows me while the cat observes. The first true change between Tess and me began because of a single photograph. Then a letter which accompanied that photograph, posted twenty-five years beforehand, ten years before Paddy's death. I'm at the sink now, scrubbing between my fingers. I feel like Lady Macbeth beset by guilt. The kitchen window is open.

I dry my hands and regard myself in a cracked mirror near the sink. North light infuses the air, revealing unmade-up skin with a concession of mascara. I wear a woolly mauve sweatshirt of a kind I'd never have been seen in, dead or alive, when younger. Now, I don't care. The body beneath it is sound. Still able. Grateful for that. Grateful for so many things. Walking. Swallowing.

Breathing. No urinary incontinence. I can be like one of those women in the TV ad who jumps energetically on a trampoline without leaking. I can still write and publish books. Sometimes I have no back pain or sciatica. Until the recent past, there were blissful, winey holidays with friends in France, long evenings in the depths of western Provence, all the stuff from the books I read in my girlhood. I can balance on one leg for a minute if I want to, which I don't, or walk five miles with only minor suffering in my joints the next day. I can beat Christoph at table-tennis and at University Challenge, especially the questions to do with literature and science.

I'm still considering the photograph and the ensuing letter I wrote to Tess. I wander out to the hall and check for sound from upstairs. Silence.

It's a chance thing, to discover such a photo. Sometimes, time and space collide, and the thing that eludes someone all their life becomes clear. My hand dislodges a photograph album from a box beside the piano which conceals a damp patch on the north facing wall of the dining-room. The chronicle of some kind of past, as if it could be held and remembered, when in actuality neither activity is possible, neither holding nor remembering. I had felt so sure of what I remembered. Yet it comes at me like the kind of blast after a bomb goes off, perhaps.

I see two of us in Dun Laoghaire in 1964. That means Tess was four and I ten. Paddy was to join us at the weekend, which meant the three of us had the first five days to ourselves. We explored the seaside town, we took the hill down past the church towards the Victorian monument, then turned right and on to the promenade, where the evening strollers of South Dublin paraded. Sometimes we turned left and took a stroll out along the East Pier. There were lemon and banana flavoured ice-creams, umbrella-shaped orange lollipops, a sea breeze, playful child voices. Sometimes we caught a bus to the Blackrock Baths, which was where the photograph was taken, presumably by Elma herself.

I recall the days, at first bright, effortless, our mother in good humour. We both wore swimming rings, being typical Irish children who had not learnt to swim when we were young. And even when we had a ring, nobody told us to keep our mouths shut while trying to swim, so there was a lot of spluttering as we floundered contentedly around in the sea-water baths. I loved that swimsuit, because at the age of ten the first swelling of breasts was tingling on my chest. I felt so proud, very grown-up or on my way to being grown-up. Tess was in a ruched dark green swimsuit that tied behind her neck, she too gripping a red and yellow swimming-ring with small, square-topped fingers. Dun Laoghaire glowed in sunshine and a light breeze played with clusters of palm trees in the gardens, there were waves breaking on the prows of yachts with merry red and green sails as they jagged along in the bay. At the start of the holiday I'd been happy. *Over there is Wales, or Cymru*, Elma said, pointing. We peered hard but could see nothing but the thin haze of the distant horizon. Sometimes she offered sparkling pieces of information about the world, about geographical space, which she had read of in childhood during the snatched hours when she was supposed to be peeling potatoes or making beds for her brothers. She told us the name of the first woman in space, Valentina Tereshkova, something which interested me.

Days passed. At the hotel, our mother greeted other guests pleasantly and they greeted her in turn, usually at breakfast each morning, where thinly sliced white toast was served with softly poached eggs and dark coffee in a silver pot, or sugar-sweetened tea for us. Sometimes they admired us, *so well-behaved*, one woman remarked, *and beautifully dressed too, what little dotes.* When Tess enquired one evening whether carrots grow on trees, Elma was briefly embarrassed as the question drew titters at the tables all around, but then she relented and laughed.

At the thought of night-time in Dun Laoghaire, I feel a weight in my chest and stop dead in the hallway. I try to blank out the images. I turn then and mount the stairs, checking the dial of the grandfather clock, which stares back at me. Only eleven o'clock in the morning, it gloats. I feel like kicking it as I pass, but don't. I turn the corner and there stands my ghostly mother, edging and staggering towards the bathroom on her walking aid, naked except for sanitary wear. My heart clutches itself with pity at the sight of her. God help her, I think despite all, God help my darling mother. It no longer startles me to see her like this, with white, dishevelled hair, the unneeded mask dangling off one ear, a twisted back with many collapsed vertebrae, breasts long and loose with purplish nipples. And yet it pains me.

'Ah, you're up!' I say. I can hear the forced brightness in my voice. Then, to tone it down. 'You might as well get dressed.'

'Did you put those maps back where you found them?'

Always amazing what she remembers from moment to moment, and what vanishes.

'I did.'

Elma pauses to consider this. 'I might as well get up, I suppose,' she finally relents. 'There's not a move from the trees. No wind.'

'Let's go into the bathroom then. Your clothes are in there.'

The large bathroom has functioned as a dressing-room for years, with a wall of high presses behind which Elma's trousers, a spectrum of blouses, and about fifty pairs of shoes, are housed. Her feet are painful, the arches fallen, toes crumpled. She can no longer wear any shoes except a stained and ancient pair of grey Ecco extra-wide sandals with Velcro straps.

My mother is making her way slowly towards the chair from which she will be dressed. Her footsteps are so tiny as she creeps forward that I am reminded of the Chinese women whose feet used to be broken, their toe-bones forced and bent beneath the ball of the foot, with only the big toe left for balance. My mother's pain may resemble their foot pain, as they advanced along the pathways, into shrines, or simply to meet their groom. With such pain, they walked when pregnant and heavier than normal. Exhausted, Elma plomps down heavily into the wicker chair.

The incontinence wear must be changed. As I attempt to pull down the padded knickers, Elma grasps my hand. 'No,' she says.

'It's time for a fresh one,' I reply, tugging again. This time they come as far as her knees.

'I — do — not — need — it — changed.'

'But you do, Mum, you do.' I'm speaking softly, so as not to arouse anger, touching her arm. 'Come on now, we can do this quickly. It's no bother.'

'Noooooo!' Elma yanks her arm away, almost unbalancing and falling off the chair.

What ensues is not quite a row, because I do the pouring forth and my mother is eventually quiet, with bowed head. Verbiage, scolding her, *for God's sake* descending to phrases like *for fuck's sake*, and *let me help you!* I'm rougher than I ought to be as I whip down the bulky knickers and Elma cries Ouch! *For heaven's sake I didn't mean to hurt you!* I quickly grasp a fresh pack and, bending, manoeuvre each awkward foot into each opening, before pulling bit by bit up my mother's legs as far as her thighs. My back is straining at the angle, one dodgy lumbar vertebra ever in danger of popping out and creating excruciating pain. I stiffen my back muscles as I take her helpless weight. I need her to stand and support herself with the walking aid again so that I can finally pull the pants around her buttocks securely. 'Please separate your legs or I can't pull it up the full way,' I instruct, feeling myself turn into a monster daughter. By now, Elma complies in silence. She is aware that she has crossed a line, one which she does not and cannot understand, and that for the next few minutes the cacophony will mount as I rant for reasons now bewildering to her. It's not just the struggle to toilet Elma, but the memory that emerges every time my own frustrated resentment spills over into a different resentment. I remember what you did to Tess, I'm shrieking in my head at such times. I saw it. I heard it. You did this and more to the child you adopted. *And you let me look on*. I remember an incident and instead of parcelling it away into a mental cupboard, it clambers out like a lobster that does not want to remain in a vat of boiling water, awaiting the fatal heat that makes it dance in pain.

Dun Laoghaire 1964 again. The three of us in a large, pale green walled bedroom that overlooked the street. A scrollwork of stencilled ivy in darker green ran just below the ceiling. I don't recall the provocation, if an adult can be provoked by a four-year old. Paddy had been delayed, although it was Friday. What I see instead are rapid hand-movements one evening just before dinner, constant whacking, slapping around the shoulders, on the face, on the bottom and legs, much shaking by the shoulders and a brutal hiding that has Tess gulping and screaming uncontrollably as she tries to escape Elma's grasp. Then, a blank. I can't see anything between the beating and the time when, as we descended the curving staircase towards the dining-room that evening, a tall, suited man stopped and murmured something to Elma. Something interrogative. I remember his face but not what he said. The words didn't sound friendly although I couldn't understand them. Nor the face. That only emerged years later, when Elma independently recalled the incident herself, and how embarrassed and ashamed she felt when the man had asked her if everything was alright with the little girl. At least back then she had the feeling in her that allowed for shame. That night, Tess threw up all over the bed, but Elma didn't blame her. I remember the stream of lemon ice-cream, followed on by chewed chicken pieces and bits of potato salad, a swill projecting suddenly all over the bed-spread. My breaking heart. To this day, my breaking heart at such things.

The black and white holiday photograph taken the next day, or perhaps the day after — because I can't recall just when — shows the pair of us, side by side. Little strangers, one the punished, one the silent onlooker, also punished through her witnessing. I wear a wan, pale smile that reveals two lop-sided front teeth as I hold my swimming-ring. There is a rubber swimming cap on my head. Tess's hair is bound in two small ponytails behind each ear. She looks straight to camera, chin tilted slightly upwards. Much later, when I scrutinise the child's face and body, I see a serious child face, eyes watchful as they look without expectation into the camera. In the photograph, there is a shadowing on her legs, the bruises. One arm also seems slightly discoloured.

*

In the end, Elma decides not to get dressed, but agrees to a fresh nightdress and insists on a return to bed. She's used to my outbursts, but perhaps I also exhaust her when I start.

'Here Jimmy, Jimmy,' she calls out to the cat, 'Where are you?'

Yellow-eyed Jimmy appears, blinking balefully at me. My

mother has withdrawn from me, enough to sing the Italian Fascist anthem from the Mussolini era. This she learned as a child when she was befriended by the local Italian family who ran an ice-cream parlour in the town.

Su, compagni in forti schiere,
marciam verso l'avvenire.
Siam falangi audaci e fiere,
pronte a osare, pronte a ardire...

It is relentless. Not the singing itself, which holds an elegant marching musicality as Elma lies propped on three pillows. An old lady who drifts from song to song, who remembers lyrics from the 1940s, words about marching and adventure, is surely charming. As I descend the stairs again, she is still singing, her humour restored.

Having found the photograph, I write an actual paper letter to Tess in New York. *So by today's standards I think you were an abused child. It was criminal. I see that now. Why did Paddy never stop her? Was he weak? I am so sorry, so sorry Tess...*

Tess's reply lands in our post-box ten days later, written in her typically heavy, broadly-inscribed hand. *You'll never know what this has done for me. There was I thinking I was mad, that I'd concocted memories, that some of it was just my mind going crazy. You know, I encounter kids at the hospital, and their speech is severely arrested because of trauma at home. I often have to bring in a psych, if the parents will agree to it. But anyway, I thought I was born crazy. The spirit moved you, that's for sure, if there is a spirit, but something has changed for me. . .such a relief to know I'm not so crazy after all, like the loon I always assumed I was because that's the message I always got from both of them. Even if Paddy loved me. O poor Tess, as Paddy would call me in an indulgent way, but at least he had some feeling for me. With her it was all For God's sake Tess would you think of someone else for a change and not be so selfish? I don't even name-call her, you know. I can't. This is beyond name-calling.*

Witness. Bearing witness. To have witnesses? The problem with witnesses is that sometimes, they arrive too late. Fear silences people. Sometimes, stupidity. Hitler flowered like the black stain on history's soul. So too Mussolini, renowned for forcing purgatives down the throats of those who threatened him, so too, Franco. Idi Amin and Robert Mugabe. Cannibalism, death by gassing, death by starvation, death by beating. Auschwitz, Sobibór, Belzec, Treblinka, Chelmno.

To see one thing, a photograph, but ignore so much else. The truth unrolls like a filthy sheet, the stains hanging before me in the dark, and there's this suffering — bloody and bare as an ancient shroud in its threadbare yet undeniable imprint.

I need to tell the story to myself, to calm me, below again in the kitchen. But not yet, not just yet.

5

Tess has been delayed. Elma isn't concerned and even looks a little surprised to see me.

'Oh. You're here. When did you arrive?'

'Weeks ago.'

She shakes her head and rolls her eyes. 'Of course. I'm dreaming! That head of mine!'

As I prepare small grilled steaks with fried mushrooms and onions, the annoyance about Tess's non-appearance runs off me. Not that it exactly evaporates, but like water off a duck's back it lingers in the emotional liquid I float in. *You'll feel better when you've eaten,* I comfort myself, realising I'm starving and have a growling belly. I shove a supermarket pack of potatoes *au gratin* in the oven. The shining mushrooms wobble in the pan, gradually shrinking in the frying butter and salt.

*

Shrooms everywhere in the damp and humid tufts of grass, beneath the elms and oaks. Tess knew them, how to turn over the golden tops and liberty caps, ate them fresh, not dried. She was all haste to ingest the magic, to get away, to feel drowsy and introspective in a good way. They never made her psychotic. They might have done, but nobody noticed. It was one of the things we shared later on, when she was fourteen and I was twenty and going off my head over a man who'd tossed me aside like a broken doll. One of my mid-70s disco conquests, all kisses and dreams himself, but only interested in hunting with hounds and selling bloodstock into Europe. Once, when I was snivelling in my room, writing secret messages to myself about him in shorthand on the back of my David Bowie album *Aladdin Sane,* Tess came in. She stood at a distance, watching, absorbing. But you never cry, she said, puzzled. And it was true, even then. I would hold the tears for my private, dark spaces, and nobody got to see. Except for this time. Now you know I do, I sniffled. Tess crossed the room, one hand in her jacket pocket. She was still damp from the rain, she smelt of fields and freshness. She thrust her hand out and opened her palm. There they were, broken but still fresh, a sacred manna from the field gods, an offering. And then she hugged me.

I tried them. How wonderful they were. First time. I'd had first time sex but was immediately abandoned. Now I was having first time shrooms and in a peculiar way that was infinitely better. The release of it, real release from pain, the patterns on the bedroom wallpaper now making sense way beyond my mother's decor choices, the curve of those flowers tethering me, the layering of some original artist's paint in a workshop, far, far, back beyond even William Morris's bramble patterns. I could see it now laid bare, how beautiful the world was and could be. Would be.

The effect lasted a few hours. During it, Tess and I sat at

Elma's new cassette-recorder, playing and replaying Bowie and Kraftwerk, then Otis Redding and after that the Jacques Loussier Trio's version of the Brandenburg Concerto. We scarcely spoke, and nodded gently towards one another as each new track appeared. We both held secrets and guarded ourselves from stuff we couldn't talk about. Now Tess knew something more about me, her mysterious big sister, and the gap between us closed a little. There were times when she gave to me and I gave to her, in the broken graces between us.

About eleven years into our marriage — when Christoph and I were trying to build some financial security — I'd decided to try my luck with savings of three thousand pounds on the stock-market. Paddy had given me the money to help furnish our home. After three months, a stroke of beginners' luck saw me double our money. Take it out now, Christoph said, please withdraw it and get off that scene. I withdrew two thousand five hundred but left the balance, then splurged on a new but battered-looking soft leather sofa, an antique pine table and, for me, a Vivienne Westwood trouser-suit. Typical of him, wise and careful, to warn me. And typical of me, less careful, more like Elma, I admit, doing what I thought was best. What *I* wanted, regardless of him. The shares plummeted. By the time I got the paperwork sorted precisely fifty-five pounds was returned to my bank account. Christoph, fuming, demanded to see letters, statements, memos, as I tried to bluff and slither out of the responsibility. That night, he moved out to the spare bedroom and slept on a futon that was too firm, too low for his bulk, and surrounded himself with Goethe's *Die Leiden des Jungen Werther* or *The Sorrows of Young Werther*. I actually *heard* him read aloud. Our walls were thin, I lay in the next bedroom only to hear him droning about *Meine Sinnen verwirren sich, schon acht Tage habe ich keine Besinnungskraft mehr, meine Augen sind voll Tränen.* Well Christoph, I thought a little cynically, your senses might be in a storm, but really? Goethe wasn't the solution. Perhaps he needed to escape me, to touch base with his own culture, with the giant literary root of it that had always, always inspired him.

When Christoph and I were sleeping apart for those few weeks as he punished me and we both steamed with anxiety and anger, I took a day away from the typewriter and headed for the city. With so much emotional uncertainty in the air, I couldn't concentrate on my writing. A dress in a vintage shop caught my eye, a 1930s silk satin dress in sea green, with a square neck, and cut on the bias so that the garment glided over my body, catching it in just the right places — breasts and buttocks. It also helped show off my collarbones, with just a hint of cleavage. I gazed at myself in the shop mirror, surrounded by old hats, handbags, paste jewellery and the faded sparkle of the past. I liked what I saw. With barely enough cash for the lunch I'd planned on that getaway-from-reality day, I dreamed bitterly and self-pityingly through the side streets of Dublin, wandering through off-beat Drury Street, Clarendon Street, to the magical narrow run of Johnston's Court and its antique jewellers, then finally, to Grafton Street. On Grafton, the shoppers were as usual, languorous, self-possessed, some of them expensive-looking, mingling with students from Trinity College down the road. Finally, I settled in a café on Dawson Street, over Hodges Figgis bookshop, and consoled myself with strong creamy coffee and a fat slice of raspberry roulade with extra cream. Afterwards, I cynically scanned all the self-help books — Turn Your Life Around, Finding Power after Menopause, and Are you Afraid to Love?, then purchased something that appealed to my frame of mind, an Irish novel about a psychotic murderer, the author of which at first denied having based it on real life but which no reader for a moment believed, nor did they care, because it was a wonderful, horrific story.

The following weekend, on a chilly summer evening, Tess visited. We sat on the luxuriously bohemian leather sofa in our sitting room while Christoph worked in his study, a little less silent with me, though still resentful. I happened to mention the dress and how I'd fallen in love with a garment, and wasn't that so trivial of me, in the circumstances?

'Don't be beating yourself up,' she said, exhaling cigarette smoke. By now, I was smoking one of her cigarettes too. We relaxed together in front of the small wood fire. I said nothing and we sat and gazed out the window towards the Galtees, as the sun began its slow descent into a long twilight.

'I should beat myself up. I've lost our money,' I replied 'I earn next to nothing on my royalties. I've no readings or talks lined up, not until September.' Close to tears, I wondered if I was crazy to have written my first novel, which, for all the publicity it had accrued, hadn't translated into hard cash, despite that dazzling label 'erotic' which a radio presenter had attached to it, which at least ensured copies flowed out of the bookshops for a couple of weeks, making it number three on the bestsellers list.

'Sounds like guilt,' she remarked noncommittally. 'You need to get over that.'

I said nothing, then, 'I hate never having enough money, that's the truth.'

'Whatever. Nothing you can do about that. You're a writer and Christoph's a teacher. But sure, I'll give you the money for the dress.'

It was so sweet of her. I still have the dress. It hangs in my wardrobe at home, still worn only on occasion, when I want to look vampish and Germanic.

When 'the knowledge' tumbled out years later during Tess's rehab at Forest Glen clinic, both Elma and Paddy were aghast about the mushrooms. They stared at me, me who had never given them the remotest cause for anxiety — apart from being ill and raising Elma's natural anxiety to stratospheric levels.

'No wonder those boys from the nearby seminary were forever in our fields,' Elma had tutted. 'It wasn't just the apples in the orchard they were after. And you're *smoking,* Tess! Since when did you smoke?'

The smoking seemed an even greater shock than the magic mushrooms for our mother, perhaps because smoking seemed ordinary and she missed it. Paddy shook his head and wondered where he'd gone wrong to have reared such a strange child as Tess, and to think that their own land had helped to sustain a drug addict! The counsellor intervened at that point and redirected a question at him. Was there, she asked, another way of viewing the situation? He was after all a health professional, she added. Surely such things were known to him? Paddy stared at her, puzzled, his lips in a resentful tight line. In his own hierarchical way, he resisted engaging with a counsellor.

*

It takes half an hour to get Elma up out of bed. The preparation of the meal must be staggered in such a way that food is not spoiled or burned in the longeurs prior to her arrival downstairs.

As the chair-lift hums its way down, Elma is singing about an old woman who was tossed up in a blanket, and Lottie, excited, barks from the hallway.

There was an old woman tossed up in a blanket,
Ninety-nine times as high as the moon,
And where she was going I couldn't but ask it,
For in her hand she carried a broom.

Old woman! old woman! old woman! quoth I,
Oh whither, oh whither, oh whither so high.'
'To sweep the cobwebs off the sky,
and I'll be with you again, by and by.'

To the air of *Lillibulero,* Elma's voice not strong enough to march it out, like the English had sung it once to mock the arrival of transferred Irish regiments. Instead, the words came slowly, lingeringly. Elma is remembering something tender from her own past. Her father used to sing this, she often tells me, often when he was towelling her and her brothers bone dry before the open fire after their weekly bath. He was terrified of damp and cold, all his brothers having died from TB.

I return to the kitchen as my mother moves from chair-lift to a second walking frame, placed strategically where she can easily grasp it. She makes her way into the kitchen, centimetre by centimetre. The tiny-toed Chinese effect. Hobble, hobble, shuffle, stop. Hobble, hobble, shuffle, stop. She is breathless but keeps going. Determined to help herself, to not be a bother to anyone. She believes she is no bother. She believes she is physically independent, queen of all she surveys.

These days I cut all meats in small pieces for her. I also cut my own meat in tiny squares for the sake of appearances and so as not to humiliate my mother, who dislikes any pandering to her infirmity. She ignores the cutlery sometimes, lifting the pieces of meat in her hands, pulling at them until she has had enough. She is still in control, after all. She slurps her soup and smacks at her cream-laden desserts. I, who find loud eating and masticating almost unbearable — there's even a word for it I discovered recently, *Misophonia* — am sometimes driven to wicked thoughts about putting an end to things. As in, killing my mother just because she eats noisily. Scrambled eggs and a crushed light-bulb would sort it out. Do the health people have the slightest idea of the danger old people unwittingly face at the hands of their own adult children? I've considered fiddling with her meds, since she doesn't count her pills. Sometimes I omit the blood-thinners, the blood-pressure tablet, and the little Nuprin prescribed by the hospital doctor after she fell down the stairs. But nothing changes. My mother's blood does not clot. Her heart beats on. She cannot cut her own meat or eat without dribbling. None of that matters. It is entirely her right to do all those things.

We chat in a desultory manner at the table. When Elma starts to remember something from the past it unlocks her speech, and I listen. I no longer say mean things like 'So you said,' or 'You told me that yesterday,' because there is no point and Elma cannot help remembering or not remembering. She has set her own mental camera, the F-stop focusing sharply on specific details from the past. Some part of me acknowledges this, tries to recall the good things. Like Elma's cooking. There were good things, but they do not accrue the same importance as the other elements, what my mother confessed to me some twenty years before about her handling of Tess. I sit up straight. I'd rather not remember that now. Instead, I turn to the small television on the dresser where Michael Portillo is taking a train ride to King's Lynn. We speculate idly on his sexual orientation.

'Those orange trousers. And the pink jacket?' Elma says.

'Part of the image.'

'What image?'

'Famous people like to have something the public will associate them with. Clashing colours in his case.'

'I doubt it. Gay, I'd say.'

'Who cares?' I reply.

Elma speculates, 'I personally believe many suicides are because those poor young men are gay and have no one to talk to.'

'It's not so bad nowadays. I mean, speaking out. Getting heard. Though it could be better.'

'Hmm. I try not to think about what they do to one another. As you know, I believe that marriage is for a man and a woman, nobody else,' Elma muses, keeping her eye on Portillo as he springs lightly from a train and greets his beaming host for the day. 'But I do know one thing and that's that I loved your father. Paddy was everything to me. Everything. That man lifted me up and made me something.'

I try to concentrate. This will go on for a while.

'When I first met him I was going out with another fella, Jack Cassidy, a smart fly-by-night who thought he was on to a good thing with me. And he said to me, because he had no car, but your father had, we'll get Paddy Esmond to drive us to the cinema. He's going himself. And some instinct in me made me think, Cassidy you're a user, you're no good, and I'm no longer interested in you. The next day I dropped him, and wasn't I right? Cassidy took it badly. He asked me to say it was broken off by mutual consent.' She pauses. 'Nose on him like a pike too, hah! Your Nana was raging. Couldn't wait to get me out the door and married, you know. I was a good enough child and young person. But when I gave up the nursing training and came home to them, she wanted me out.'

She laughs at the memory. I laugh with her, waiting for the

tale to continue. How normal she sounds, remembering her own youth. Her past is over-crowded by brothers, by two uncles and a granny also living in the same three-storied house in the town. The dominating note is one of masculine needs. It is no accident that my mother remembers Mussolini's anthem by heart. And had she been born in Germany and not Emergency Ireland, it's easy to imagine little Elma, a fair-haired child with plaits, in a brown jacket and the insignia of the Bund Deutscher Mädel.

After the meal I ask her if she would like to use the small bathroom just off the kitchen. No, she replies scornfully, as if to say why on earth would you ask me that? Already she is hobbling off towards the sitting-room, where the television is blaring and will be turned to Emmerdale and an evening of ITV programming. She will sit in her incontinence wear, those bulky knickers and the lining pad, as urine leaks all evening but even so she will resist the bathroom. When she stands up to go to bed, when I haul her to her feet because she cannot raise herself off her sofa, her trousers will be damp.

'Have you been speaking to Bernard?' Elma calls back as she struggles into the hallway.

'Bernard?'

'Your *husband*? Bernard!' she gasps.

'His name is Christoph.'

'Oh, there I go. I was thinking of that chap Tess used to see. Or maybe I'm thinking of Martin Bormann from the war, and how we loved to listen to Lord Haw Haw's broadcasts. Made our evenings when we'd sit around the kitchen fire,' she titters. 'Anyway, you know, that nice man, the one who fell into the Danube. Bernard, wasn't that his name? Of course, if Tess had been with him, his fate would have been different. It wouldn't have happened. And little Alison? How is she without her

Daddy? Bernard or whoever he was?'

'Her name is Allegra,' I say evenly. 'She celebrated her twenty-fourth birthday ten days ago. Tess and Bernard divorced ten years ago and he drowned swimming in the Danube eight years ago. He did not fall in or throw himself in as you keep saying. Allegra is fine and still in college. Remember now?'

'There I go again, mixing them all up. I can't keep up with your generation. Well anyway, I hope Tess is safe in that apartment in New York.'

'Safe as houses.'

'But living with a fella, isn't she? Not a boyfriend.'

'A room-mate. Allegra no longer lives with her so she rents out the room.'

'A room*mate*? What's that when it's at home?'

'He's a doctor in the same hospital.'

'Oh.'

'It's an arrangement. Rent sharing.'

'You mean they're sharing a room and they're not dating?'

'They have separate rooms, Mum, and he has a girlfriend of his own. It's New York and not everybody is a rapist. It's rental income for Tess.'

Elma gives a little shoulder twitch. 'Even so,' she says hopefully, 'he's a doctor. That's something I suppose.'

Tess never expected to become pregnant with Allegra. After years of trying, she'd stopped using contraception while continuing to have sex. The man she was with back then was one of the constant ones, with a closely trimmed head of dark curls and round tortoise-shell spectacles. He invited her to his parents' summerhouse in the Hamptons, introduced her to sailing during one long summer when Tess used to occasionally phone home. One morning, when her man was planning a beach jog, something made her drag him back into the bed again and they had sex. A month later, she was pregnant. She knew it the moment she found he was beating her for the first time in their regular game of tennis. She felt weak and almost out of her own body but with an unspecific ailment. That was now nature worked, with post-post-modern slickness, primed, smooth, unquenchably attentive to chance.

I could never face the prospect of having children. It wasn't that we couldn't have them. We could have. But I was afraid of it. Afraid of history repeating itself, afraid that I had ingested too much of Elma not to have internalised her behaviour. And so, the one time I became pregnant by accident, I went to London for an abortion. It was a time when such an action was a criminal offence in Ireland. I never regretted it. I am puzzled by the women who say they are traumatised by their abortion. To be traumatised by it, and not liberated, is to me incomprehensible. To feel trauma, the foundations must be deep and historic, where the traumatised person has or has had no control of their life.

*

After dinner I remember a call I'm supposed to make. I'm mentoring a new writer, Jason Bergman. I message him and wait. *Emmerdale* has begun on the kitchen television and two blonde women are at one another's throats, a frightened child is looking on from a door opening, and in the pub the female vicar is flirting with a farmer half her age. Then, a swift reply. *Yes. Just thinking about the book actually. Quite nervous about publication!* Me, then. *It's all in hand. I wanted to ask you more about that section you sent.* Again, like lightning. *Shoot. I'll give you a video call.*

I have questions for Jason, because so far, I don't fully trust his account of himself in his own story. Though, does that matter, I wonder? Any account is likely to be flexible once memory is involved.

Before daily life changed, I'd arranged to meet him in person in Dublin. The sight of Jason did me good, still does me good. I've mentioned this to Christoph, also to one or two female friends, as if this imparting confers innocent interest. A man in my position couldn't say the same about a young female whose work he was editing. The national agenda, in its attempts to cleanse society of misogyny, has worked hard to suppress all forms of flirtation. Now, there are no grey areas, no equivocations, no winks, nods, or good-humoured gropings to be slapped away. One mouthy poet's social media post referred to another better-known poet as the Harvey Weinstein of Irish Letters because he'd invited a female student from his university workshop to go to bed with him for a few hours. Horrors. But I could do this unproblematically if I wished. It is, after all, my right as a free and sexual woman. However, and in the first place, I'm not having an affair with Jason. Secondly, he is not remotely aware of me as a female because I'm old enough to be his mother. Thirdly, I believe myself to be in control of my feelings about everyone and everything in life, except my mother and sister. I can't think of a fourth reason.

Before Jason's call, I rummage in my handbag for my YSL lipstick. I apply a quick slick to brighten an evening-tired face, left to right on both lips, then I rummage for the small perfume spray also inhabiting the depths of the bag. Perfume? He can't smell me. But even online there's a place for perfume, which in my view makes people behave better.

At the kitchen table, I open the laptop and the call comes. Click, expand screen. There he is, staring at me. Looks happy to see me, wide eyes and a wide smile too. I mean, eyes and mouth match. They're both smiling. He's glad to have me cast my critical eye over the work and improve it with him. That we get along well is a bonus, and until recently I was happy to enjoy the occasional coffee with him as we'd tussle over phrases and misappropriations.

'Hey'.

'Hey,' he answers. Then, 'Ready, yeah?'

Not so quick, not so quick, I think, wanting to decelerate. I note that he's not at home. Not isolated.

'Where the hell are you?'

'Donnybrook. Outside a shut café.'

I say nothing for a moment. 'I can hear cups clattering,' I insist.

'That's because we self-starters like to get out and take our socially distanced coffees in the open. I brought my own mug. Chill, Frankie?'

I say nothing

'I had to get out,' he says apologetically. 'I'm sanitised, y'know? Haven't touched anything except this laptop. Wiped the table with antiseptic before I so much as touched it.'

'You're freaking me out Jason.'

'Ah go on, I'm not!'

'You bloody are.'

'I'll be careful. I'll stay home after this. Promise.'

As if I was his mother, and he the son.

'So. How are you?' I enquire, leaning back in my chair.

'Grand. The finishing post seems a long way off.'

'It'll happen. It always does, you know.'

'Yeah but will the book come out? I mean isn't everybody panicking?'

'Is that what they've told you?'

'No.'

'My understanding is that we'll still have an autumn launch. With or without actual bodies breathing all over one another, It may be online, right?' In my gut I know there will be no more book-launches à la mode for a while, with sweaty, boozy, enthusiastic bodies crammed and clamouring in one of the big city bookstores.

'I just want to get it out. Virtual is fine.'

It's a good book for the market, approaching final polish and rendering. Another fine work from another fine author who might be asked, if interviewed, about Irish identity, about whether he considers himself to be an Irish author or a European author or a half-Swedish author and what this means. What does Europe bring to Ireland? What does Ireland bring to Europe? Is he influenced by Scandinavian writing? To be an Irish author, I've come to realise from years of floating around the scene and launching my own titles, is to consider oneself special in the world of books, whether or not this is true. It is to believe that Irish + author = mystic-Celt-with-insights and the burden of the repressed past still riding you like a succubus. It is also the burden of active misogyny, but it's all burden, burden, burden. God help Jason, I'm thinking. He has no idea what's ahead of him and how his startling baroque landscape could be misunderstood.

On the other hand, he's a young man and young men are due their time in the sun again. It's been a period of women basking and even welcomed by the stalwarts of the literary community. I know. I too have benefited. But tides always turn. All going to plan, the literary world should open its portals to him. But first things first. Jason, who is smokingly, cinderingly, social and civil, still hasn't delivered the final revisions. This is the man whose vision of a novel had him wandering the backstreets of Bucharest, searching for excitement, adventure, but also perhaps something a few leagues deeper in the ocean we call experience.

I watch in silence, setting my face to a disinterested neutral expression. For a blonde man Jason is a cool fox, but I don't want to look like a grinning fool.

'I had to move through the country, looking. My notebooks were crammed with new passages and ideas when I got back home,' he says

'What were you looking for? Or do you know?'

His eyes flash at me. 'Isn't it obvious to you at this stage? Looking for The One.' Pause. 'The One!'

My turn to pause now. 'Er, do you mean something like love? A meaningful encounter?'

He inhales slowly and closes his eyes, before opening them again and gazing into the distance. 'That too. But I have a story. You can see that, right? It's not all love, love, love.'

Like all good writers, he's fixated on his own work. He's a Narcissus, gazing at his own beauty in the water, his inner beauty. But none of this interests me. No, that is untrue. It interests me as stories go, the idea of a guy who may be imaginative to the point of delusional, on the loose in post-Ceaușescu's Romania, with little enough money but enough to keep him going as he moves through the country villages living on his wits, scribbling observations, making small illustrative line drawings of bridges and rivers.

'Did you find what you were looking for then?'

'Eh, actually I did find something close to it,' he replies eventually.

'Eastern Romania, right?

'Yup. Jurilovca. A fishing village. Unreal. But too hot for me.

I used tube after tube of sun-protection.'

'What?'

'Can't you see I've practically got albinism.'

'Ridiculous. You're fair, that's true, but —'

'I don't like open sunlight. So I slip-slap-slop the sunblock?'

If anything, he's a hypochondriac. 'Tell me about Jurilovca. Would I like it?'

He talks about the traditional houses. Fishermen on the Danube delta. Local music. An ancient settlement. How he spent more time out at night than during the day on account of the fierce sunlight.

'I don't do that very much in Ireland for some reason.'

'What? Go on the razzle?'

'If you want to call it that.' His expression is amused in a slightly superior way. He smiles, tolerating the word razzle.

'So, what do you do here?' I know I'm wandering off the subject, but a little digging into his private life might throw up some connections.

He starts to talk about the girlfriend he met just over a month ago, who now lives with him in his four-bed Ringsend house which he has all to himself. They're not getting along, he adds. But that's not what I want to discuss and now I'm in that odd situation of trying not to think about the girlfriend at all, about the fact that Jason is in a relationship.

'I might as well admit I'm not all that keen on the pointedly gothic elements of your book. Why did you set it in Romania, for example?'

'It's not that gothic,' he smiles in a surprised way. 'And it's a bit late to rethink the location!'

'But why Romania?'

He hesitates and looks sheepish. 'I suppose I'd been there. I knew parts of the country.'

'But surely you could throw in some sense of modern Romania and cut some of the quainter touches? This is a country that produces doctors, academics, great artists, it has an educated middle class. There's more to it than meets the eye.'

I've annoyed him. He says nothing for a moment, then starts up again. 'People call anything and everything gothic nowadays. They just throw that word around as if it's cool. All you have to do is piss in a doorway at night and some arsehole will call it a gothic event down a dark alley,' he scoffs.

'All I'm saying is that you need to get your protagonist Oscar out of Jurilovca and maybe heighten some of the other elements of this country and his experiences there.'

'Oisín! He's called Oisín!' Jason snaps, and for the first time his pallor has gone and his cheeks have pinked up in anger.

'Oh, I'm sorry. Of course I know his name. Slip of the tongue.'

We sit a moment, neither of us speaking. I am digesting his justifiable anger, and I don't know what exactly he's digesting but it's surely something.

Looking into the screen at Jason, with his thick, wavy and very blond hair, dense brows and pale, untainted skin, my mind wanders and I imagine myself thirty years younger, or that I have a picture in the attic which tracks my age while below in the everyday world I play and learn and understand how a whole new generation thinks and feels. I wonder if Jason tints his eyelashes and eyebrows, because unlike most very fair people, his blue eyes have definition, indeed the lashes are long and thick, but brown. Under a battered black leather jacket, as far as I can see, an indigo blue linen shirt droops towards his collarbone, site of passion, site of tenderly laid kisses is what I'm thinking. I really am an old luster. There are no nice, gentle, accepting, non-comedic words to describe older women who occasionally want to go a level younger. Hag, crone, bint, battleaxe, cougar, hormonal. Frustrated. Matron. No beauty to be found, apparently, in the ember desires of age. But what do I care at this stage? The world thinks it knows all about women, when it grasps nothing of our natures, or that there are skilled men — a few — who do comprehend this. I pause to wonder why I'm even considering this question.

'Maybe have another look at chapter seven and the night where your Oisín is in bed with that woman Ana?' I try to keep judgement out of my voice.

'I'll do my best,' he replies.

'I take it this is a fictional account of a sexual encounter?'

'Does it matter?' He frowns.

Am I his mother, for fuck's sake? 'I guess not, sorry I asked. But I think you need to sharpen the writing. By which I mean make it more accessible. Make it palatable. People like stories,' I emphasise.

'I'll do my best,' he repeats. Then, entirely unrelated, 'I'm not feeling the best lately. Nothing to do with the virus by the way.'

'What's up?' I'm uninterested and not about to entertain a health melodrama. He really is a hypochondriac.

'The doctor doesn't know yet. I got tested.'

'When will you know?' Nor do I wish to enquire as to the nature of the tests. Between Elma's, and my own, and the knowledge that most people don't give a shit about anyone else's health outside their own cosy circle, I no longer enquire with any sincerity. People in my world speak about postmodern and post-postmodern. In that spirit, I am a post-post-hormonal hag.

'Maybe next week. I get a lot of pain these days.'

'What kind of pain? Have you a temperature?' For chrissakes

stop acting like his mother.

'Bone pain, I suppose. Best way to describe it.'

'Take paracetamol.'

His eyes are averted from the screen. He is thinking of something he would like to say, but dares not.

'Anyway. . .' I shrug.

Suddenly, he comes to. 'You think I can rescue the book?'

'I can't believe you're even asking that. Of course we, no, *you*, can do it. Idiot.'

There is another protracted silence between us, him looking at me and me looking at him.

'I'm delighted to be working with you,' he says.

This is unexpected.

'It's a brilliant book.' I want him to feel encouraged. His face breaks once more into a happy smile, the kind that only young people can pull off spontaneously, showing orthodontised white teeth, the fine nose with the skin tight across the bone. He scratches his head.

'Ah Jaysus,' he jokes, 'I didn't know you really thought that.'

6

Elma is still sitting where I left her, on raised cushions, the walking aid pushed aside. She is watching television without seeming to follow the plot of anything. She follows movement. Colour. Big wins in a game show with lots of noise and clattering coins coming down a chute. It wasn't always like this.

I pick up the Weekend section of a newspaper and attempt to concentrate on one of the columnists. Formerly routine topics have vanished from the pages, among them starvation in Syria, Armenians being murdered, misogyny, equality and #MeToo. They are replaced almost uniformly by accounts of Covid 19 and what is to happen to the economy and to schoolchildren. In some countries there are packed container-loads of citizens' bodies because the morgues are full. What happens in the care homes anywhere is a mystery that will provoke tribunals in the future. Some of the people who own them are business people, and advertisements offer 'a home away from home' and 'a boutique vibe'. But a boutique vibe isn't much use when you're sat in wet underwear and can't talk, when your swallow has weakened, when you can't manage your own hearing aids.

Thoughts intrude. How do I feel about the house now? It was always easily identified from the north road below. People would say, *So you live in that house on the hill?* And *Oh yes, the house with the tower, the county surgeon's house.* At the foot of the long avenue, rounded white stone pillars with black capstones and a white iron gate. Then the rumpling, gravelled avenue of leaning oaks and laurel hedges, a few larches, some unhedged sections pitted with burrows and the entrance to a badger set. The house, arrived at after a final upwards sweep and a lilac-edged lawn, sat happy as a woman in wide skirts. My mother's house really, because she made it hers in so many ways with touches both beautiful and philistine. For years, Elma hated the house, which was too far from the town. She refused to cycle like women from further out the country who would regularly pump along on the far side of the lake on their way to town, wicker shopping baskets at the front of big, high bikes.

I scan the view from the window. If the house was a poem it could speak of losses, absences. The gate pillars at the entrance are long gone, replaced by a curving, white, pebble-dashed wall and modern pebble-dashed gate-pillars between which a pair of black wrought-iron gates are permanently and lopsidedly open. Four long downstairs front windows were ripped out in the late 60s and replaced by two huge bowed front windows. It was an attempt at a chateau on Elma's part, I imagine, a well-meant move to create something more out of a rambling old dwelling. People did admire the windows, although they were all wrong for the architecture of the house. The glass winked in the evening light, especially in winter during the hard frosts and big snows of those years. I used to think of Louis MacNeice's lines from his poem 'Snow'.

> *The room was suddenly rich and the great bay-window was*
> *Spawning snow and pink roses against it,*

By the time I was ten or so, I was spending an hour a night staring up at the stars. What do you want to be, people sometimes asked me in front of Elma. I want to be a meteorologist, I would reply shyly. But I was silent with most adults. I liked to read, head down in a book while the adults talked, though often I listened to their mysterious chat.

*

'Would youse stop fightin', stop fightin,' I hear my own voice one day, home from school for dinner as the parents go at it over the kitchen table like dogs, snapping and snarling in argument. My sister sits beside me, crying because Elma has struck her on the face for giving cheek. My father has just witnessed this and for once is barking mad and telling her she goes too hard on the child. Tess is four and I am almost ten. I try again to speak. *Stop fightin' would youse,* But they don't hear me. I push my plate away and say nothing as Elma now shrieks at me to finish that dinner, *there are children starving in Africa, do you know that Miss? Finish it! Finish the damn thing!* I force one more mouthful of mashed potato into my mouth, then gag. *Oh for God's sake don't tell me you're starting that carry-on again! Potatoes? Good mashed potatoes? What's wrong with you?* I throw up then, a glutinous mess of potato, peas, carrots and pieces of meat all over the dinner-plate, dripping onto the blue table-cloth. *Get out of my sight while I clean up this pracas!* Then, my father's voice again,

deep, more gentle now. He catches her by the wrist and holds it. *Enough Elma. Take it easy. Can't you see the child is upset*? Too little from Paddy, so often too late.

Aged eight, I listen to tales of Elma's childhood. She was a sensitive child, and although she says this self-referentially and continually, I know it's true.

'Your Nana got me to help her in the house from the age of seven,' she tells me once when I object to helping her with drying the dishes after tea. I'm eleven. 'She had me upstairs at the top of the house changing sheets and making beds, even though we had a maid. But she wasn't going to spoil me, she used to say.'

'She was cross,' I reply.

'She meant well. Maybe she meant well.'

'Well did Uncle Stephen have to make the beds? Did he help with the washup?' I ask defiantly.

Elma shakes her head. 'Never. No, never. The boys had it handy, like most boys back then.'

This, I remember, is on the exact day Elma has told me about periods, so I believe us to be on an equal footing, like two women together in the world. She's advanced for her generation, informing me in good time about the blood I would see one of these months. I'm quite physically developed, she announces, so she wants me to be prepared.

'Did Nana tell you about. . .about that?' I ask hesitantly.

'You must be joking,' she replies with a touch of regret. 'No, I had to find out from other girls at school. And the science teacher Sister Eucharia mentioned it in a roundabout way. Something to do with the human life cycle. My periods didn't come until I was fourteen. I was a wee one really, a slow developer'.

I'm enjoying this intimacy. Just the two of us. She's at her best when she has a chance to be liberal. Tess is out on her own with her small pony, walking it up and down the low field, Paddy at work.

'When my period comes, does the blood stop at night?'

Elma scrutinises me, amused. 'At night? What do you mean?'

'Does it stop when I lie down in bed?'

She laughs at this, then hugs me unexpectedly. 'No pet, once your periods come, they're with you for four or five days. And nights. For a long time. All it means is that you're a woman.'

Pleased though I am at Elma talking about me being a woman, I don't much like the sound of this. I wipe all thoughts of periods out of my mind there and then, happy to still be a tall, leggy child with no women's problems to deal with. I return to thoughts of her brothers and one sister. It seems as if Elma was sometimes dealt the unfair card, as if people picked on her. Brothers favoured. Smaller sister Elizabeth favoured just because she was smaller and the baby in the family. Nuns taking spite on her alone because she was giddy and wouldn't listen. Nuns criticising her clothes, which were good quality, always fashionable. Cross, busy voices in her home as pigs were driven up the yard to the slaughter-house before being prepared for export to Birkenhead during the Emergency. The English had little meat. Elma's father prospered right through the war. But Elma tells me also of being skelped by a thin branch from the garden beyond the yard, and how her own mother, Nana, was able to hold anger all the way up the garden to pluck just the right, stinging branch and return to their kitchen to lay into Elma, or one of her brothers. But usually Elma.

Good old Philip Larkin has the hang of it with fuck-you-up Mums and Dads who hand on every fault they had *and add one extra, just for you.* Sometimes, Paddy and Elma do a silly-sweet thing in front of us, she perched in his lap, lounging in his arms when they forget we are present, or perhaps don't care, and she pretends to pull his thinning hair as he grips her and tickles her. She loves that. Attention. But at other times they're at one another's throats as if blaming is a solution.

*

After Tess's arrival, I grow wilfully silent. At four, I could perform in front of Elma's tea-glugging, bun-guzzling women friends, could hold my hands obligingly in front of my tummy, one clasped within the other, and sing in my pretty dress, Doris Day's *Que sera, sera.* I could sing. Then, I wasn't shy. But later, no more singing. Nor will I smile for the local photographer, invited to the house to do a formal family photograph. He is one of those men who tells all children to *Watch the birdie, watch the little birdie!* to entice them to smile. There we are in the rectangular, mottled silver frame, like any family. Paddy on the left, Elma on the right, with me in the middle and Tess on Elma's knee. Behind them, the loaded book-cases of the big dining-room. Paddy and Elma smile, both still in their thirties. I decide that I will *not* smile under any circumstances, and say so to Elma. Power. Elma loves smiles. Neither is Tess smiling. She is a small, serious-faced toddler with short-cut, still unpermed hair, staring at the camera, a small rubber duck held between her hands.

Silence deepens at school, depending on the teacher. Fourth class and Mrs Bunty McGrory, a little wasp of a woman. The Bishop arrives to examine the class in their catechism prior to Confirmation. He is an elderly man, known for occasionally hectoring sermons from the pulpit. Bishop McMahon, tall and aged, sweeps in. He moves along the rows, pausing in front of some girls, ignoring others. He stops in front of me.

'*Dia dhuit!* And what's your name?'

'Frankie.'

'I see.' He tilts himself up and down on the balls of his feet. 'I know your Mammy and Daddy. Sure didn't I marry them! And your Daddy's a Wexford man?'

'Yes, your Lordship.' I don't actually know who married them, but Paddy is from Wexford, and travelled long ago, I think, in the freezing winter of '47, from the rich fields of South Leinster northwards to our poorly drained hills. That's how he would describe it to me when telling of his journey north.

'Well now, let me tell you, I did. And perhaps you'll grow up to be a nurse in a big hospital, or even a doctor like your Daddy!' He exclaims this, as if I'm supposed to respond in some way. I nod.

'Now dear, an easy question from the Catechism. You've been a good girl, haven't you? You're a responsible child, ready to accept the gifts of the Holy Spirit?'

I consider that I have not been a particularly good girl, and the many omissions in the confessional, including how I have never mentioned the number of times I called my mother a bitch. In my head, of course, always in my head, or into the curtains, or into the pillow at night. Name-calling and cursing are venial sins, and should be confessed, but I never do. I hang my head.

'So now, wee Miss Esmond! Frankie or is it Frances? After St Francis?'

'It's both.'

'Well then, I shall call you Frances, after that great saint himself. I'm sure you love animals too, don't you, Frances?'

Another nod.

'Now, a wee question, which I'm sure you know the answer to, child.'

I, standing, look up. The Bishop's lips are loose and wrinkly. Horse-faced Mrs. McGrory stands close to him, pink-rimmed eyes boring into me, nodding to encourage me, one eyebrow flicking nervously up and down. She wears absolutely no make-up. Unlike Elma, who is at home in bed but will get up the moment the Angelus bell strikes on the radio to make the dinner.

'Now tell me this, does God know all things?'

I know the answer, I definitely know the answer. It is an easy-peasy one and I know it. But the silence draws me to itself again. I can think the answer but I cannot speak it. Now, I hear it in my own head as if the Archangel Michael, the wingy guy I believe can fight for me and save me, as if he is whispering it. *God knows all things, past, present, and to come, even our most secret thoughts and actions.* But it lies congealed within my brain and I cannot liberate the words. Lips are sealed, tongue is struck dumb.

'God knows? What does God know, dear?' Mrs McGrory encourages me in a scratchy voice as her eyes widen and bore into me.

Still nothing. The rest of the class are not fidgeting. A mid-morning thickening of nervous air has descended. The other children watch. Mrs McGrory stands stock still. I see her little grey-stockinged muscled legs with their narrow ankles, and her knobbly toes pressing up against the leather of her brogues. Whatever occurs within adult shoes is another of God's mysteries, all those hammer toes, things called bunions, and thick, disgusting toenails.

'God knows all things? And what else?' Bishop McMahon tries again after a glance at Mrs. McGrory. 'Come, child, what kind of things does God know?'

'Stuff we done,' I ventured.

'Did,' Mrs. McGrory corrects, lips tightening.

'Did,' I repeat.

The Bishop blinks slowly and turns to Mrs McGrory, who has begun to redden. 'And God, yes, that's the past, very good, but what else might he know about us, this God we are all preparing to meet on Confirmation Sunday?'

Then it emerges, as if spewed out of me. 'Past, present and future, secret thoughts and actions.'

'Very good, very good,' he affirms mildly and he must think I'm a thick plank, really stupid, like people often do when I fall silent. 'I'm sure you're as ready for the big day as anyone, and sure the Holy Ghost will help you to avoid evil and to do good for the rest of your life, isn't that right Mrs. McGrory?' He turns to the teacher, and I could swear she is trembling with rage at the delay in my answering the question.

At home, Paddy tries to help me with sums and Catechism, but has no patience for teaching, so as often as not I say thank you Daddy, I understand it now, when I don't. My silences infuriate Elma, who wants me to be outgoing and talkative. I have friends, but not always the ones Elma would have chosen. I'm friends with the girl my mother says is a step up from a tinker, but is actually the funniest girl in the town. We both show one another our thick wintery knickers and laugh at the colours chosen by our mothers. Later, I become best friends with a girl whose mother has a short leg, whose father does nothing, and whose younger sister is also a silent girl, like me.

During school holidays I prefer winter to summer. In winter, I sidle close to the walls of the different houses as I walk the streets of the town, where it is darker, shadowed by the lighting system. I will not be noticed, nor engaged in social conversation. Summer is a different matter. The town cranks itself up to become a spinning-wheel of events and festivals: the band festival draws pipe and brass brands from the North and elsewhere, taking over for a few days of piping, drumming, marching and drinking. Feral boys roam, and the local girls, including me, turn feral and squeal with excitement at the sight of newcomers, shrieking with nervous laughter as we follow one another in clusters after school.

Once, a boy who chases me, shoves his hand right up my dress in my grandmother's back yard, just at the moment when Paddy arrives, finding me struggling with the boy. I am twelve. Shocked by the hand, by this invasion of myself when I know nothing about invasions of the female body. I roar crying in the car all the way home, pleading with Paddy to understand that I did nothing, we were only talking and laughing and then the boy wouldn't stop following me and I ran to Nana's yard but the back door was locked and I was stuck there, battling, pulling the boy's hair in an attempt to push him away. But Paddy says nothing at all. To my astonishment, he drives, thin-lipped and silent, smelling slightly of hospital and something antiseptic, but saying nothing whatsoever, neither blaming nor not blaming. But I take his silence as a reproach. When we get home, Elma, who grew up with seven brothers and is used to boys and their carry-on, makes light of it.

'Why can't you be like Marie O'Driscoll?' she enquires one day when I'm yet again in the chorus for the school play. 'She's not afraid to speak up for herself, she'll go places in life.'

'We're not in the same class,' I reply.

I have no wish to emulate Marie O'Driscoll, even though I quite like her, but she is a know-all, now playing the part of Old King Cole, that merry old soul in the school dramatic production. The O'Driscoll's came up from Cork and are very go-ahead. They play golf at the local club near Rossmore Park. Their mother has a strong accent which Elma and Aunt Elizabeth smirk at together.

At the same time, their own local accent embarrasses them with its northern tilt, and they do everything possible to smooth it out and sound a little more BBC. Marie O'Driscoll is a year ahead of me, so we have different friends. Then Mrs. O'Driscoll, who is friendly with Elma, invites me for tea. Marie and I get along fine and go hunting for birds' nests along the Rossmore Park hedgerows. Marie knows many secret places in which to be alone, just as I do on the far side of the town. But there it ends.

'How did you get on?' Elma enquires when she collects me.

'Fine.'

'Is that all you have to say for yourself? *Fine*?'

'It was nice.'

My mother sighs. 'So what did you do together? Did you enjoy yourself? Is Bridget a good cook? I don't think she is, but she makes out she is.'

I tell my mother about hunting for birds' nests, and how Marie showed me how to make an actual nest to put into a hedge and which a bird might adopt as its home.

'Now there's a girl showing initiative. No wonder she got the main part in the school play! Of course everyone knows a bird won't nest in something that has been touched by human hand,' she laughs. 'I'm surprised Marie doesn't know that.'

'Well she doesn't.'

7

'You're like Princess Anne,' Elma announces pleased, having fixed my fair hair in a floppy blue ribbon, to match the blue and white broderie anglaise dress, the white leather shoes, the neat ankle-socks. The progress of the Royal children is closely studied, especially Anne, four years older than me. Anne on her pony. Anne going to school. Anne playing with Queen Elizabeth in the gardens of Buckingham Palace, beds of summer roses in full bloom. Tartans, Shetland wool sweaters, and a small string of pearls for the twelve-year-old Anne. None of this is admitted to other Irish people except Aunt Elizabeth. I never speak of it for the sheer, instinctive shame of it. Does my mother not realise that in our country now, attention to the Royal family is seen by some people as ludicrous? Even as a child, I know this. Even at eight, I know that we live in a republic, and that a republic takes a different position to monarchy. Paddy tells me quietly that we're finished with kings and queens.

'They do things better in England,' Elma informs me one

evening after we've watched the changing of the Guards on BBC television news and the Queen sitting side-saddle. 'The uppers over there have a bit of style. Not like us, half the country still bog-trotting. I think we should have stayed with England and not become a Republic.'

'What's a Republic?' I ask, testing Elma, even though I know, fidgeting with a scab on my knee, 'And what's contraception?'

'It's what we are,' she replies, ignoring the second question, 'it means everybody is supposed to be the same, there's no Queen like in England, but we're not really all the same, which is how it should be. Some people are uppers, some are lowers, if you get my meaning.'

'Why?'

'Because people are not all the same. Some are *better* than others.'

'Is the Queen better?'

'I don't know,' Elma considers. 'Maybe. She's two years older than me. She's a very strong woman and she has that Prince Philip to handle on top of everything else.'

'What's wrong with Prince Philip? What did he do?'

Elma frowns slightly, then smiles. 'I'll explain when you're older. He's supposed to be a handful, that's all I can say. A woman running a nation as Queen should not have to contend with a cad!'

'What's a cad?'

'When you're older, Frankie, when you're older, I'll tell you all about cads,' my mother smiles, 'and a girl with your looks will meet plenty of them,' she adds mysteriously.

Later that day, Elma cares about the Dummy Man as much as goings on at Buckingham Palace. I watch as my mother becomes charitable. She pities the Dummy Man, who is mute, his mouth a gaping space of crooked, yellowed teeth, the corners of his lips crisped with dry saliva. On crutches, he painstakingly makes his way along and up the avenue to see Elma, as he does every spring. He knocks on the door, signals with his hand.

'Oh. It's yourself,' she says, 'hold on now. Would you like tea?'

He shakes his head. He wants a few coppers.

'Are you sure you don't want tea? Or water? I can bring it out to you and you can sit yourself on the bench.' She points to the pale blue garden bench, its yellow cast iron snakes supporting the planks.

Again, he shakes his head. Elma goes to the kitchen to retrieve her purse. She trots back to the door again, her stilettos clicking along the hall floor. 'Here you are. Get yourself a few drinks.'

The Dummy Man nods and something like a smile widens his mouth, revealing thick tartar.

'Wait!' she calls as he begins to turn. I see kindness in her eyes. 'At least let me drive you down the avenue.'

But the Dummy Man shakes his head at her and moves off slowly, crutches beneath his arms as he snail-trails his way down past the laurel hedge, under the lime-trees, and along until he descends to the road beneath its overhang of oaks. I watch from the east side of the house, slightly scared of him. Beside me a spicily scented cream rose creeps in a frail way upwards.

All the old plants are forgotten and eventually stop growing for want of attention. The Turk's Cap lilies, the peony roses, and the rhododendron, all gradually fade, then die, but the philadelphus survives. Someone from another generation put down these plantings, heeling them secure. Early one summer Paddy plants tomatoes in the old glasshouse. He waters them in the evenings but asks Elma and then me to do so in the mornings while he is at work. He is in the hospital theatre from eight in the morning until two o'clock, after which he conducts ward rounds. But Elma won't rise from bed before noon, and after a while I tire of the weight of the slopping water-cans as I make my way downhill to the glasshouse. So I stop. Paddy understands. Again, he asks Elma if she'll do it.

'Think of all the fresh tomatoes we'll have! That rich smell, eh?' He winks at her. 'You'll be able to do stuffed tomatoes with basil.'

'Is that what you'd like?' she asks, amused.

'Yes. I'd love some stuffed tomatoes.'

'Oh dear. Stuffed tomatoes? I think not, Paddy! Life's too short.'

Sometimes, Elma is decades ahead of the game.

That summer, Tess and I play separately but together. Mud-pies made in Paddy's old *Mick McQuaid* tobacco tins. Water ferried down in glass bottles from the rainwater barrel outside the kitchen, then mixed carefully with soil, turning it to a rich, chocolatey brown. I send Tess off to gather flowers for decorating these cakes, and she returns with small violets, wood-anemone, lesser celandine and blue-eyed speedwell. Before the mud dries, we tear the petals free and create patterns on each tin of tamped-down mud.

Once, we really do play. Tess believes these are real, edible cakes. She trusts me so much that if I put them in the magic oven beneath the laurel hedge nearby, they will emerge baked and delicious. I watch my little sister, her round head and tatty brown hair, the retroussé nose, the small hands with even fingers and bitten nails which make such lovely patterns in the half-dried mud using only a twig. The remains of the denatonium benzoate Elma paints on nightly have left Tess's fingertips yellow and dry.

I'm not sure what these feelings are, but I have new feelings about my sister that I have not experienced before. I wonder if this is what my cousins feel together as brothers and sisters, and if there is a name for it. Playing along, we decorate four tins of mud: anemone leaf, a trail of speedwell around the edges, then yellow spatters of spring jasmine.

'Put it in the oven Frankie!'

I slide the four tins beneath the laurels, then draw the laurel leaves down and place a large stone on them to hold them in position. 'That's the oven door shut,' I tell Tess. We wait a few minutes, settling some dandelion heads along the grass, then rolling in them.

'We'll both wet the bed tonight,' I tease. Tess laughs at this. 'But I won't tell Mammy if you don't.' Tess nods, accepting the words, eyes bright as speedwell.

'Open the oven, open the oven!' she shouts after a while with excitement. 'They must be cooked now!'

Slowly, I remove the stone as if opening the tomb of the resurrection. The laurel leaves spring back, revealing four tins beneath the hedge. Tess reaches in, pauses, then pretends to pull back. 'Ow! They're hot!'

I withdraw the four tins, lay them carefully on the yellow brickwork outside the glass-house. We look and examine. Tess lets out a gasp. 'They're lovely,' she sighs. 'I'm hungry. Are they ready to eat?'

'I'd say so. Want to try a slice?'

'Yummy! Will you?'

'Of course!'

I withdraw a pen-knife from my jeans pocket, pull the blade open and begin to cut with a surgical precision Paddy would have been proud of. Tess looks on as a triangle of chocolate tart is removed from a *Mick McQuaid* tobacco tin. Then another. Seriously, we both begin to chew. The dried mud moistens and crumbles tastelessly in our mouths. 'Mmm, yum. . .' We chew thoughtfully. Tess nods as if in approval and bites in a second time. We keep going until we finish a slice each, both ignoring the bland and alien taste of mud as it fills our mouths, sticks to our tongues, grits up our teeth and gums. Later, we take water from the rain-barrel behind the kitchen and swish our mouths clear, grinning briefly at one another, displaying mud-caked teeth, then swishing and spitting and laughing again.

*

Finally, the glasshouse falls into disuse. Bored and in a fit of pique one afternoon, I fling stone after stone at the roof glass, smashing it. Incredibly, nobody hears. Nobody witnesses. Nobody responds to my delinquency. I wonder if I really exist. I wonder why nobody notices what I have just done. It appears I could chop my own head off and nobody, meaning my parents, would react even to my spewing blood, because all they talk about is Tess. They imagine I am a good girl, a good daughter.

Later, during the hour or so of doing homework at the table in the front room, I can't resist inscribing long fangs and devil's horns on both my mother and sister in the photograph which rests on the table before my open copybook, on which lines of fractions await my attention. When Paddy finds my handiwork, he is perturbed. But, incredibly, a little amused.

'Frankie, I don't know what kind of a mind you have. To think that a golden girl like you, my *Niamh Cinn Óir,* would do such a thing? Where did we get you from at all, I wonder, eh? From the fairies, is it? Are the Tuatha de Danann working on you in secret?'

He strokes my head for a moment and asks if I am alright. Now the silence rises in me, a bubble about to break and flood. Are you alright, he repeats, are there things you'd like to talk about?

He is whispering. His Indian friend, Dr Desgupta at the hospital, would listen. But Dr Desgupta, I know, is the Nutcase Doctor. I do not wish to speak to the Nutcase Doctor. Only my Daddy. But I nod anyway, and lean against his tweed jacket, then say that I am alright, knowing this is not true. What is alright anyway? Who is alright? I ache to lean in even more closely to his jacket, to be enveloped by it so that I can smell the aroma of pipe-smoke and hospital antiseptic that impregnates the lining, to dream into the safety of my mild Daddy, to let it all spill out and tell him everything, though what it is I would tell is a mystery, because it is such a jumble in my head and I cannot assemble the right words.

Yet the world sometimes makes me happy despite its fractures. I have my own child's fiefdom, know life to be a teeming, cellular condition to which I am tuned, as to a musical instrument. I am tree-climber, dog-racer, girl-on-a-swing, mud-pie maker, field walker, nest seeker and squirrel spotter, tolerant of rats, bats, mice and frogs. Tess fears these things, struggles along behind me. Secretly, I fear something far beyond and much worse than rats, mice or frogs. Something isn't right.

I'm mostly what is called a good child. Obedient enough. Pleasant, apparently. One April in spring Elma has the gardener make three rhombus-shaped flower-beds in the lawn below the limestone block front steps. In these he plants tight-leaved begonias which will flame orange, red and yellow from July. There is something almost brazen about their leaves.

One day in the shed, I examine pots of old paints. A plan nudges into shape. I'm old enough to understand weed-killer and its treachery. Rubber gloves whipped from behind the kitchen taps while Elma is out and Paddy's nose is in JP Dunleavy's *A Singular Man,* bought one day in the Eblana Bookshop in Dublin's Grafton Street when I was with him. My parents would take me with them on their forays to the city and leave Tess behind at home with Nana. I preferred Paddy's company to the slow trek through the shops my mother favours. Being with Paddy in the Eblana is to feel released into a new and enticing world, where I learn how to browse books and take my time. Whatever I fancy he will buy for me, and a picture-book for Tess. Now as he reads he chuckles to himself at intervals, lost in the novel. I slip from the house. Gloved and back in the shed, I locate the necessary, then set out on the lawn to the three flower beds. The blooms remind me of Elma's skirts, red or orange, big loose skirts that float as she walks. I swish the spray here and there, making deliberate decisions about which begonias are to live and which to die.

'You! Die! Die!' I whisper, then 'You? You can live!'

I'm without hope. I know that no normal child would do such a thing, that I am partly mad or wicked, or both. No one will ever find out what I have done. I feel sick in my stomach. Why would I do such a thing to my parents? The plants will wilt in a day's time or less. My parents will look on in dismay, with no clue whatsoever that their daughter is so delinquent, that the urge to destroy has awakened and may never be shut-eyed in the sub-conscious again. Even still, they'll continue to consider me a good child, even if I'm not chatty or pushy enough.

Elma blames the gardener. Three days later she stares hard at the begonia beds. Paudge is a serene man. But now he's flustered. Already, at twelve, I note his beauty. Dark hair and dark skin. A man's clean and warm sweat-odour wafting from him. A countryman, he reads books and keeps a shed filled with prize roosters. In his few acres are Falabellas, miniature horses, creamy and impudent, which he invites Tess and me to see every spring when Paddy drives us down to Paudge's farm. Scratching his jaw, he stares confounded at the plants in their death-throes.

'Troth, I don't know what's after happening. If I didn't know better. . .' his voice fades and he turns in my direction. His eyes fall on me briefly. *He knows, he knows*, I panic and move away casually. I'm acquiring cunning.

'If you didn't know better *whot*, Paudge?' Elma turns to him, her accent altered as she speaks. She's his social better, she can enunciate, she doesn't speak in the local accent. *Forget about up the bray, girls, it's up the hill. Am I clear?* she'd say. And the response of, *Yes, Mammy*. Two voices, Tess's lighter than mine.

Paudge doesn't betray me. He shakes his head. 'Must have been a bad lock o'plants. I'll have a word with your man that sold them to me.' He understands something isn't right, and it comforts me. Men are so much easier, I realise. They are softer than the two women I have mostly known, Elma and Aunt Elizabeth.

The following spring, at his house further out the country, I accompany him up and down one of his hill fields as his big horse with the hairy feet pulls the plough. I hold his hand and he clasps mine carefully. It's a good, roughish, gentle hand, and I inhale the aroma of brown soil, enter briefly into Paudge's life for one afternoon in quiet rhythm with the worms and the beetles, and all the whirring, busy creatures of springtime. Paudge mentions the begonias casually, how he thinks my mother should give them a miss for a while.

'Mebbe some things just don't settle right, isn't that it?' he murmurs, clicking with his tongue as he draws back the reins and the horse slows to a standstill, lowering its massive head, grinding its teeth on the bit.

'It is,' I reply shyly, averting my eyes.

I wondered about the people I can speak to and those I can not, and what the difference was. The people who can get me to talk are the ones who listen and watch, but in a different way from Elma's listening and watching. They are never stern. They don't cut bacon at a slicing machine and drill stupid, cackling questions into my face. They talk about other things, remarking on them simply. Birds and animals, and why rain on St. Swithin's Day is said to be bad luck. Paudge knows all about the Devil but laughs at him, advising me to fling a spoon of salt over my shoulder if ever I feel afraid.

'He's scared of salt, and he doesn't bother with childer like you, because childer have no sin,' Paudge says gently.

The Devil looms large in my life.

*

Saturday night close to midnight. I help Elma to her bed. She has perched on the sofa too long, watching television movements and colour. Now there has been an accident which she is ashamed to admit to, but which I swiftly attend to upstairs. I try not to add to her humiliation. Eventually, I guide her across the landing, tiny step by tiny step in her battered sandals, her stiff toes protruding crookedly, then into the bedroom, around the bed. Slowly now, telling her to lean on my arm, trying not to wince when her weight pinches my own tender muscle. I'm in the middle of a flare-up, which means my own muscles are electric and tight, my bones and fingertips often cold. Plonk onto the mattress. Legs lift-up, encourage to bring bottom to the centre of mattress, draw up duvet. I don't always kiss my mother good-night. That was a childhood ritual with both parents, who were physically expressive, even to Tess. Now it depends on my mood, and how angry or at ease I might be. I don't always possess the gift of chivvying Elma along. Tonight though, a mother-kiss on cool cheek. The old woman looks up and squints.

'Am I imagining it or have you grown taller?'

'No, Mum, I haven't grown taller.'

'You look taller every time I see you.'

She settles herself on the pillows, then lifts the television remote, her hand shaky. As I leave, the sound is very loud.

'Do you want Jimmy with you?' I call back.

'Yes. Is he in? I sincerely hope you didn't put him out?'

'I did, but I'll call him. He'll want to —'

'What? You put him out and closed the window? He'll go down on the road and get run over, oh find him!' Panic in her voice. 'What were you thinking of? Find him Frankie!'

I charge downstairs. Into the kitchen. Open the window, sure enough old stripey-skin is there, slinks in purring, whiskers spread wide in expectation of being fed. I open a pack of cat food, squeeze it into his bowl beside the sink, and leave the kitchen door ajar. Jimmy will find his way in his own time to Elma's bed.

'Did you find him?' she cries out. There is a loud thump which I assume is something being thrown at the wall. A book or even her prayer-missal.

'He's fucking coming!' I shout upstairs.

'Well fucking good for you! If anything happens to that cat I won't be responsible for —'

'Yadda-yadda,' I mutter, not listening to the rest of the rant, climbing the stairs to my own room.

When we were young Elma didn't curse and swear the way she does now. Occasionally she'd use the word bloody or damn. I discovered the word fuck in the primary school yard where someone inscribed it in six-foot high chalk lines. Now, her language is strong and occasionally what her doctor describes as abusive. I think the doctor is being a little too uptight about that. Elma is an old woman whose sense of social inhibition has fallen away, and maybe it does the doctor no harm, herself no slouch when it comes to plain speaking, on the one occasion Elma tells her to get her fucking hands off her legs.

In my own bedroom I strip down, and in an effort to change my mood take a photograph of my naked self to send to Christoph. He'll like that. For a change, the room is entirely silent. I can hear the silence and peace, my eye travelling up the slanting ceiling and across to the window. It's a windless night. I lift my rib-cage and take another shot at a different angle. Never face on, slightly sideways to conceal my paunch. Satisfied, I zip it off to him with a short text. *Night night.* It's the sort of text that shocks him as much as it amuses him, my casual dart of the funny-erotic, which, by the way, mostly eludes us, though I still pursue it and wonder about it. For God's sake, I am alive.

I then lay myself down to sleep, switch off the bedside lamp, and pray to the cosmos to keep my quaking soul safe, for it's in shreds, and that's also the truth among all the truths in my head. Already, I'm drowsy with the warmth from the electric blanket. All of a sudden my head snaps to the right. A disturbance close to the bed. I feel as if I am being closely observed. I reach out and switch on the lamp again. Above, the yellow lampshades in the centre of the room have begun to shiver, as if a distant earthquake is rattling the old house, whittling at its roots, stirring the soil. No, that's not it. I'm being watched. I know it. I feel it. Just as always. The ghosting of my bedroom is as alive and present today as it was when I was a teenager and first encountered it. Christoph has experienced it many times, but only when I'm with him, never when he's alone. In his pragmatic way, he explains it as a representation of youthful, disturbed spirit, an emotional pattern laid into the airs of the room, now set to repeat itself in my presence.

It's true my head is racing with cross-currents tonight. With thoughts of Jason, his writing, his young life and its direction, of which I know little. With thoughts of Elma, about whom I'll always fret even as she irritates me and tries me. And with thoughts of myself, blaming thoughts, guilty thoughts that I know have no place in my consciousness at this stage in my life.

For a while, I prop myself up observing the light fitting. Swing, swing, back and forth very gently. There is no draught. The air is entirely still and warm but then yes, that scent peculiar to the manifestation is gradually rising around me, imbuing the air with cumin, spices. And something sweeter, a perfume, perhaps. Am I frightened? Not really. Watchful certainly, but this is nothing new. I admit to having held on to this down the years, as if it was my secret alone. It has never harmed me, so much as responded to me.

'Oh room, behave yourself and let me sleep!' I grumble, adjusting my phone on the bedside cabinet before switching off the bedside lamp and turning roughly into the pillow. Yet I can feel my bladder contract, my bowels churn, my heart pump so that it hammers against my chest. I'm frozen to the mattress, but sweating. I tell myself yet again that this is not badness, but strayed memory still attached to a particular place, a residue of another time. The swinging lights don't bother me so much. That's a common enough poltergeist manifestation. It's the sequel that always gets me. The sounds. The scratching sound, the scraping that moves around the room and which I can't pin to a particular area, neither the table below the west window, nor the chair, nor any other surface. Tonight, the scratching is faint, as if the presence can't be bothered, or cannot feed off my energy. Now, some subtle stirring begins instead in my head, an emergence in images, almost like the layers of a C-scan displaying the self-regulating body, section by section, except this memory is on its way to torment me, forcing me to explore it thoroughly, sliver by sliver. I can't sleep and instead, my mind drifts back and forth, agitating itself in its useless rememberings. As I wrestle with memory, the scratching sounds increase in volume and speed and in no time, my nightdress is drenched with sweat. Finally, I fling back the duvet and stomp out to the bathroom, have a pee then rinse my face in cold water.

*

Caning is a form of corporal punishment and most canes in the British Isles were made from birchwood, but out in the colonies they were made from rattan and, in some cases, from bamboo. But I wasn't living in the colonies, and so I got to look at our very own birchwood cane every day. Purchased by Elma, it became as ordinary and casual as a toasting fork, or a soup ladle, hanging as it did in the kitchen between the dresser and the stove. Pale yellow, on a thick nail. The more I think back, the more I wonder about Paddy. Did he not see it? What did he think? He came from a gentle home, had never known physical punishment. So I'm confused. I fear it, although at home I'm not the recipient. Only in school, where the nun in sixth class uses it liberally on our hands if we haven't learned our Irish poetry verses by heart, or the daily *combrá*, or conversation piece. When I'm older, I read of other punishments meted out to children, but these are usually applied to boys in boarding schools. James Joyce writes explicitly about the use of the pandy-bat, a many layered torture implement made of leather, supple enough to deliver the most stinging, welt-inducing of marks along a boy's naked bottom. There is no pandy-bat in Kilnavarn House, but there is a birchwood cane. To think that a once living plant, now cut, has had part of its former living turned into this! Later at university, I memorise a section from Joyce's *Portrait,* and his description of the pandy in action.

— Up, Fleming! Up, my boy!
Fleming stood up slowly.
— Hold out! cried the prefect of studies.
Fleming held out his hand. The pandybat came down on it with a loud smacking sound: one, two, three, four, five, six.
— Other hand!
The pandybat came down again in six loud quick smacks.
— Kneel down! cried the prefect of studies.

Lying in the dark now with my eyes still tightly closed, the airs around me criss-crossed with amelodic scratchings, as of claws or metal, I recall a contemporary whose novel describes what happens to a young autistic man confined in a mental home in the '40s, and how the severity of the electric shock treatment he received breaks his back, and how the opened eye of Balor has fallen on him. Balor the one-eyed Formorian god who destroys whatever is before him when he opens that eye.

God or whoever, save us all from the eye of Balor, I think now, pulling the duvet closer to my neck. It is not the eye of Balor that makes the lamps move in my room, the source of this disturbance is not malignant. But I believe the eye of Balor fell on our unfortunate mother in 1960, after Tess's arrival. Elma would not have considered herself unfortunate, but I had always understood her to be unfortunate, without knowing precisely why. I don't recall the cane being used, but assume it must have been. I cannot remember. No doubt some therapist could unearth a memory, but the question for me would always be, what is the real memory and what the false? Many incidents are also lost to Tess, blocked out, a chaos of strands she cannot always frame to form a whole image of an incident. Tess was good, not bad. Elma was good, not bad. Paddy was good, not bad. I insist on the primal innocence of each, but the adults should have known better. The adults were in charge. And what was I? Was I good or bad? Have I ever forgiven myself for the involuntary act of seeing, of witnessing? Have I ever forgiven them for neglecting both of us? The temporal and the spatial continue to dazzle and confuse us, each in our own way.

Sleep, now sleep, I soothe myself, wondering again if I'm mad. Lately, I sometimes think I'd like to be admitted to a hospital where I could be 'adjusted'. Tranquillisers and nice chats on tap. Past experience of therapists and head-shrinkers? Let's face it: variable. Some are flaky, getting over their own personal problems and divorces and gender reorientations, while others, having listened to me for months and months with expressionless, non-judgemental faces, offer fuck-useless non-directive counselling. Others again suggest CBT. As good as it gets.

But in my ideal institution there would be stories from the other inmates. Material too, my scavenging writer's head reflects. Lots of long sleeps. Above all, no responsibility for anyone else. Vaguely, I wonder if there could ever be places for people like me. Not quite a mental hospital, but not an ordinary hospital either. A pain-resolving zone for exhausted adults. The chance to lie in bed and sleep for as long as necessary, in order to heal and face the world again. I wonder if I should go to the doctor the following week and ask him to increase my dose of antidepressant, which is pretty useless beyond keeping me sort of calm. Not totally frantic. I never get the zing and energy I used to get when I was once on Prozac.

Occasionally I feel unsafe about my own degree of incipient and unexpressed violence towards Elma. People speak on radio about elder abuse, the cliché which none of us likes to think about. Us. That's any and all kinds of people. Neighbours. Friends. It's a bit like domestic violence towards spouses. Happens all the time, mostly nobody can tell.

The times I have imagined, on Elma's death, flinging her walking frame down the garden as far as it will go; I have imagined choking her, I have imagined smothering her with a pillow as she slept. Instead, and despite these thoughts, I try to be gentle. And Tess's own daughter, as far as I can see, has been raised without a hand ever lifted by Tess.

I switch on the bedside light again and note that the lights in the centre of the room are once again completely still. A slant of moonlight lights the foot of my bed, the old house settles, the black grandfather clock outside the door ticking, ticking, and next to it my mother's wig on the head of St. Joseph like a grey, uneven hat. If I could have one wish, I'm thinking before sleep finally envelopes me, it would be that Paddy were here to intervene in a way he never did when alive, that he could come back. Impossible. If he never intervened while he was alive, why would be do so now? But if he came back, how would I ever explain the world to him? So much has happened. So much between me and Elma, two women negotiating the business of justice, as women, and not always as mother and daughter. So much also, to the riven world itself.

8

When Tess was in boarding-school, she and her friends liked to escape at night. They legged it up and over the wall, removed their uniforms and concealed them beneath the shrubbery that spilled over from the sports grounds. Down along the South Circular Road in Limerick then, heads averted until they got their lift with a boy from Crescent College. They wanted out of the city, to course through the flat concrete suburbs and on out to the countryside.

By this time, we were in irregular contact. I was at university, and spending summers in Germany. I wrote cards and letters to Tess and advised her to dispense with her virginity sooner rather than later, especially when she went off to spend a summer in Copenhagen working in a canning factory. Tess wrote back, both of us being deliberately comical as a communication strategy. I didn't need to worry about her virginity, she assured me, it had long been dispensed with, adding a stick cartoon that showed her and a boy kissing, little round breasts pressed up against the stick boy and hearts and flowers floating above their heads.

Later, in Forest Glen Rehab, I was twenty-eight and Tess twenty-three. Everything tumbled out, how hard drinking became a thing on those nights when she and her friends made their way to a country shebeen in which a single light bulb dangled in a smoke-stained room and where the silent old men ignored them and which allowed them to drink. They had the best time, she told me, it was one long drink-and-snog with the local boys. Lucky you, I replied, envious of her nights out, the crazy night drives with gay Gus as the crowd referred to him, every girl's best pal, zooming along close to the course of the Shannon river, sometimes driving as far as Dromineer, rising and dipping in a low red sports car, overloaded with five girls, two in the front along with Gus, sticking hard to the road as they took the sharp bends. But ironically, she said, it was what got her into Speech Therapy. Only through recovery from addiction did she learn how to speak. Really speak, she said, and understand the importance of speaking out, and how, if a child had a speech impediment, it had even less chance of speaking out if bad things were happening. She wanted to see children freed from all kinds of tyranny, she told me, and that was what brought her gradually into the work of speech.

She also reminisced during group sessions about how the nuns sent the friendlier, chattier girls out weekly as company for the young, disabled men in an institution nearby, overlooking the river. The rehab therapist usually looked on, not saying much, occasionally asking a question about how Tess felt. After a time, Tess admitted, her services were no longer wanted by the institution, on the grounds that she was upsetting some of the young men, making them unhappy.

'And what were you really doing? Did you really have sex with that young guy?' I asked.

'Mostly we were only messing. Having wheelchair races up and down the corridors, which the guys liked.'

'And?'

'And *what*?'

'Hardly reason for dismissal, is it?'

'I was only trying to be nice, and one particular guy was so nice to me, shouldn't have been in that place had his couldn't-give-a-fuck family been bothered.'

'Nice about *what*?'

'So I had sex with him. Oh, nothing much. Just a bit of harmless fumbling now that I think of it. I mean, I didn't have much experience either!'

'Jesus Christ.' I laughed like a drain, 'Bringing joy to the world. No wonder they let you go.'

'Hmm. Paddy and Elma were pretty shocked though. No wonder, given the decade we were in. Tail end of old Oirish repression and all that?'

Paddy and Elma had listened to the disclosure, he pale-faced and tight-lipped, she leaning forward in genuine interest, frowning, as if watching a piece of Greek theatre in which blood would surely spill.

The counsellor insisted that it wasn't a comedy show. 'But you, Tess,' she went on, 'thought it quite okay to take advantage of a really disabled young man and provide him with *sex*? Correct?'

At this, Tess had shrugged and looked out the window.

'I asked you a question, Tess. What were you thinking?'

'I didn't think I was providing anything. I was thinking he should have a good time just like everybody else. *Fuck*, why shouldn't he enjoy himself too? What's wrong with *that*!' Her voice rose, and as she stood abruptly, her chair fell back with a slam to the floor.

The therapist stood too, and two muscle-bound men shifted to their feet at the back of the room. 'You do not stand or leave this room without my say-so! Do you understand that? Now pick up that chair, sit down, and proceed with your tale of how you felt this young fella should have a good time. Because what I — we — need to know is, were you drinking? Were you sober? This is all about sobriety, your *sobriety*!' she spat.

Listening to her, some part of me suspected that therapists weren't really supposed to get that angry, but what did I know?

That evening when Paddy and Elma got back to Kilnavarn, Paddy rang through to the hospital and cancelled the next day's theatre schedule. Then he hit the bottle in his little private whiskey room and got plastered. Eventually he staggered upstairs to bed and cried for an hour into the pillows while Elma looked on and felt helpless. She phoned me in a panic, outraged that Paddy should be so upset. I felt that distinctive pain which has tracked me from childhood, pain at my father's broken heart, pain at his inability to do something for us.

'To think that Tess has caused her father such pain!' Elma spoke in a low voice, 'I've never seen him so upset in his entire life, may God and St Joseph help him.'

I'd already been on the phone to Tess, congratulating her on her courage, telling her not to mind the counsellor and anyone else who disapproved of what she'd done with that boy. I think she was glad to talk to me. I think my response came as a relief.

*

The Health Minister is on television, hectoring the whole population of Ireland as Elma and I look on. A half-eaten toasted cheese sandwich sits limply on a plate in Elma's lap. It is reported that a Cork youth spat in his face on the street and told him he had Corona Virus. He holds forth on how some people are still not complying on the question of physical distance. We are in the middle of a war, he tells us in a tight voice, there will be sanctions and stricter monitoring of activities in highly populated areas in the country.

'Shocking behaviour,' Elma shakes her head, 'that poor young chap, he has a wife and family too.'

Half an hour later, I walk down the avenue, turn into the bottom field and make my way around the lake in hiking boots. There's a light drizzle. Aged eighteen I learned to swim here in very shallow, muddy water, the smell of the lake rising in my nostrils, little wavelets spreading out as I dog-paddled my way along, moving in careful circles, never so far out as to be unable to touch the lakebed. It was Leaving Cert year, after I had been ill. For the first time in ages I was without pain, and my bones, muscles and tendons were less inflamed. I had energy. I was young. But frenzied Elma watched me like a hawk — what I ate, where I went, if I visited the bathroom at night, whether I was warm enough and properly dressed for cold and wind. Had I been able to really swim, I had the energy, it felt to me, to swim from one side of the lake to the other. I was a pent-up young animal, bursting with life.

I glance up at the house on the hill and think again of the rule-breakers Elma admired. Dame Freya Stark, travelling through the desert on horse or by camel. Amelia Earhart on her solo trans-Atlantic flight, and later, the broadcasters Joan Bakewell and Kate Adie. My mother's life would have been different had she been born in England, or America. Or even in Dublin. But then, so would mine.

What a house of sounds it was. Especially nocturnal sound. The ferocity of storms that hammered in fists at the window at the western gable often kept me awake. In the pitch dark of the unlit countryside, and the cave darkness of my room, I feared the house would collapse, imagined I could feel it shiver in its old foundations. Tess's wood-panelled room was quieter, and once infancy was past she slept soundly. But that unidentifiable scratching sound in my room continued, as bad as the swinging lampshades which sometimes accompanied it, at first scarcely detectable, nonetheless present and on those spring and summer nights it tormented me.

*

For forty-five years, the traveller Roddy Boyd had occupied Kilnavarn House with his local servant Tom Macklin and a tamed Caspian tiger called Finn. Boyd, a rebel and dreamer by nature, who was supposed to have aided some of the Bedouin tribes in their battles for autonomy, even if this was never quite secured, bought the beast on the shores of Muscat from a man who was in need of money for his daughter's dowry. He returned a hero to his home county, with the tiger. Tanned, dark-haired and unshaven, he was a man for himself with no known interest in women. Boyd had adopted the use of an opium pipe, or what he termed his dream-stick, and he was known to settle himself in a leather armchair in the vaulted, wooden-ceilinged attic beneath the oculus window he installed. Tom Macklin wrote in his diary, now preserved in the local heritage museum, how he would often see the sweet smoke drifting upwards on many an afternoon. He also recounted how the tiger wandered through Kilnavarn House, squirting its tangy, male taint on the furniture.

For years, Elma claimed to smell the funk of a big cat around the place, an idea Tess and I enjoyed, believing we too could smell it. Then, into my teenage life came nocturnal visuals and auditory disturbances. I knew them to be poltergeist activity from the outset. It has come and gone and returned again over the years. *Scratch, scratch, scratch*, in my bedroom, especially on summer nights, when I awaken in what was once Boyd's bedroom. *Scratch, scratch, scratch*, beginning quietly, then increasing until it is like an urgent scribble, a marking of ink on old paper.

The first time it happens I turn on the bedside light, my eyes scrutinise the room's darker corners, roll then towards the centre light in the room, with five candle-like shades, which begin to tremble, then swing gently, back and forth, the sound creaking and rippling gently around the room, casting long-reaching fingers of shadows. I freeze, sweat breaking over my body. I am seized by a strong urge to pee. I fling the blankets back and charge for the door, twist the ceramic handle and head for my parents' bedroom. But I hesitate. From within their room, sounds. A creaking of bedsprings and some low moanings. I don't wish to investigate this. I turn back, disgust overtaking fear, and gradually retreat as my parents' lust advances in the half-light. For God's sake! At two o'clock in the morning, and at their age? I go to the bathroom and sit for some minutes on the lavatory, head in hands. What is this about, what is this about, what is this about, the words repeat. By the time I enter my bedroom again, the lightshades are still. All is silent. I hear no sound.

I come to recognise that the more conflicted I feel, the stronger the swing of the light, the more violently its back and forth, back and forth. It continues to make me uneasy. It doesn't terrify, but neither am I happy in the presence of this phenomenon. Inexplicably, not once did either parent suggest I move into another bedroom. There is a maid's room, beside Tess's old room, also a maid's room from the old days. I could have slept there. Yet I'm certain Christoph is correct when he suggests that the phenomenon is an embedded memory that originates with Roddy Boyd himself. In my mind's eye, it's him in front of my bedroom fireplace, writing the poetry of rebellion, fomented by the memory of the struggle of the oppressed tribes in the Empty Quarter. Boyd was surely loved by his man, Tom Macklin, who tended his own inner fire, I like to think.

I hope I have convinced Elma that there is generally nothing to be concerned about regarding my bedroom, and its haunting. She probably forgets all about it most of the time. By now, I've pulled my own logic together. Has anything ever happened to me in the bedroom? No, it has not. Have I been always safe? Yes, I have been physically safe. It's not the supernatural that threatens me. But at sixteen, the sounds persist, and continue at seventeen, eighteen and nineteen. In the pitch dark that fills that room even in the middle of the summer nights after returning from a disco or a dance, I click on the bedside cabinet lamp. The surging swing in my ears isn't caused by the blasting rhythms of disco fever and sound systems, but an unsettling pulsation and scratching in the air around me. I then pull blankets around ears and shut my eyes tightly and whilst fearing no evil from the long dead Boyd, I'm nonetheless afraid.

Still, I sometimes feel the lightest of air currents stirring, detect an odour of cumin, paprika, the barest whiff. Above my head, the light fitting swings from the ceiling. I dare not switch off the light. *Scratch, scratch, scratch,* comes the sound. Then rustling. Roddy Boyd settling his papers. But where is he in this room? Eye-swivel around the walls. I swear out loud as I so often do. The sound ceases. He is aware of me then. No more writing, no more scratching of ink on paper. Lamp off eventually. I try to sleep. In an instant the sound returns and the scribe is busy. If this is a spirit, it's a good one, I tell myself. Somehow, sleep comes.

*

My phone rings. I've done a full circle of the lake, squelching in the shallows, photographing birds, weeds and one dead crayfish for my Instagram page. I enjoy the shadows and reflections, a stillness that looks as if I might enter it, right there, and enter another world.

'Hi.'

'Tess?'

'How're things?'

'Just checking in.'

I'm waiting. I know exactly what I'm waiting for, have known from the moment Tess decided to divert to Stella's place.

'Um, things are looking bad, aren't they? Don't know if I'll get back to NYC anytime soon, way things are going.'

Keep calm, bleyb shtil, the Yiddish I remember from some book on the Jews in Krakow. I'm freezing up. I'm freezing for the sake of my survival.

'The skies have gone silent,' I say eventually. 'And it's bloody great. I don't miss anything about the noisy world.'

'So I was thinking,'

'Yeah?'

'I'm nervous about the situation. I'm actually afraid to go to Kilnavarn.'

'It's a long trip,' I say, trying to keep my voice softly neutral. 'Four or five hours?'

I'm thinking of the many times Tess has driven through deep

snow along the motorway to get to a holiday lodge with Allegra in Upstate New York, even further in summer, a good five hours to reach Provincetown for a two-night break with friends.

'Yeah, it is,' she agrees.

'Though you can still get through to see an elderly person who can't look after herself. It's not really so far.'

'But —'

'I know what you're going to say.'

'You do?'

But I shut up. The years of arguments are over. I'll only be accused of guilt-tripping, of judging.

'Stella's on her own too.'

'And?'

'She's a bit isolated,'

How can Tess give a shit about effervescent Stella when she could also care about un-effervescent me, locked up for weeks at Kilnavarn, even if voluntarily? And Elma.

'So you won't be coming?'

'I think it's too risky.'

'Elma was looking forward to seeing you.' And I don't care if that makes her feel guilty.

Neither of us speaks for a moment. Young shoots of wild garlic are already pushing up below the trees, greening the long swards on either side of where I stand.

'Do you really think she's looking forward to seeing me?'

'Of course she is. She loves to see you.'

'Do you really, really, think so?'

'Yes.'

'Maybe you're right,' Tess relents.

'What?'

'I should come.'

I try not to respond with too much brio in case my enthusiasm makes her change her mind. 'That's great,' I say all the same. 'She loves you to bits, you know.'

Curlews call in the background, a light wind rustles the bulrushes near where she stands.

'Can we still have a conversation about this?' Tess goes on. 'I know you don't always get this, but already I feel myself seizing up at the thoughts of *being* there. With *her*. After two hours under that roof, something happens. You know —'

'Perhaps this one time? It might be different? We could share it, couldn't we? And as I say, she loves you. She really does.'

Something prompts me to ask Tess if she ever thought Paddy could have done a better job of intervening, if he too had some role to play. 'I mean, you've always put him on a pedestal, as if he was a saint.'

'He was on my side. He was there. He'd come into my room and comfort me.'

'But he never stood up to her, did he? How can you forgive that? Because I can't.'

'I just do. I know that's weird of me. He never stood up to her properly. He wanted to please her too, which is why he went crazy once and beat the shite out of me, remember? The bath episode?'

Paddy losing his rag in an attempt to side with Elma, pursuing Tess up the stairs and beating her hard, with his hand, so much that ten-year-old Tess jumped into the bath and slipped, hitting her head off the chrome taps. Elma and me at the bottom of the stairs when all goes silent. Paddy emerges from the bathroom, holding Tess in his arms, tightly, himself sobbing and Tess sobbing and roaring as he slides onto the top step of the stairs and rocks her over and over, *I'm sorry love, I'm sorry my little love, I'm so sorry, so sorry, so sorry. . .*

Elma murmurs something about him having gone too far, that it's a bit much, and retreats back into the kitchen, looking guilty. Transfixed, I stand staring up the stairs at the pair of them, a strange shape, a big man holding a slumping, shivering, shocked girl in his arms, it reminds me of Michaelangelo's *Pietà,* a distorted version, but something about mercy filters through to me, even if it's all twisted and my own stomach knots from the sounds and the sights that momentarily lacerate my brain like spinning knives.

'I remember it all. That afternoon. He went berserk or something.'

'You were only fifteen or sixteen,' Tess whispers. There's forgiveness in her voice.

After Paddy's death, I vent my turmoil in *Graveyard Tango*, a five-stanza piece in which I solo-tango up and down our father's grave, stomping stiletto heels into the earth, triumphing that I'm alive and that, being dead, what he thinks or did or didn't do is irrelevant. The poem is published in an English magazine rather than in Ireland. Now though, I wouldn't think twice about publishing it anywhere, and wonder at my own caution back then, as if Great God Daddy was beyond criticism.

Elma couldn't let go of him. She grieved and she wept. In the house. In the car. In the bank, where she didn't know how to conduct her business, and I had to teach her how to lodge a cheque. She cried in the supermarket. On the street. In bed, where she could be found accusing herself, telling the air above her head and below the peculiar, green-tinted, luminous crucifix gifted them for their wedding by Aunt Clara, that he was too good for her. Although they weren't particularly religious, it had always hung there.

My eye falls on a cluster of cyclists making their way along the road on the far side of the lake. I hear them before I actually see them, six men shouting to one another, laughing, pushing along down the road in the direction of the border.

'What's that?' Tess breaks in.

'You can hear them? All the guys are out on bikes these days. Everyone's discovering sport.'

'Not me,' Tess snorts.

'Me neither,' I laugh. 'Like fuck am I going to start running and sea-swimming. *Sea-swimming!* Can you believe it? Everyone's out in force these days, toddling into the freezing sea and then out again to sip their lattes beneath their little fluffy-wuffy beach-robes as they dry off. Or hadn't you heard?'

'Nope. In New York it's still skate-boarding and jogging.'

I'm pleased to be seeing Tess soon. My sister's energy is different from mine. I often wonder if it's because Tess is a Capricorn, and naturally gregarious, revealing new slices of herself all the time. As a strong-headed Arian, I still feel inadequate, although self-contained and outwardly confident, banging my head into stone walls instead of leaping over them. I'd be ashamed if anybody knew that I did actually believe there was something to astrology. We say goodbye and hang up, and I feel better than I did earlier. My sister still fascinates me.

Back at the house, I sit on the edge of the ornamental stone trough, and regard the place with a briefly cold eye. In one way, I can't wait to put the property on the market and sell it, and not for reasons to do with money. In another way, that thought is unbearable, like red hot blades in my heart or wherever the peculiar pain of loss is felt.

I feed Lottie and as ever the dog is grateful. She has relaxed around me. She knows she'll be fed at the right time, that her water bowl will be replenished, her dark head stroked gently.

Hilda is not known to remember the needs of animals, and hates cats especially. I haven't hectored my mother up out of bed at all today as I'm making life easy for myself. I look into the room, enter, then perch on the chartreuse coloured chaise longue at the bottom of the bed. Elma is shut-eyed.

'So how are you?'

My mother stirs. 'Oh. You're here.'

'Yes, many weeks now, remember?'

'Of course I remember. So today is Saturday?'

'It's Sunday.'

'I suppose Tess will phone today.'

'Even better. Tess is coming,' I announce with a certain triumph.

Elma's brows twitch in surprise and she lets out a small gasp. 'Oh. That's something to look forward to. You mean she's flown over here to see *me*?'

'She has,' I reply, touched by this humility. But then she spoils it.

'Not that she ever has any news,' she sighs and yawns. One of her front teeth has chipped badly. 'I don't know what kind of a social life they have out there. She seems to know nobody, doesn't do anything. Of course in America, families keep to themselves, not like our ones, spreading themselves around everywhere and doing the friendliness thing we're famous for. Hah! Makes me laugh that does!'

'Why does it make you laugh, Mum?'

'Because half of it's for show. Doesn't fool me one bit.'

'People like to have friends. Especially later.'

Elma's head turns, her eye has fallen on me. 'Why, *especially later*?' she asks, mimicking me. She has always mimicked people when feeling defensive.

'When you're old, is what I mean.'

'Is that what you mean? How wise of you, Frankie.'

My patience goes. 'Well, you never cultivated too many friends in the neighbourhood. If you had, they'd maybe visit you from time to time.'

Elma looks at me calmly. 'Oh that's charming. Thank God I have Tess to look forward to.'

'I'm sure Tess will be a great help to you,' I remark ironically.

'Really? Oh, by the way, is she still involved with that women's group over there? She mentions that sometimes. I think that's her social life.' Elma chuckles, amused at her other daughter's folly.

'You mean the feminist group? Yes of course.'

'*You mean the feminist group*?' Elma mimics back.

'Billions of women are feminists.'

'I never had any need for it.'

'Didn't you?'

'I was married to your father, so really, I could do as I pleased, as I've told you before, and isn't that what it's all about? I was free.' She draws herself slowly onto her side and sighs. 'Honestly, I don't know what half of these women are on about.'

Nothing will ever convince Elma that there are women whose husbands are complete bastards who beat them up, kick their stomachs, break their teeth, who crush them by word and deed.

'Oh, I've been as free as I wanted to be,' she drifts on.

Annoyed, I get to my feet. 'So what do you want for dinner tonight? Chicken?'

'Any food that's handed to me is a blessing.'

Downstairs, I switch on the television. Sky News shows a Spanish woman, barrel-shaped and with heavily sprayed vermillion hair, who sits gasping for breath on a bench outside a Madrid hospital. There are other scenes, exponential statistics, and a stream of stories about people not keeping themselves physically separate. But for now, we carry on pretty normally. Food must still be prepared. Chicken in a roasting pan with some oil, herbs, butter, smoked paprika slipped beneath the breast skin, half an orange up its rear opening. Place in oven at 180 degrees centigrade. I peel the spuds. We both love roasties sprinkled with a rough twist of Maldon's salt.

Once on a train to a town in Essex, where I was to speak at a literary festival, I admired the different bulk and beauty of the English landscape as the train passed along the river Blackwater, from which this salt is harvested. Everything on a greater scale, somehow, with a different weight of the soil-poetry than in Ireland. In such places, I felt released from doubt, from the voice of childhood, the voice of home, pushing me, telling me to choose modern languages at university, but at the same time advising me to *take it easy at school, don't work too hard, I never did and I got on fine.* I scrape the potatoes angrily.

I'm sick of hearing about the virus. *Springwatch* will be on soon, so I change to BBC1 and settle down to wait for that. Nature heals. Even watching it on television heals in its way. Those jolly and very pleasant English presenters make life seem so easy. In an ideal world I'd have them around a table for dinner, to discuss the state of the natural world, for example, and advances in protecting certain indigenous species of pig, frog or newt. I'd also like to have the company of one of those shepherds from high up in the Pennines, a different kind of man or woman who could talk in a rich regional tongue about the challenges of the seasons. They feel real, I reflect. What they have to say counts and seems far closer to the world I inhabit. Not that I want to go too primitive. But there's an appeal to the notion of having a good bed and bathroom in, say, a cosy croft in the Scottish Isles, perhaps, and getting on with my work within the passage of the planet's rhythms and seasons.

*

My phone vibrates. Jason. I'm ready for bed and sitting in the kitchen, whiskey in hand. Elma is in bed. The house is blissfully quiet. What does he want at this hour?

'Hi.'

'Am I disturbing you?'

'No,' I answer in a tone that lets him know he is disturbing me.

'I've redone chapter seven. The night sections in Jurilovca, okay? It's all very liminal, right?'

No shit Sherlock.

'I've emailed you an attachment. Maybe you'll have a look?'

He sounds out of breath. He is unusually pale. I scan the background behind him on the screen. He's at home, sitting to the right of a long, uncurtained window, and in the window, a blue glass vase of crisped, almost dead daffodils. Even on the phone, I see the line of cellular decay at the watermark.

'I'll get back to you tomorrow. How's that?'

'Cool.'

'And hey?' Curiosity about his living space erupts.

'What?'

'You at home? In your own place?'

'It was my mother's. She left it to me.'

'Lucky you. No rent pressure.'

'I do still need to work, you know.' He sounds mildly indignant, as if defending himself against someone who thinks his life is too easy.

'So?'

'I work six weeks at the Post Office before and after Christmas. The amount of crap that people buy. . .they love their boxes with the Amazon smile.'

I smile guiltily, thinking of my own on-line purchasing, the pristine wrapped boxes that arrive occasionally from Saint and Sofia, and more regularly from ASOS, and how I enjoy opening each one, breaking the little sticky black tab, unfolding the whispering tissue paper, lifting a new garment from its scented bedding.

Jason carries on. 'Then from February to June I'm in The Sitric. Accommodation Porter.'

'New hotel?'

'It's down the Liffey estuary at Grand Canal Harbour. It attracts an unusual clientele. Diverse, I mean.'

'So what do you actually do?' I couldn't care less about his diverse clientele, but what he works at piques my curiosity.

'I port.' He tells me how he wheels vast baskets of bedding from each floor every day down into the basement of the building, where purple laundry vans drive in and collect it. I wouldn't believe how much alcohol gets spilt on the sheets. And other excrescences. Semen, menstrual blood, urine. Shit-streaks too. And tea, coffee, wine and egg yolk. 'They think that just because they pay for something, they can do what they like. I wouldn't even call them animals, because that would insult animals.'

'Sounds awful,' I say. I did such work in Munich in the summer of '75, cleaning rooms and changing sheets. It was true. The filth of others. But people were not like animals, because animals were pure, animals were where God resided, so people should never, ever, be compared to them in a negative way, because people always fell short. People were like something else, the worst possible version of themselves perhaps. Disorderly, dirty, passive and therefore wicked. Helpless too.

'It is,' he responds, 'but I get through it.' There's a pause. 'How're things your end?'

'So-so,' I respond in an attempt at sounding sane. I don't want to start ranting.

'How?'

'I mean, I'm here for now. Away from my husband. The Four Horsemen of the Apocalypse are galloping and guess what? My mother is lying up in her bed unawares and I'm drinking whiskey late at night, need I say more?'

'Do you need her to be so aware, or something?'

The question stalls me.

'Is she dying?' he probes more gently.

'Not imminently. At least I don't think so.'

'Like the rest of us then. So she's an old lady with a rambling mind. You'll be glad someday that you spent this time with her.'

Gimme a break. 'You're not minding her, you don't know her, and she isn't any quiet old lady sitting over her knitting in the corner of a kitchen.'

'Would you want her to be like that?'

'Yes, actually.'

A very traditional, crocheting or knitting kind of a mother with not too much to say except to emit occasional wisdoms about the state of the world and how great the young people are today. Who would not need to be so central, pulling the ground from beneath me, with her joking, teasing and jeering. I'm aware of my own restrictive wishes.

'Yes,' I repeat for the sake of it.

'Maybe I'm speaking out of turn. Both my parents are dead, but I still miss them.' A silence. 'And by the way, I'm still not feeling the best.'

'What's wrong with you now?'

'Dunno. I'm waiting for blood-test results. My bones ache and the balls of my feet feel like I'm walking on marbles.'

'Arthritis? You're a bit young for that.'

'Maybe. I'll know soon enough.'

'I hope you find out. This isn't the first time you've mentioned it.'

'It's on my mind. . .' He shrugs and is it my imagination that he looks even paler than he did a few minutes ago?

'Curiosity now. When did your parents die?'

As he responds, his face becomes blank, as if he is reading an inner account, as if he has found distance within himself. His father Olaf, he says, died in the North Tower of the World Trade Centre on 9/11.

'You said both your parents were dead. What happened with Alice?'

'She took an overdose.'

'Oh Jesus. That's awful.'

The silence between us fills with the sound of background traffic. A dog barking somewhere near him, its voice-map reaching my ears.

'I'm sorry.' It's all I can think to say, wondering why I'd even asked him in the first place.

'Thanks. But you know something? I think I'm going to have a lie-down and do fuck-all for a while. Admire the ceiling.'

'Do that. We can talk tomorrow. I'm looking forward to reading this.' I click on Leave and the screen blanks out.

The following day, by the time I finish reading Jason's writing and save it back into its folder, I've forgotten to make lunch and Elma is shouting from the bedroom. I switch off the oven and sit for a moment, face in hands. The book is a compelling account of a young man's odyssey through post-Ceauşescu Romania as the country recovers from the ravages of over forty years ago when images of twisted, crazed or starved children and babies lit up the screens of the watching West like a nightly horror movie. Vivid writing. I am confirmed in my sense that Jason has found that elusive quality known as voice.

I text him. *It's fine. Keep going. Read my notes. I'm convinced! F.*

Tess's daughter Allegra tells me that only older people sign off on their texts and use emojis, so my compromise is to use my initial. It seems bald without one.

9

No sooner have I stuck my head around the bedroom door to get my mother up than Elma asks about *that noise.*

'What noise?'

'You know. The *noise.* Of course you know.'

'I don't know. What are you talking about?'

Elma moves her hands in little circles as she struggles to remember. 'Don't be obtuse Frankie, you *know*!'

'I don't.'

'The noise. . .the noise, for heaven's sake?'

She is sighing heavily, rolling her eyes, trying to whirl the memory into action. 'That thing that. . .long ago. . .in your room. . .'

'Oh, that. That ended well, didn't it?'

She stares, head tilted to one side on the pillow as she struggles to recall. 'Yes, it did,' she gambles. Then, 'No seriously, I can't remember what happened. Tell me again.'

I begin. 'One summer morning long ago when I was about fourteen, it was quite early but bright and I heard it. I'd been awake, because in those days I found it hard to sleep.' I am speaking in my storytelling voice, the one I use when giving public readings from my fiction.

'Why did you find it so hard to sleep?'

'Between one thing and the other, I hardly slept,' I reply evasively. 'The songbirds in the garden, for one thing.'

'But what else? What things?'

Elma is elsewhere. She is quite innocent now, she gazes at me with wide, expectant eyes and in that moment I know I still love her. Her innocence perplexes me, and I wonder who is innocent and who guilty, who says they remember something, but do not remember correctly. Or who forgets, or claims to forget, because remembering is too painful.

'Frankie? Are you listening? What are you talking about?' Elma persists.

Have I forgiven myself as un-acting child witness? I believe in sin, in the form of ignorance, the roots of every black and poisonous flower that infects others, I believe that even when the worst of people are aware of their own evil, they are not truly aware. Such people have somehow grown up devoid of a pain barometer and as such their awareness of their own evil is stunted. Does this mean that they should go unpunished? No, I decide. Because although they are naturally born in this way, it does not mean they are innocent. And so I come full circle again. Who is innocent? Who is guilty? And who remembers anything in a way that will make any difference to the procession through a material place we are more physically attached to than we can ever really imagine?

'I was suffering from a child's broken heart,' I announce dramatically, flinging my arms in the air. 'No, not quite. But I was disturbed by what was going on in this house.'

'Oh really, is that a fact?' Elma drawls, totally pissed at me now.

'Yes it's a fact,'

'You're talking nonsense.'

'I'm trying to answer you.' Every so often, I attempt truthfulness and not brutality. 'I was disturbed and unhappy. No wonder Tess turned to drink. And you and Paddy were clueless. Remember that?'

Elma shrugs. 'Oh be honest, why don't you! How could I forget? Sure it nearly killed your poor father. I never saw him so upset in my whole life, though I wasn't bothered by her antics so much as the annoyance she caused. Imagine how we felt having to go to that drying-out house in Dublin, to see her like that and to hear all our family business paraded before a roomful of strangers, all hand-holding in a circle and that stupid Serenity Prayer at the start of each session? Serenity? Nobody could be serene in that set-up! How do you think we felt about that? She never did one single thing to make us proud.'

'She became a speech and language pathologist, or have you forgotten?'

'What's that when it's at home? An American way of saying speech therapist?'

'That's not the point!'

'And what is?'

'She did it all herself. She sorted her life out once she left. She slaved to get to where she needed to be. She really worked. Whether or not she made you proud, as you call it.'

For once, Elma has no response, instead turning her head to one side, shutting her eyes as if to blank me out of her sight.

*

How our mother smirked and seemed bemused during some of the addicts' testimonies, or their families' testimonies. A young fellow off his head with drink, a truckload of his father's prime cattle, ready for export, driven along Dun Laoghaire promenade, scattering Sunday morning strollers, then braking so hard the truck tipped over, half the cattle fell into the harbour and drowned. A pity the driver didn't drown, Elma said later as we crossed the city in the car, which heaved and stalled in the evening traffic. Oh yes, very comical, Elma. And comical too, the boy who stole from his impoverished mother's purse, and the man who frightened his children and beat his wife every Saturday night. It was all so very comical. Elma enjoyed being allowed to write down her own testimony about Tess, about all the terrible things Tess had done, not staying in touch, ignoring letters and phone calls, stealing from Paddy's wallet, refusing to help with housework when she did put in an appearance, borrowing money from Paddy and never giving it back, losing job after job, fees paid for a university course she rarely attended. Elma was very happy to provide such a written account to the counsellors and still retains a copy of her testimony in one of her jewellery cases.

Her reading aloud — as we all had to do with our testimonies — was perfection itself, the care she took, as if rehearsed for the local dramatic society. I stared aghast, my throat tightening as the need to sob filled my chest, then looked at Paddy, who was studying his knees, his mouth tight. Afterwards, I returned home to Christoph in Tipperary and cried for an hour in the deep warm bath he filled for me that evening. I could not understand how Elma found the tragedy of all that had happened to all these people such an amusement, people born sweet, fresh and with hope in their little bones and blood as they emerged wetly from between their mother's thighs.

But Tess is perceptive in ways I'm not. I mentioned it to her a few months into her recovery when we met in a coffee-shop on Westmoreland Street. She was on her office lunch break. She said that Elma had never been exposed to so many people speaking openly and in a group about the mess of their lives, allowing others to hear it.

'It's possible,' she said, 'that she was so shocked that her tittering was more of a nervous reaction rather than outright amusement? And if I'm honest,' she goes on thoughtfully, 'some of the stories are. . .were. . .mad. . .'

*

'Mum?' Silence. 'Mother? Can we return to your original question about the noise in my bedroom?'

'Do, sweetheart.'

'Remember how, that morning when I was a teenager I listened and listened. In the daylight the sound no longer seemed —'

'Supernatural? No longer supernatural? Go on!'

'Yes, I sat up in bed quite a while trying to locate the source of the sound. It still went *scratch, scratch, scratch,* of course.'

'But you were no longer afraid.'

'True. Well, not much. I was determined.'

'You always were determined, I'll grant you. You had things to overcome.'

'Was I determined? What things?'

'Oh, I can't remember them all.'

'Thank you, Mother.' I am gratified by that vague acknowledgement. 'Anyway, I realised it came from near the window, from behind the shutters. And I crept across the room because I didn't want to disturb the creature, or thing, or whatever it was. And I stood by the window-shutter, the left-hand one, and waited and listened.'

'And it having frightened the life out of you!' Elma, completely absorbed by now, her small hands gripping the top of the bed covering, eyes bright.

'So, I opened it slowly.'

'You did. And?'

'Of all things, there lay a small bat.'

'A *bat*!' she repeats, as if this was new knowledge.

'A tiny brownie-black fellow with his big wings spread, and a terrified, mousy face on him as he froze in the sudden light and me staring in.'

'So what did you do? Did you kill him?'

'Of course I didn't kill him. Why would I kill a bat?' My voice rises. 'I like bats. Remember we had the bat experts here, checking out the colony? I closed the shutter quickly. I didn't want to frighten him. I wonder what it's like up in the attic now? I haven't been for years.'

'Oh,' Elma says loftily, 'full of bat-shit I suppose. Black. Silent as the grave.'

'You know I used to go there when I was a teenager?'

'Really? Whatever for?'

'Just to pace up and down the length of it. There was so much junk too, old baskets and boxes, toys and books. But you wouldn't know, you didn't bother going up there much, did you?'

What I don't say is that it was a place to feel myself open up and out, a bit like the oculus window, which was comprised of many panes, a few of which could be pushed open by a flange; it was a place in which I could calm down and slowly expand the map of myself and know there was so much more to unravel and travel within.

'I felt calm there. Maybe because I knew Roddy Boyd once wrote beneath the light of the oculus window, and scribbled about adventures.'

Boyd would have watched as I have done, the fields of Kilnavarn falling away below him to the long lake and its shadows. To think Elma has only a few times in all these years visited this part of her own house, her kingdom. Vast, eerie, another world hovering above our daily world, where different things happened and animal and insect life reigned.

'The story of the bat. A good story,' Elma says reflectively.

'Yes. But it didn't end there.'

'Why? What do you mean?'

'It's true, but not the whole truth.' I'm staring at Elma, trying to gauge her reaction to this information.

'You mean. . .there was never any bat?' her expression drops, her mouth slightly open.

'Oh there was a bat alright, but the sounds have never gone away either, even after we closed up the hole in that shutter and the bats left.' I'm quite enjoying myself, marvelling at my own teasing.

'Does that mean the room really *is* haunted? No wonder I always got a strange feeling in your bedroom. . .and the strangest of smells sometimes, a mixture of cats and foreign cooking. And you only told me the bit about the bat. But why would you do that to me, Frankie, or what kind of an oddity are you? Sure we should've had the place exorcised!'

I grin at the idea of having the priest calling to perform an exorcism. The local priest probably wouldn't have done it I tell Elma. They'd call in an expert, exorcism news goes straight through to the Vatican and is taken quite seriously. A Jesuit would be called, someone trained to take these things seriously.

'Anyway, it isn't — wasn't — an evil presence, Mum, it really isn't.'

The bat in the bedroom, the bat behind the shutters. A way of sparing my mother further anxiety at a time when she was worrying herself to a frazzle over my health. She smothered me, but I still felt sorry for her. All was more or less quite bearable in that haunted bedroom air, which I had grown used to, with its occasional light waft of spices I couldn't at the time identify but which I now know to be the essences of Arabic cuisine: cardamom, cumin, coriander. In that room, I read the *ABC of Communism*, Mao's *Little Red Book*, and a sex manual from England which referenced Mao by being called *The Little Red Schoolbook*. The book told me everything I wanted to know about sex, contraception, even when there was none to be had in Ireland, and about masturbation which, being a bit obtuse, I hadn't had much success at despite my best attempts to follow the book's instructions when locked safely in the bathroom. I never tried anything like that in the bedroom. In case Roddy Boyd was watching, so to speak. I lived permanently in an unreleased ache of lust. Even though Roddy Boyd himself was an experienced gentleman and he would have approved, I imagine, of the how tos and whys of everything for a girl in 1971. So, in the spirit of Roddy Boyd, and from time to time still feeling uneasy in that bedroom, I read very widely indeed. I tried to keep myself calm, so as not to raise his ghost.

'You were very anxious, Mum. I wanted to make you feel better after I was sick. You didn't need a haunted room along with everything else.'

'Everything else?' My mother looks at me, surprised.

'Need I say more?'

'You were worried about me.'

'That's true.'

'You were fucking insane, in fact.'

'No need for that language.'

I love the way she accepts my calling her insane yet dislikes my swearing.

'But it mostly stopped.' I feel the need to dial things down a bit. 'It's hardly ever there now,' I lie. 'I'll never know why. Yes, after I returned from college it had mostly stopped.'

'Is it still stopped then?'

I pause. 'If it hasn't, it doesn't keep me awake very much. I sleep there peacefully.'

'If you say so,' Elma says, suddenly complacent.

'Do you remember the days when a picture falling off a wall was an omen?' Elma begins again. 'Or the footsteps your Nana heard before your uncle Peter died. Came to the door they did one night, but ne'er a one knocked nor entered. He died two days later.'

'We're better off without superstition,' I say.

'Are we? But that room is uneasy.'

'Uneasy? How so?'

'I mean that there are places that never feel right. Harmless, most of them, rooms that are built in the wrong shape and where the wrong things happened. But don't mind me, my head's wandering. . .'

'People shouldn't be afraid. We need logic. Even if we can't understand what isn't quite logical. No room for superstition or fear.'

'I can't follow you now, you've gone all intellectual on me. Anyway, I think I'll get up,' she says suddenly. 'Fetch me my wig, the light blonde one. I don't want to scare any visitors, but I like the smell of that dinner. Well-cooked, I'd say.'

I go out to the landing and slip the wig off the head of St Joseph, and return to the bedroom, twirling it on my hand. I remind myself to start disinfecting the door handles. Better do that than have Hilda back sprinkling more Holy Water around Elma's bed to protect her from things tailed, forked and horned and other agents of the night. She's an almost extinct kind of Catholic.

*

At eight thirty all television programmes are interrupted by another bulletin from Government headquarters. A two-kilometre walk is allowed, alone or with a family member from the same house. Now I'm fretting about my return to Christoph. With absence, my heart hasn't grown fonder. It just stops growing in any particular direction, and I suspect mine measures temperate to cool. There's nothing to heighten it's temperature. I should travel home soon. On the other hand, Christoph might also have come up here, demanding something of me. Like what the hell I'm doing staying away from Tipperary so long, for example, or don't I want him anymore? If he cares for me, he should make a few demands instead of being so tolerant. Kilnavarn has stolen enough from my life, has often had my best when Christoph did not, when he might have had more, but rarely complained. Does Elma need me? I can't be sure of that, except in the most rudimentary way. Elma doesn't really care for company unless it entertains her.

While she watches television, I am in the kitchen. Lottie and Jimmy are pacing and slinking between both rooms, the dog wagging her tail and looking questioningly at me, while the cat sits and stares, occasionally licking a paw. The cat, of course, is signalling hunger. *Feed me now.* I move from the kitchen towards the hall. The sound of a television gameshow pours out into the house. I hear a competitor answering a question with absolute confidence that the capital of Sweden is Helsinki.

My attention is held by the view, my eye moving slowly along each tree, beginning to the left of the house where a large, awkward-shaped oak hangs over the east wing, elevated on the first rise to the upper field. Other trees have always been there and are the most interesting by virtue of age, shape and my attachment to them. The newer trees are planted in the lower garden to the right of the house and down the bottom of another slope: maples, a weeping ash, a small, twisted hazel which always annoyed Elma because it has remained miniature and stunted. To these, I have no attachment. But to the other trees I feel like a relative. These trees are my childhood kin, known all my life since we, the Esmonds, moved up into Kilnavarn. How I will ever leave these trees behind is a prospect I cannot even begin to deal with. On our travels together, Christoph and I have photographed trees and more trees, from the ficus and clown trees of São Paulo, to the tea-trees and deep eucalyptus forests of Australia, and on to the teak forests of Laos. I can say that our interest in trees is inexhaustible.

I feel a pain right in the centre of my torso — probably somewhere between my heart and my gut — when I contemplate leaving the trees, handing them over to someone else for good. And when I think of the gap between the desire I feel for Christoph and the desire I actually want, I feel something else: a passion-seamed emptiness, a deep mine into which I have sunk, wanting to be caught, drawn up and away, tussled and turned, loved to death.

Growing old is so hard.

*

More than half my travelling life has been spent with Christoph, the rest by myself or occasionally with other writers, attending some literary festival or other. It is the characteristic of our generation. Travel at will, whenever and however possible, shoestring decisions and economies.

Christoph has also been my best friend and lover. Despite my occasional closeness to others — men who have briefly become muses, one or two female friends whose artistic sparkle makes of me a bee to their honey — he is the man to whom I always freely return. When he got his holidays and the university closed, once the papers were marked, and he'd filed an essay or two for publication, or sent in his abstract for some conference in late summer in a pleasant destination, we did the Irish thing of heading off. The thing was to 'head off.' To get ourselves off the island. To set our feet on some great continent and at the same time feel ourselves sprout powerful wings.

Although I have never kept maps in quite the same way as Elma, there are some, piled untidily at home in my study, which also contains my old stamp collection, a world atlas, and travel guides on France, Northern Spain and Sardinia. Life with Christoph is marked by an inventory of locations, and few of these places have disappointed us. I fetch far back in memory and raise them up. Places like Torremolinos in 1978, where I first read Cervantes, Yugoslavia in 1980, where I read Bruce Chatwin's 'In Patagonia' and where I noticed a heavy, silver-haired German who never took his eyes off Christoph. That was not unusual and happened also in Crete, where several young men trailed Christoph around Knossos with quiet, ardent eyes. Then work in Heidelberg, both of us translating at the university. Later, Tunisia, Turkey, Morocco, Egypt, Portugal. A break in Achill Island during Italia '90, when Paddy and Elma also joined us for four nights. Elma, astonished by the fierce, summer gold and purple beauty of the island, its high cliffs and rushing tides. She enjoyed herself and even went cycling with Paddy from village to village along the ribbon roads. Christoph and I had frantic sex in a high wind half way up Croghaun sea cliffs, using my green raincoat as a bed. Later, we shouted and cheered in the pub at Packie Bonner's penalty save against Romania.

But travel changed and like everybody else we became fussier. It wasn't just Spain or Torremolinos now, but the Costa de la Luz and the undiscovered towns around Cadiz, it wasn't just Brittany with the rest of the happy campers, but Rocamadour, Domme, Belvès and the prehistoric caves at Lascaux. And America was no use unless we crossed the border into Mexico, spending two nights in Tijuana with Allegra, whose flight from New York was Tess's birthday gift to her daughter that year. Tijuana the despised, Tijuana the pharmaceutical haven for anyone who wants to stock up on uppers, downers, sleepers, wakers, whatever it takes to get through life. Being with Allegra for those days made us wonder for the first time if it had been a mistake not to have children. Grace-filled, wonderful Allegra, managing her own life thanks to, or in spite of, Tess's hands-off parenting style — a little too hands-off in my private view — because Tess never advised as a mother, but as a teenager Allegra wrote occasionally to me, airing her views on friends, teachers, and what her Mom said about everything.

I remember watching Allegra move along the streets of

Tijuana. It was Mexico Day, and the locals were celebrating with flags and music. Allegra was grown up, a young adult of twenty-three, beautiful, brown as a berry from the sunshine, with long hair stained to golden strands that twisted and danced as she moved. As she drifted along the long main street, men and women looked at her, some called out cheerfully *Hola tũ, hermosa niña! Quiero casarme contigo!* Even so, if she was a girl alone in Tijuana, I knew, a migrant girl for example, it wouldn't be a question of marriage, it would be gropes or even rape by any of the clusters of men hanging around that day. At the thought, I shiver. We and our like — Christoph, Tess, Allegra, Elma, the whole of white Europe even — are the minority of the sometimes relatively safe. Allegra can afford to be beautiful. To believe that she is free, at least for a while. There is a better chance that she will not be raped in New York. She is white enough, not a migrant. But she is female.

If I were to look at the planet and if it showed my travel path-lines and not just the ones on Google that my phone presents every so often, I would find a web of journeys, away from Monaghan, from Tipperary, from Ireland, away from myself, while in Christoph's company. Because we were always running from something and towards something else. Isn't that the nature of living for most people? Restlessness, ambition, the drive for knowledge. Knowledge was everything to Christoph and me. Not of the facts, but of what lay behind facts. And that is why we took the weirdest steam-train journey ever into the heart of Sardinia one day in summer 2014, the air blasting in hotly through the open windows as we rattled along.

Arriving in the small town of Soddì, where a crowd of visitors had been expected but only we arrived to be hosted to a feast of hospitality by the Mayor and assembled dignitaries from the local museum. The little crowd concealed their disappointment at the non-arrival of tourists other than us, but made us feel special, so that as they walked us slowly towards the fossilised tree-trunks exhibited in front of the church of Santa Maria Maddelena, we felt an extra pressure to be responsive and interested. But it was no pressure. The awareness of such things sits in such unequivocal opposition to my life and conversations with Elma, because although Elma enjoyed knowing about famous people who achieved greatness and overcame obstacles, she didn't much care for the quieter elements. So, fossilised tree-trunks are a memory of a time in which other, dramatic things occurred. Not rapidly, but slowly, due to climate and attrition. Fossilised tree-trunks are a visual holograph carried from the far past. They announce themselves without pomposity, so far removed from Michaelangelo's graceful David, or his Pietà, as to be practically invisible, far removed from obelisks and Pharoh's heads, from the Valley of the Kings and Queens, from the said birthplace of the infant Jesus Christ, from the Giant's Causeway and its legends about Fionn Mac Cumhaill, from anything exclamatory.

So what was all that about, I ask myself. And will I still want to do it? Somehow, it seems as if life has offered me and Christoph so much, and that we have actually sometimes known how and when to enjoy it. With Christoph by my side, I could learn the things I needed to learn in order to largely depart my younger self. All this was true and incontestable.

It would be a lie to say I never found him boring. I can tell that some of his dearest male friends find him a little heavy. Even his mother had announced unceremoniously before we married that, *Du wirst dich mit ihm langweilen*, you'll get bored with him. She was right about that. I remember her resting her steady, brown gaze on me, recognising the desperately giddy joy which

I appeared to be taking in her son, before deciding that he might not always be a match for such joy. I tell him his tendency to imagine disaster where there is none reflects a lack of confidence by him. And, like most people who rationalise the behaviour of a spouse, I also blame his too-sensible mother, just as I blame my own for a different spectrum of breaches.

If the world ever returns to itself, it will never be the same as before. Because everything changes, there can be no exact replay of the way we were. At this thought, my sadness is like an unburst fluid pressing against my soul. It's possible, after all, that travel as I have known it, may in the future not occur at all. Instead, we may resign ourselves to tilling our own garden, like Voltaire's foolishly optimistic Candide, and perhaps agree, eventually, that some things happen for the best, balancing reasons.

Except that they don't.

Not always.

10

It takes me most of the first two years to unlearn my silences. Boarding school is for my own good, and the company of girls from other places will take me out of myself. I often wonder about being taken out of myself, and how to take someone out of her own self, and how that is ever possible, because surely the *self* inhabits the space within and cannot be distanced from the rest of you.

In first year, all class results are posted on the notice-board on the school veranda which shelters us from rain as we parade from one part of the school to the chapel. I feel very stupid as my weekly marks slide gradually downwards. This isn't like Top of the Pops, and yet it is. The bacon factory manager's daughter always tops maths and Latin, the Dublin girls from the all-Irish schools, as well as the Donegal Gaeltacht girls always wrestle for the top five positions in Irish. Marie O'Driscoll in the year above has just won the European Schools Day Essay Writing Competition, which makes her briefly famous as someone who is definitely a future writer, something the nuns respect. She becomes an engineer. In my own class, another girl vies with me to top English, then sulks when I hold my position. But everything about English comes automatically. In this alone, I am quietly confident, soaked in an understanding and grasp of words, meanings, imaginings that is far ahead of the others. I know this without vanity.

Perhaps I have not been such a bad sister after all. Tess misses me! Paddy writes that she has been getting up in the middle of the night to play with the cat, and also to play Monopoly with herself, being player and opponent at once.

I get up around 4 to check on Tess and often she is below in the kitchen, the pet. But we'll get over this little bump on the road, he wrote, *and everything is in your mother's capable hands and all will be well. She is bringing Tess to see an optician to have her eyes checked, though her eyesight seems good. But some children fall behind at school if they're not seeing the blackboard properly so perhaps her eyesight is defective. I'm busy as ever at the hospital, with new theatre equipment due in from Frankfurt, a better anaesthetic machine for one thing, three new ECG monitors and a surgical table that slides the patient back onto a stretcher. Can you believe that? I'll bring you up during the holidays and you can try it out! It's useful with heavy people. We're also getting some blanket warmers and new surgical lights. But someday, if you do well in your Leaving Certificate, perhaps you might go on to the UCD School of Medicine yourself. Well, dear daughter, do your best and God will be good to us.*

Take care and know that we love and miss you,
Your loving Daddy x x x

I love Paddy's letters with their hope for my future, despite some of the content and my worry about Tess, which at the time brings an uncomfortable pain to my stomach. I inscribe my feelings about her in a little diary, in tiny hand-writing, always in different coloured inks. Elma's letters, on the other hand, are funny in their way, though they are often critical of other women. She and Aunt Elizabeth are locked in life-long rivalry. They hold petty secrets from one another, and live either in a state of secretiveness or its opposite, when they are the best of friends again and tell each other everything. I note how my mother's letters change in tone and energy, though those are not the words I think of. She writes often about the town's new musical society, and how it is run by a man from Athlone.

The Director is a musical genius, right to his fingertips, and he has given me my chance to sing in the next musical. That'll be New Moon, *you won't have heard of it, but it's a lovely show. I went shopping today. Met Mrs. Connolly from The Rectory and we chatted. She spoke about a new recipe for stuffed peppers, though where she got those in our town I can't imagine. She didn't say, and anyway I'm sure Auguste Escoffier (if you know who he is) needn't worry, haha! After that in the new supermarket I met Mrs. Chatterjee. Her husband the dentist is very busy since he's come to town. He also does orthodontics. Might be able to straighten out those two front teeth of yours, she said, though not in those words, haha again! She also gave me Indian stamps for your collection, they're in my jewellery case and in case anything happens to me and your father gets fed up and throws me out, big joke! Very nice of Mrs Chatterjee to think of you. She's in the ICA now and was all talk about that and you know my feelings about that crowd.*

Over the next year, Elma's time with the musical society

increases. There are two rehearsals a week, but these increase to four or sometimes five times a week. Paddy encourages her from behind *The Irish Times* to go and enjoy herself with the *artistes.* During the Christmas holidays, I once awaken to find Elma slipping into bed beside me. I sense the energetic and restless approach of an over-heated body. I tell my mother to go away, to go to her own bed, but she ignores me and after a few moments rustling the sheets falls fast asleep on her back.

Gradually, I piece it together. Some nights she slides into my bed instead of hers and Paddy's, because, she claims, it's late and she doesn't want to disturb him as he has work the next day. There is something unpleasant about my mother's body heat. But I remain silent. Not the old silence, but a new one which involves much thinking on my part. Even a little exciting, this other life I sense, although I wonder about Paddy. Surely he couldn't be so blind? And the other man, the musical genius, is very handsome, and once, admires my hair and touches it gently. To my surprise, I am not outraged, although I feel that I ought to be, even if out of loyalty to my mother. It says something about his weak and untrustworthy character, even I can see that. I watch him conduct the orchestra throughout *New Moon,* and the next year *South Pacific,* and yet another year for *The Gondoliers.* I admire the taut pull of his dark evening coat across his back as his arms rise to prompt the first violins or the brass section in the orchestra. I envy the singers, coming together, different from their street selves, people playing lords, ladies, peasants, wandering players, gypsies, belly-dancers, drummers and wicked witches. I also admire Elma's performances, her warm mezzo voice, and the fact that she must be a good performer because I am completely able to forget that this is my mother. At such moments, I feel proud of my talented mother.

When I am older I am taken out of boarding school and attend as a day-girl. I have been seriously ill with an as yet unspecified condition and my parents no longer entrust me to the care of the nuns. One day, I arrive home on my bike to find the musical genius's metallic pale blue Scirocco outside the house. It is half past four in the afternoon. In the back door, I make my way to the sitting-room, which has a piano, following the sound. There they are, he playing and Elma singing. *Take my hand, I'm a stranger in Paradise.* From the musical Kismet. Her voice is rich, her eyes are shining with a light I hardly recognise. Such happiness is a revelation. Alexander Borodin's original melody shows a thing or two about love, I think, but so, I think, does Elma, and I recognise in the song something I have not yet known. Transcendence. Rapture. Elma and the musical genius are enraptured. They *are* Marsinah and Caliph.

'I pray night and day for forgiveness,' she confides to me years later. I tell her not to be silly, and ask if she thinks the musical genius lies awake praying for forgiveness, he with his poor wife and six children in another town far away? When Elma reads my first published short story, *Bone Picker,* she discovers that I've known all along, even if I depict a single mother and her lonely daughter, both drawn to the alcoholic musical genius, with a wife and six neglected children, and relocate them in a seaside town with a sonorous foghorn sounding through the night.

*

I open the press where Elma used to keep her emery boards and nail polishes. They are still there, long dried-up and unusable, a rainbow of tones ranging from pale pink to coral and on to orange and red. 'It's a mood thing,' she once told me. 'Colour reflects my mood.'

'So what does red mean?'

'I'm either very happy or very angry.'

'And pink?'

'Oh bored, so bored, just getting on with it.'

Boredom. Indolence. The plight of the middle-class women of Elma's generation. Not quite qualified for anything because they married immediately after school or before finishing college. All along the border, a baby producing line of Catholics, with Protestants having smaller families. Catholics who are not cowed by their religion buy contraception in the North, and it is assumed that those with a mere two or three children are being smart, crossing over to get the Pill or some 'French Letters'. It's a world of Omo and Daz, when kitchen crockery is washed in sudsy water and not rinsed, and women shave their legs but never wax. A world too of Fry's Chocolate Cream bars, or Emerald sweets in a crinkling packet, of quarter pound bags of Cinnamon Drops, and Instant Whip. Margarine comes into vogue, and the world discovers hydrogenated fats. Paddy, who constantly treats coronary patients at the hospital, tells me and Tess that a hydrogen molecule added to the natural unsaturated fatty acid molecules of vegetable oil make it more saturated, and then transform oil from liquid to solid. It is far more dangerous to the health than butter, he emphasises, which is good in moderation. Margarine raises the body's cholesterol, he informs us. Occasionally, as relaxation, he turns his hand to bread baking, serving it up thickly buttered and with a spoon of blackcurrant jam. Although faintly amused by his efforts, Elma does not object. He has domesticated traits and used to try knitting when he was a child, she tells me in an indulgent voice, because he was his mother's favourite, her white-headed boy *Pádraig*. Since he travelled up to our town in '47, nobody has called him by that name, because Elma so dislikes Irish names, finding them unsuitable for modern life. It had to be Patrick or Paddy, with none of the shame of the old language.

Where the hell was Paddy during the mid-years of his marriage to Elma? I ask this constantly. He often thought about our diet as children and used to buy a big crate of eating apples which we could take anytime we liked during the harsh Monaghan winters. It would be left on the floor of his study. He believed in the value of fruit for growing bodies. That room smelt of apples, whiskey and books. But where, in his head, was the map of where he and Elma had come from and where they were to go? Because it seems to me that if Paddy had had a map outside of his life as one of the hospital's male deities, or some coordinates on how love can proceed without harm to others, many things might not have occurred. First, do no harm, as the Hippocratic Oath states. There should be a similar quite specific oath for people intending to have children. Elma might not have been the tyrant she became, she might not have fallen for the musical genius and might have made some lasting friendships. She might also have been a decent mother to Tess.

I half listen to the sound of the television gameshow from the other room across the hallway. In the dining-room, I root through two cardboard boxes with impatient, searching fingers. My fingers have a sense of purpose although I don't know what this search is about. I am sick of old photographs, because they awaken memory. Afraid of them perhaps, because I might remember even more. A black flower with a poisoned stem and root system. Such images pervade the present and represent to us what we think is the truth. Sometimes it is the truth. But this evening, I don't seek.

My hand slips beneath three copybooks. One of them is red-covered, with feint-ruled lines, and beneath, two lines of the copybook owner's name and address. *Padraig Joseph Esmond*, I read, *Fernvilla, New Ross, Co Wexford.* On the inside cover, Paddy has pasted a photograph of the Taj Mahal, photographed by Dorien Leigh. It is 1936. Opposite is pasted a colour-shaded photograph of a ship, described as *a four-masted barque,* Pamir, *leaving Dublin Bay on her return voyage to Australia*. Paddy inhabits our baby-bear shaped Ireland, with its front paws flung out towards the Atlantic, its truncated aspirations and the twinning of Church and State, but at the same time he is out there, in the world, all the time observant of the build-up to war. Other interests include the motor car, with newspaper cut-outs of a 5 cv. Decauville photographed in the Bois de Boulogne in 1900. Another, pasted to the copybook in 1937, in an article headlined *Scotland for the Motorist,* shows a Ford which has just made the climb to the top of Ben Nevis, with a snowy summit in the background. A thirty-year-old veteran war horse, a hero, is brought back from Belgium to Ipswich on December 13th 1937, the expense borne by local children who collected farthings to ensure that such horses ended their days in comfort.

The war is what mostly interests Paddy. Through 1937, 1938, he is reading, cutting, pasting his chronicle. *Absorbment of Austria by Reich, March 13th 1938,* he writes beneath a map which depicts the German offensive from Passau to Linz, from Rosenheim to Salzburg and from Rosenheim to Kufstein. Another picture shows the first German troops and horses pouring into Salzburg over the Salzach Bridge. Christoph will want to see this, I'm thinking, even if he knows it all already, but the hand-created chronicle is irreplaceable. On March 11th 1940, Paddy writes how Herr Hitler declared, 'I live now for one task alone — to concentrate day and night on victory, to fight for it, to work for it, and, if necessary, not to spare my own life, realising that this time Germany's future will be shaped for many centuries.' Beneath it, a photograph of his hen's-ass, anal, face. No wonder he suffered from life-long constipation. Winston Churchill is photographed smiling in May 1940, with a clipping from June where he is quoted saying 'the news from France is very bad, and I grieve for the gallant French people who have fallen into this terrible misfortune. Nothing will alter our feelings towards them or our faith that the genius of France will rise again.' That appeals to me. Genius attached to France.

I continue to search for something else, a hint of the real meat, but the Irish newspapers are reporting over-generously on the Germans, and the man referred to as 'Unser Hermann', Goering of the Four-Year Plan and Speaker of the Reichstag. *Come on, Paddy*, I urge. *Where is it? Where's the stuff we needed to know*? He has glued in a report on the killing of Trotsky by Ramón Mercader, a Soviet agent, and I happily note what I already knew, that the guy managed to fracture Trotsky's skull in the process. The brainpower of evil to be reduced where possible. Still nothing on the most important thing. Where is Paddy's *Holocaust* news? Because that is what I care about. Instead, I read of Italy's entry to the war against France, an earlier photograph of Herr von Ribbentrop signing the Four Power Pact with Mussolini in Munich. There appears to have been some romance between Ireland and our idea of the Germans. Interspersed with this are articles on Bird Life on the Saltee Islands and a report of the death of the tenor John Count McCormack, but finally — finally — *Surrender by Germany*, I read, *Total Capitulation signed at Rheims*. Perhaps now, discoveries of what went on will be depicted in his chronicle. But no. Paddy is like a hare and has veered off course yet again, instead turning to literary and blood-sport musings, reports on the beloved national Bard of Scotland and the Irish Independent's readers' tributes in doggerel after the death of the poet WB Yeats.

I don't believe that Paddy was unaware of what was happening, just like I don't believe he was unaware of what was happening in our house. Perhaps he thought it would all sort itself out, like the self-regulatory mechanism he believed the human body to be. Perhaps, as during the war, he felt helpless and without agency. But that too is a mere excuse. He couldn't have felt without agency during the war, otherwise he wouldn't have been collecting the harmless little poems and fragments along with his war clippings, and interspersing them so carelessly throughout his chronicles.

If I keep looking, perhaps there will be something. Too little, too late, as so often, and later, as with his wife.

11

At nine o'clock in the evening, we watch the news. Another government directive, the strictest yet, but food suppliers remain open. The news ends and the weather forecast begins. Elma comments on the meteorologist's tight-fitting dress, with an asymmetric neckline that slashes to the left. There's a week of north-easterlies ahead. But no rain.

One winter when I'm still in boarding-school, the government decides to stick to Summer Time throughout the winter. As a result, the world is in darkness every morning until almost ten o'clock. After the first class, we cluster around the radiators at the back of the classroom, watching the outside night although it is 9.40, making jokes about how people who sit on radiators got piles. Outside in the town, cars edge along Canal Road, headlights on, nudging through the frost and the fog that rises from the Ulster Canal.

Later as a day-girl, I troop with the other girls to the corner of Canal Road, where water pools heavily in wet weather. By now I no longer have close friends. Being away in hospital in Dublin for so long has changed me, and I no longer feel much in common with the girls I knew formerly. I have gone in one direction, they in another. We are all the girls we were, but different, so there is no one to blame. I persist in the theatre of friendship, as in, a performance I must go through for the final months of school and until the Leaving Cert. We push and skit, pedalling as fast as possible into the giant puddle, legs-spread high, hoping to emerge on the other side. Once, I wobble and the bike skids. I fall off and into the water, arriving home drenched and shivering. To my astonishment, Elma only smiles and does not scold. In retrospect, I know that Elma's concentration is elsewhere.

I am seventeen, the year Aunt Clara sends me the most wonderful poem I've ever read, The Song of Amergin. Aunt Clara found it in one of her favourite journals, *The Druid,* which Elma remarked was one of those weird magazines read by crackpots.

I am the wind on the sea for might;
I am a sigh of the deep for length;
I am the sound of the sea for fright;
I am a stag of seven points for strength.
I am a hawk on a cliff for lightness;
I am a tear of the sun for brightness;
I am a salmon in Wisdom's fountain;
I am a lake that afar expands;
I am Knowledge and Poesy's mountain;
I am a spear in a spoiler's hands;
I am a God who fashions smoke from magic fire
For a Druid to slay with.

I understand now how this might not appeal to Elma, whose

family has been reared differently: her father was a big man locally. It was a house of speedy movement and busyness, of floor-washing and range-polishing. Men gathered and smoked in the kitchen until the air curdled blue and the chat was sharp and humorous. There were two long deal tables, one on each side of the kitchen, and old newspapers and Sacred Heart Messengers, stacked in the deep window-ledge. Laundry was a white and creamy downpour from the third and second floor rooms, of cotton and linen sheets, bolster covers and night-shirts. Fifteen people in the house. Ten children, two parents, one demented grandmother with whom Elma shared a bedroom as a child, and two virgin uncles. Because the lavatory was out in the back yard, every bedroom was furnished with a guzunder. Eleven-year-old Elma awakened many nights to find her grandmother fully dressed and hatted to go out, hammering on the bedroom door which had been locked to keep her in.

Elma's role when not at school was to peel spuds, run wet sheets through the mangle, make beds and not read books she loved, on the myths and legends of Greece and Rome while upstairs, away from the kitchen. She later told me how much she really enjoyed myths and legends, but was interrupted constantly by her mother, Mary Ann, my Nana, who would tell her to get a move on, and to take her head down out of the clouds. It is a pity that Elma's head was removed from the clouds, leaving her no time in which to spin more tender dreams. Mary Ann planned for her to be a domestic economy teacher when she left school. Elma wanted to be a singer or an actress but was told to get those ideas out of her head. The stage was not the place for a respectable girl, and she would never have any money to call her own. Elma believed her mother was relieved when she got married and was off her hands.

Later, a few years after Paddy died, she confided to me how she cried the first night of her honeymoon in 1953. The couple did not have sex just then, because she was too nervous. She had never seen a penis that wanted to do something to her before, she said. That's one difference between my generation and hers. At least for me. I never saw the penis as an object of threat, like an implement of potential torture or even rape.

*

Just like in the story of the old woman tossed up in a blanket, something still needs to be swept clear, as cobwebs do. Tess, who should have been a treasured child, is not even certain that her birthday really is the date on which she was born. The Cork orphanage destroyed some records and altered details on others, so that adopted adults would not be able to trace their birth parent. Tess has managed to trace her own blood mother. She imparts this to me sometime after receiving the Dun Laoghaire photograph that helped her remember so much. She has had a series of meetings with the internecine keepers of secrets, those who decide what may and may not be known. She manages to prise a name, a mother's name. Her mother, she discovers, is fourteen years older than her. She later married and had four more children. Two boys. Two girls. Tess's half-siblings. I wonder if they resemble her? Does one of them have Tess's retroussé nose, or her wide mouth with its even, strong teeth? But the mother refuses to meet Tess. Tess can only surmise why. A rape? Even an incestuous rape. Or Tess's grandfather may also be her father, or her brother may be her father. Or it is all simply too much to bear.

'How did you feel about that?' I once asked her over the phone to New York.

'It was what it was. What more could I do?'

But a week later, a letter arrived for me in Tipperary.

In the end I decided to look no further. Anne Bishop, if that was her real name? I think it was Bishop, and she was from Cork, didn't want to meet me. And you know something? I think I understood why. She must have gone through hell on earth in early 1960, pregnant with me at that age, between the place where she had me and then having to give me up. Knowing what we know now, not all those nuns were angels of mercy. My mother was only a child. So I've let that go, because I have to, and after all the work on my dependency problems I'm in a few really good fellowships over here, I have to go on without her. Imagine! I have siblings somewhere in the world! Well, it doesn't excite me anymore, if I'm honest, because I've closed all that off having no choice in the matter. The bottom line is my mother doesn't want to meet me, see me, or have me in her life. I hope she's happy now, I really do. And another thing, I have a few First Nation friends in the fellowship and they've taught me SO much about acceptance. You wouldn't believe it. And oddly, I sometimes feel their lands are connected to our lands at Kilnavarn, places of natural sanctuary, even if I didn't always have sanctuary in the actual house. I loved the place outside, it calmed me. And it grew shrooms! And as for the bitch of a nun in the orphanage, I finally got to speak with one of the older ones who may have known something. I suspect she really did. All I wanted was my actual birth date, as in the right *one, you know? Because those bitches collaborated with a system which wanted babies, yet didn't really want them. Once they got rid of us into adoption or sold us overseas to America, they erased some dates and mixed up others. They knew, they damn well knew they were doing something* so *wrong, that they had to cover their tracks...*

*

It strikes me, ironically, given that I was the daughter of a medical person, how my physical wellbeing may have been ignored. Elma's teeth are strong, if uneven. She often recounts how the dentist she saw when she was sixteen assured her that she'd have all her teeth when she was eighty. And how true that is, she puffs happily, recently smiling at herself in a mirror so that I can see her now stained but mostly intact teeth.

'Your own teeth look lovely, Frankie,' she remarks suddenly. 'They've turned out so well in the end, though there was a time when they kept rotting.'

'Because you never brought me for dental check-ups,' I huff impatiently.

'What are you talking about? Anyway, nobody in my family had weak teeth, that's for sure.'

'Well I had. And I've spent a small fortune on them.'

She frowns. 'You probably inherited Aunt Clara's teeth. A bit crooked and gummy. But your father and I always had great teeth. What are you on about anyway? What money did you spend on your teeth?'

Later, after I begin seeing Christoph, but before we married, I often believe that people do not quite grasp my sister's true worth. I also ignore her drinking, her constant lateness at work, her admission to Jervis Street hospital with abdominal pain, caused by a severe case of Trichomoniasis. *Lifestyle*, the harassed staff nurse on the ward snaps at me. Promiscuous sex, a parasite protozoan, flowering in Tess's vagina and uterus. 'She's an addict, you *do* realise that?' the same nurse thunders. 'I don't want her on my ward, so we're discharging her.' Outraged, I turn my back on the nurse. Staff nurse flounces off, calling back that it's on our own heads, but she wants *her* out, *today*. 'No space for the likes of her in this ward!' she repeats.

A month later, Tess calls me. She is very polite. Could I collect her and her luggage from her Rathmines flat? The flatmates are freezing her out. Recently enough on the phone to New York, we laughed our heads off at the memory.

'What a crowd of wankers,' I spit.

'Completely up their holes,' Tess snorts.

'They were so sniffy when I arrived, I felt like a bad smell in their polite little nostrils. I remember some guy working away at a drawing-board, like, he was a draughtsman? And this girl in really cool clothes studying at a table. They barely spoke to me. They were very into themselves.'

'So who did they think they were?'

Tess pauses a moment. 'You know, they probably had a point? I'd tried to cut my wrists one night and there was this trail of blood all the way up the stairs. On the white carpet. I guess that clinched it.'

A silence.

'I guess it did.'

Then we talk about the very together people who are always in the right place, in the right flat, at the right time, with the right people, doing the right college courses, mixing with the right golden circle guys and girls who they will later marry when the time is right, because they are just like their parents before them and will produce a set of children to continue the mirroring of middle-class dynasties. And we laugh our heads off again.

Sometimes I used to rescue Tess, when we were both in Dublin, both of us temping. I believed her to be brilliant, just not acknowledged. Everybody was looking for work at the time, and half of our generation was emigrating. It never struck me that there might be a reason for all the sackings, things to do with alcohol and just not being able to get to work on time. It never struck me how easy it was to replace someone. Lateness once or twice was okay, but everybody in Dublin who had work was working hard. There was no room for slackers in the already risen big legal firms who employed temps, or in the architects offices, or in the quantity surveyors.

I discovered I had the knack of writing polished, defensive and high-handed letters to Tess's snotty employers, people I believed hadn't an ounce of brain-power in comparison to my brilliant sister. Had such a post existed, I might have been employed professionally as a letter-writer and complainer, a general defender of injustice wherever it was found.

Perhaps the whole daily narrative is so erasable that none of it matters. I often protest that memory is no true compass. People mis-remember things they believe happened to them when young, or else they suppress it entirely and never recover a true image. But it is all stored image in the brain's archive, to be flipped up at will, an essential-seeming 3-D airing when the moment is right and, like the Cyclops in its cave, or Balor in Celtic mythology, it may be prodded into action. We adhere with fidelity to the contours of a holographic life, recalling images that rupture the equilibrium every so often. Among them, Elma confessing her shortcomings, without using that word. Elma admitting to child cruelty and later — pathetically — seeking forgiveness from both of us. Now, by being here, by minding her, this is how I grant it. I grant it to myself too, for my helpless witnessings.

12

My hospitalisation results in a diagnosis of Stills Disease. At the age of sixteen, my blood pressure has soared so much that the GP takes it several times, and swallows while trying to look calm. I'm whisked off to Dublin the next day where I am immediately sedated. Over the ensuing days I croak like a toad in that hospital bed, dazzled by a jumble of print when I attempt to read Walter Macken's *Brown Lord of the Mountain*. Finally, four months later, I return home, half mended but feeling fine. Elma instructs me to remain in my bedroom at night. When I tiptoe furtively out to the bathroom, this activity is noted as an accusation, a confirmation that my kidneys are failing me badly.

You were out in that bathroom last night! Desperate, I retrieve a long forgotten vessel from the back shelf in the larder, rummaging behind tureens and the Royal Albert Christmas plates, the oval turkey platter, the trifle bowls, behind cruets for salt, pepper and for oil and vinegar from the time a French girl stayed with us for a few weeks and vinaigrette was necessary for her evening salad. The large swan vase with an open back into which Elma sets flowers at Christmas. This white, shining porcelain is from Elma's home, where once a bisque porcelain egg nestled within the open space and on which the words *Easter 1922* were inscribed. Now it is put to innovative use, secreted beneath the bed in my slope-ceilinged bedroom. Let me say this but once: it is a joyful experience to piss powerfully into a vessel intended to mark the founding of the new Irish State in 1922.

All commentary on my nocturnal activities at an end, I continue to piss in privacy into the Easter vessel marking the founding of the Irish State until I leave school for Dublin. By then, my life is all about privacy, about surviving Elma's anxious commentary and observations on how I am looking. *Too pale, thin as the pull-through for a gun, you need to eat more.* I want to eat, I am starving and thin, but my throat seizes up, my body in protest at the indigestible material that lodges in my mind. It rebels. I fret about Tess, and the occasional scratch-mark on her face from Elma's rings. Food will not go down.

In Dublin, I can piss as often as I like during the night. I gain weight, make new friends. I discover I am liked, that some people listen to what I have to say, and find me funny ha-ha as opposed to peculiar. I am away from Elma and from conversations of Tess.

*

I fetch Elma's supper of hot milk and biscuits, *mind it's hot, not lukewarm.* I jab the microwave on and heat the milk until it bubbles. *That should certainly be hot enough*, removing the glass on its little saucer and bearing it and two fig rolls back to my mother, who thanks me profusely as if this was a surprise, which makes me feel mean for over-heating the milk.

As Elma sips and sups, I raise the Sunday newspaper and open it, tilting the page towards the nearby lamp. There is little to read in the main section except Covid commentary, so I fold the newspaper and put it down. Elma sighs luxuriously about nothing in particular. I click my fingers towards the dog.

'Come on Lottie, time to go out,' I say softly.

Lottie is in the process of rising when Elma interjects. 'Leave the poor creature alone, she doesn't want out.'

'Mother, she needs to be allowed out at night for five minutes at bedtime.' I am using my schoolmarm voice. 'Come, Lottie,' I repeat softly, grasping the dog's collar, 'come with Frankie.' To my relief, the dog rises and moves easily from the room and out into the kitchen as far as the back door. In recent weeks, I imagine Lottie to have grown calmer. She scoots off into the dark. A lamp at the far end of the deep garden shows her moving like a shadow, following a scent. I watch, feeling the night stillness enclose me, the scent of grass and earth rising to meet the crescent moon, on which I would like to perch, one leg hanging free, dropping a fishing-rod down into the world.

My phone pings as a long text comes in. I glance at it and swear quietly. Hilda has decided not to come in for another wee while, she writes, convinced that it is too risky for Elma. *I'm afraid I could be a carrier as I've been working at the nursing home and we've lost ten already. I'm sorry but I think the best is for you to stay wit your Mammy til I'm tested.*

I head down the lawn in my socks. I will have to stay until I can get someone else, with or without Tess. We need extra help. I can call the HSE in the morning. Elma is getting heavier, stiffer and more immobile by the day. I reread the message. It is unambiguous. I text back: *That's fine, Hilda, completely understandable. When this is all over, come back and E will be delighted to see you* :)

In the garden, Lottie snuffles through the undergrowth near the arching beech tree on the first downwards curve of the avenue. That old mental holograph again, and now I remember wonderful birthday parties, even the shared ones when Tess got to invite perhaps two friends but no more. The weather in the past is so often sunny and pleasant. We do not remember the cold breezes, or perhaps when young we do not feel them. On this lawn children rolled down, down, down the slope to the end, crash-landing into the trunk of the beech-tree. It seemed vast then. I glance up and see that it is not so vast after all. The grass beneath my feet is drenched with night dew. But how inviting it is. I lie on the ground, stretching out full length. I will remember something, even in the dark and it will be more than a three-dimensional holograph concocted from an idea of memory. *Roll, roll*, I instruct myself. I raise both arms above my head, pull my body to the left, shut my eyes and roll, faster and faster, the past flinging itself away from my core centrifugally as I spin, growing dizzy, towards a feeling of release and freedom, a feeling of unburdening body and mind. I stop, brought up sharply against the rise of roots from the beech-tree. A knuckle of ancient root bites into my right hip, another at my back. Not even Christoph has seen this side of me, this need to fling myself flagrant, wanting the skin of the natural world to soothe my body. I want to remove jeans and knickers, to rub myself against the earth in ecstasy. I think of the ancient Egyptian farmers who, I once read, would masturbate onto the planted fields to ensure a fertile crop. It is primeval. Impetuous in a young person, dotty and perverse in an older one.

Clothes drenched now. No point returning to Elma's sitting-room. I click at Lottie, who is by my side and keen to return to the house. Together we head back up the lawn, Lottie eager, pausing occasionally, tail wagging hard.

Elma hasn't noticed my arrival.

'Be back down in a tick!' I call as I head upstairs, 'Just changing for bed.'

There's no response, so I switch on the electric blanket after removing my clothes, brush my teeth, and pull my dressing-gown tight. I drape the wet garments on the bedroom radiator, where they start to steam.

Elma has decided she would like to go to bed. I switch off the television, then the lamps, but leave the door open. I haul Elma to her feet and wait until she can balance herself sufficiently to grip the walking aid without collapsing backwards. Then the walk across the room, shunting the walking aid ahead, feet following, my hand resting lightly on her arm. Finally, in the hallway, Elma makes her way towards the chairlift. I lay Elma's spare cardigan, kept for extra warmth, on the newel post, as my mother turns slowly and releases her grip on the walking-aid to sit into the chairlift. She presses the release button and the chair begins to drone upwards. Again, she sings that anthem, and despite having lost my sense of humour about most things, I have to smile.

Su, compagni in forti schiere,
marciam verso l'avvenire...

The chair ascends. I follow slowly.

'You know, my Italian friends taught me that during the war years,' Elma calls back over her shoulder. 'For some reason, I was the only one they would invite upstairs in their house, and we had good times. They were fond of me and I was fond of them. We liked to sing.'

'Singing makes people happy. We should do more of that.'

'Do you know something?' Elma turns amicably when the chairlift stops. 'I don't think I've ever heard you really sing in my entire life.'

'No?'

'I haven't.'

After midnight, Elma has been put to bed surrounded by her objects: small radio, television remote, prayer-book which belonged to Paddy and which he never used, a glass of water and one sleeping-pill. The house settles. I wonder if Tess is still up, then call her. Stella picks up. The voice is breezy.

'Um. . .hi? Is that Stella?'

'*Hiiiiii*! This *has* to be Frankie, right? Looking for Tess? She's right here if I can catch her attention for five minutes. Hang on!' Stella calls out to Tess, '*Te-essss! Phone!*'

Then Stella speaks again. 'You're probably ready to kill me for hanging on to her for so long. She wanted to go, but I persuaded her to stay on. I hope that's not awful of me.'

She's killing me with niceness. 'It's fine,' I reply.

We chat for a while. The new house. The labyrinth. Stella asks about Christoph's retirement. Is he under my feet now? An unbearable sentence spoken by most women about most husbands.

'Ah no, we have a good routine,' I say, 'and I'm up here anyway. Christoph and I haven't had a mutual sighting in quite a while!' *Ha. Ha. Bloody ha.*

I'm hopeless at being light and breezy with people like Stella, though there's nothing particularly wrong with her. There's an exchange of some kind going on between the two women and I feel as if I'm disturbing something.

Tess, breathless as if she has just been running. 'Hi Frankie. Everything okay there?'

'Hilda isn't coming back,' I announce bluntly. 'She's afraid of carrying something from the nursing home.'

'I'll be there the day after tomorrow. I promise.'

'Only then? Earlier, you said tomorrow.'

Then, hesitation at the other end. Tess is deliberating.

'I'll try to make it. It's been so long since I've seen Stella. . .You should see her house, and she has ten cats, can you imagine?'

'So you've said. It's not all about having a good time, you know.' Even as I definitely strike the wrong note, I wonder about the universe Tess inhabits. How self-protective it seems.

'God you're narky. You sound just like Elma too.'

I fail to ignore this. 'Look, I'd love to play with the cats and be in that house. Maybe one day I will too, but guess what Tess, it's late and I'm tired and you're needed here.'

'Oh, don't start the big sister shit. I'm sorry that I'm over here and not there, but that's how it is.'

'You're not one bit sorry.'

'Fuck you Frankie.'

'Fuck you too.'

A pause. 'Seriously. . .I'll be there day after tomorrow. And the Gardaí are out checking, in case you didn't know.'

'Not up here they're not. And they're not going to stop someone home from the USA, who's been cleared through customs, had her temperature checked at the airport, been in the country ten bloody days already and allegedly wants to see her elderly mother.' *You absolute cunt.*

'I've said I'm coming and I *will* come, you know?' Tess replies in an upwards inflection.

'I'm leaving soon. I'll have to see if I can get someone to come in later this week if you don't arrive soon.' *Cunt. Cunt. Cunt.*

'Your choice, obviously.'

'I have to go now. See you soon.' She hangs up.

I pace slowly up and down the hall in semi-darkness, fantasising about how things might turn out in a different life between me and Tess. The closing pages of Alice Walker's novel *The Colour Purple* is the kind of thing I envisage, when Nettie finds Celie again, where the two sisters see one another and Celie stirs on the porch, recognition dawning, then the two of them, clinging to one another in tearful reunion. *Stop*, I tell myself. Tess is not going to arrive suddenly up the avenue, carrying a backpack, a light sweat on her peachy cheeks, cigarette dangling in mouth. There will be no reunion of that kind, no falling together as the past is obliterated. Sometimes when Tess comes home, there is a weakening, as if by being in the same country as Elma, Tess's instinct is to avoid the family culture that almost broke her. That did break her, I amend. Tess, the broken child. Tess, the mended adult. She got herself fixed, and the mending marks are like the wavering rivulets of liquid gold that create a Kintsugi vessel, where the initial break becomes an art-form in its own right. Or as Leonard Cohen might say, *Forget your perfect offering, There is a crack in everything, That's how the light gets in.*

13

Two days later the cheerful presenter on the radio breakfast show is wishing us all a great day and to love one another and stay safe. I'm in the middle of changing Elma's nightie. A soggy pad is bagged and awaiting disposal. My mother is protesting as the fresh nightie is drawn down over her head. I notice her bare legs, their thin, smooth skin, I see how puffy her ankles are. Her small feet are swollen and stiff. She can barely drag herself along using the walking aid. I straighten, distracted by the roar of a car engine coming from the front of the house. Grit has scattered with the squeal of brakes. Doors open. Laughter. Voices. The thump of a sound system.

'Who the hell's that at this hour?' Elma wonders.

'No idea. Tess maybe?'

'Is she in Ireland?'

'Remember, I told you?'

I rush downstairs, check my appearance in the hall mirror, then cross the kitchen and out to the back of the house. Something I said or didn't say directly must have struck a chord with Tess, as she is there with Stella, car doors flung open, music still pumping from within, something retro that sounds like the Clash but I can't be certain. I calculate they must have left Killaloe at five in the morning. I cast my eye over the car as I move towards them. It's a red Audi Sport Quattro SI E2. Christoph would approve. A noise machine, the engine still turning over, growling happily. Tess springs out. We embrace. It's a long, silent hug.

'Fuck. We shouldn't be hugging!' she pulls back suddenly.

'Fuck, yeah.' The tension of our previous claw-fest has evaporated. Tess's hair is drawn back, twisted in a soft effulgence of chestnut and blonde, fine tattoos on her bare arms, neck, drifting down to the bulge of her right breast. Bright-eyed, her irises tremble slightly.

'I know, I know,' she murmurs as if reassuring herself, or me, or both of us, then stands back, taking me in. 'You're looking good. You actually look like a writer too, in that red shirt and your hair in a mess.'

'Oh.'

'No, I mean you look different somehow!' she amends.

'Thanks. Older, I guess, no wiser but hanging in.'

Suddenly we're chatting about everything and nothing, but mostly nothing, in a nervous theatre of approach, pushing suitcases and a rucksack around, dragging them inside.

Tess then turns towards Stella. 'Coming in for a while?'

'Tea? Coffee?' I add, trying not to stare at Stella, who is extremely beautiful. She is tall, strong-boned, and dressed entirely in black. She has changed a lot since girlhood. Gone is the blond teenager. Now, needle-straight black hair cascades silkily around her shoulders and down her back, and a sulky fringe edges just above her blue eyes.

'I won't, thank ye kindly,' she jokes, 'I've got to get back to the beasts, they'll be restless if I don't get home before late afternoon.' We chat for a few minutes about the nuisance animals can be, what a bind they are, all the responsibility.

'They're worth it though,' Stella concludes. 'Kind company and no criticism.' Which is what most animal lovers say.

Stella helps Tess with her luggage and they push it further along into the kitchen. 'Nice house,' she remarks approvingly to Tess, 'I'd forgotten your parents had such good taste.'

Tess and Stella exchange a look which I can't decipher.

'They liked collecting old things,' Tess says. 'We used to get dragged from one market to the next, from one antique shop to the next bric-a-brac dump in some out of the way farm in the back end of nowhere, remember?' She looks at me.

I nod. 'I actually didn't mind it too much.'

'Of course you didn't,' Tess scoffs.

Stella helps Tess to carry her cases up the stairs, along the landing and into her old room. Tess is sweating, then pauses to wipe her forehead.

'Come on,' I joke, 'it's only a few pieces of luggage.'

'We're not fit,' Tess says. 'Not the way you are.'

'No, not the way you are,' Stella agrees. 'Must be all that lifting and moving of your mother, eh?' I pull a face.

'Bad taste joke, I know,' Stella nudges me with her elbow, 'Been there myself. An old aunt I used to mind in Galway ten years ago had Parkinson's. I, being the family singleton, got to spend not one but *two* Christmas Days alone with her, spoon-feeding her, changing her, listening to her try to speak, mopping her drool. All that.'

'Great fun,' I reply.

'Awful, isn't it? For them, I mean, more than us,' Stella goes on, standing in the doorway of Tess's bedroom while Tess begins to open cases and shift things around. She appears to be half tuned-in to the conversation, without saying anything.

'Yes,' I respond, 'it is awful.' I had no idea Stella was so sensitive. Tess has never referred to this part of Stella's earlier life. 'And nobody cares enough for all the old people,' I say. 'Can you imagine it when we get there? There'll be even fewer young people to mind us when the wheels finally fall off our wagons.'

'Who'd do it? Look at some of the people who end up as carers,' Stella agrees breathily. 'Mind if I smoke for a moment before I hit the road? Please?' She winks at me. I nod.

'The great strong women of any county, overworked and underpaid, that's who'll do it. And a few of them are lazy cows who couldn't care less,' I add. 'I've met them too.'

'I bet you have. Personally, I plan on having a pill. I'll get the stuff I need.' Her blue eyes are sympathetic and she touches my forearm lightly. 'Anyway, it's a long drive back to the Shannon shallows, if I can keep my foot off the floor. Don't want to get fined for speeding.'

A few minutes later she drags her seat-belt on, the cigarette waggling between her lips, the car roars to life, reverses noisily, then baritones its way off down the avenue, growling past the beech-trees in flashes of red.

I turn to Tess. 'Not what I expected.'

'No? What did you expect?'

I shrug. 'Dunno. Someone. . .a bit different.' That's all I can say, because I honestly don't know quite how to express what I thought. Airhead? Perhaps. Country bohemian? Maybe. Someone careless and indifferent. That's really what I expected. Indifference.

Tess enters Elma's bedroom. Elma is sitting lopsidedly against her pillows. She has fallen down slightly to her left and the bedcover is thrown back, exposing her right thigh and the edge of her nappy. I move to cover her up but Elma stops me.

'I thought I'd get up to see Tess. Where is Tess? Tess? Is that you?' She squints towards the doorway, from which Tess hasn't moved.

I sense Tess inhaling the air, taking in the scene. Her mother. The room. Even me. I am unbelievably glad to see her. I am happy that my sister is finally home, here, with us.

'Yes, Mother, it's me,' she says pleasantly, crossing the rug and moving around the bed to Elma's side, where she puts her arms around our mother's shoulders and hugs her. She steps back and looks down. 'Good to see you,' she smiles. She is calm, chilled, as if she had just returned after a few days in Cork or Galway, rather than absent for many years.

'It took long enough to get you home. But you're here. That's the main thing,' Elma says, folding her hands across her stomach. She squints up at Tess again. 'What have you done with your hair now?'

Tess looks discomfited. 'Nothing. I mean, it's just the way it usually is.'

'No, you've done something. That colour is too harsh for you for one thing. At your age. What age are you anyway?'

'Thanks Ma.'

'Don't take that the wrong way, I know you're easily offended and I mustn't offend anyone, must I?'

Tess and I exchange looks. They chat for a few minutes. The flight over. How is Allegra? Is Tess still living alone with a strange man in the apartment? Fine. Yes. And yes.

'I have a present for you.' Tess disappears from the room. I follow on her heels. In her bedroom she turns over various wrapped packages in one suitcase, feeling each one to identify it. Then, triumphantly, she lifts two items free, turns to me and mutters 'Hope she likes these. I never know what to get her.'

'I told you before. She wants nothing. She needs nothing. At least, she doesn't need presents.'

In Elma's bedroom the unwrapping has begun. Tearing and stripping, Elma's fingers fumble weakly with the paper and ribbon.

'Here, let me,' I move to help.

'No, no, I can manage, if you don't mind!' Elma reprimands.

More pulling and tearing. Then the white protective wrapping beneath. Finally, from one package, a blue ceramic elephant with thick legs and a comical trunk. Elma stares at it, puzzled.

'Oh. I see. How funny! Hmm, well, that's all I needed, a blue elephant.'

'It's *meant* to be funny,' Tess explains.

Elma's eyes roll up and then bore into Tess. 'I didn't come down in the last shower, you know, I know it's meant to be funny. Now Frankie, put it in the window there, where I can see it.'

'Would you like to open your second gift?' I ask, positioning the elephant on the window-shelf beside a limited edition, leaping bronze impala.

'Oh. Something else, is there?'

Elma wrestles with the larger, softer wrapping, as layer after layer is exposed, until finally she reaches the tissue paper, and tears and tears. A delicious waft of sandalwood rises up from the paper, rosy and warm. It is a poncho. A large Native American poncho. Elma struggles to hold it up as she examines it, fingering it carefully.

'It's a poncho, Mother,' Tess explains, 'and it's alpaca wool. I thought it would keep you warm in winter.'

Elma is laughing outright at the poncho, as if it's the most comical garment she has seen in a long time. 'Oh *Christ.* I love alpaca wool. But me in a poncho? Are you in your right mind?' She laughs on, her upper body wobbling. 'What were you thinking of?'

Tess's face has closed down. 'It's a gift, that's all.'

I almost feel sorry for Tess. But I too have to wonder what she was thinking of bringing such a beautiful poncho to our mother, who has never worn ethnic clothing.

'Oh well, if you don't want it I'll have it,' I jump in.

Elma arches an eyebrow. 'You're welcome to it. I suppose it's the kind of thing you'd wear with your bohemian friends. Now I'm tired. I need to rest.'

We sit in the kitchen at the big table, mugs of steaming coffee and a platter of shortbread before us.

'Still unreformed, I see,' Tess remarks.

'Sometimes. Though to be honest I don't think she realises it or means it half the time.'

Tess looks at me. 'You're making excuses for her.'

'Not really.'

My sister spends most of that day in bed, which I don't understand but don't question. The hours slide by. They will never be lived again, no matter how we have passed them. That night I go to bed early and leave a note for Tess. She can get Elma ready for bed. The night passes with no disturbance for me. The room is seemingly content. But then, so is my head. Its anxieties have been temporarily stalled. A mercy.

14

Tess and I eat breakfast together. It is half past nine and I am repressing my irritation. She didn't check on Elma the night before after all and has settled breezily with a mug of coffee and some well-buttered sourdough bread. Just when I'd begun to think my sister is eccentric, was always eccentric, and not bone lazy and indifferent. I go up to check and Elma's sheet is drenched right up as far as the pillow-case, but she doesn't appear to notice. I open up the bedroom curtains a little and lift the sash window to let some air in and then return downstairs to enjoy my Lavazza Gold coffee, toast, bitter marmalade, two squeezed oranges. Tess reverts to childhood pattern and fills a large porridge bowl to the brim with sugared muesli and milk. The morning radio show is in full swing and its presenter mentions that Boris Johnson has had the virus. But the Queen is alive, and so is Prince Philip, although Charles has had it and come through. Elma will be pleased to hear that on the Royal front all is well. The presenter then moves on to children's literature, the importance of reading for everyone.

Tess complains about the mattress on her bed, which sags in the middle. But the mattress in my bedroom is no better, it too is old.

'Did you sleep at all?' I ask.

'Eventually. The quietness is bizarre, but then I gave in to it. When I stopped thinking.'

'Did you hear the fox calling?'

'You mean that chilling scream? Sure. Actually, I thought it was coming from your room, like you were having a bad nightmare.' She sniggers, then shivers quickly.

I pause. 'From my room? I heard nothing.'

'Well it was one fucking strange fox, if that was a fox,' she replies, 'not to mention that lightbulb. Even when I switched off my lamp it kept flickering. Like, ten minutes later?'

I don't really want to pursue this conversation. I nod in a conciliatory way, and say I'll check the bulb.

'Anyway,' she drawls, 'I suppose I'd better put my shoulder to the wheel and give you a hand.'

In the bedroom, Elma is drowsy at first, then exclaims as she catches sight of Tess. I feel like walloping Tess for creating the extra work of complete sheet and mattress protector changing. It has to have been a gesture on her part, even if unconscious, a fuck you to the lot of us. The smell of urine is potent. To my surprise, Elma does not resist being changed and washed, but stares up at Tess, as if with a sense of wonder. Her blue eyes radiate child-like innocence.

'You're a great girl, do you know that? Coming all this way just to see the old lady.' Tess doesn't react.

Tess draws a fresh nightgown over Elma's head and draws one arm, then the other, through the armholes. 'That's you done,' she announces. 'I'll bring up your breakfast now. Hot tea, a bit of toast?'

While Tess is downstairs, I clear up, collect the wet sheet, wet pillowcases, a damp blue cotton nightie, unpeeling surgical gloves, finally a bottle of sanitiser and some Johnson's baby powder. I dump the sheet in the laundry basket and arrange the other items along the window-ledge beside the ceramic elephant and the impala.

Outside the bathroom window, laurel hedging has begun to send up shoots, and in the field beyond the first buds have nudged out on the oak trees. The place is bursting with birdsong and I wish I could wait, stand, stare and listen and not feel annoyed.

An hour later, masked and gloved, we drive to town to pick up groceries. We head to Tesco, not Lidl and have to queue to get in, it's like life in former East Berlin, waiting outside while people shop in a half-empty building. I want to quickly whizz around and get it over with, but Tess drifts slowly, examining this and that product. Elma used to enjoy shopping with Tess, they could spend hours riffling through the clothes shops together, because Tess was more easy-going and liked to dawdle. Gradually, we stock the trolley with dog and cat food, enough for a month at least, and plastic bags, packets of baby-wipes, toilet-paper, as well as tins of beans, mushy peas, a super-sized bag of muesli, some fresh asparagus and broccoli, and packets of pork chops and lamb, a few steak fillets, three packs of crumbed frozen cod, some grated cheese and tomatoes.

'People are more careful here than they are in New York,' she remarks. A masked and gloved man has just circled around us. He waits until we move away from the cheese cabinets before bending down to reach for a pack of Gorgonzola. Further down the aisle someone sneezes. Heads turn.

As we leave we pass the queue of people waiting to get in, which is by now snaking around the corner of the building.

People stand patiently. Some are not wearing masks.

'I find it hard not to march up to people like that and ask them what part of highly infectious they don't understand,' I say.

'Conspiracy theorists,' Tess replies. We titter as I open the boot and we load up the heavy shopping bags.

Back in the car again, we're still jeering at the paranoid element in our society as I spray both steering wheel and car door with alcohol. Tess then removes her plastic gloves. The phone rings, and it's Jason, on WhatsApp video.

'Hey.' I turn to Tess. 'I'll take this, if you don't mind.'

'You out and about?' Jason asks.

'Yeah. Are you sick?' He looks like death.

'No, I'm fine. Still waiting for blood-test results. Everything is delayed now. They tested me for you-know-what. Bloody thing rammed up my nose and then swizzed around the back of my throat like the spin cycle on a washing-machine. *Uh*! I almost gagged!'

'Stop exaggerating.'

'I'm *not*,' he protests, laughing.

I start the engine and fix the phone to the dashboard. 'I'm driving, I can still see you. My sister is with me, by the way.'

'Well if she doesn't mind listening to me yammering on that's okay.'

Tess calls out to him. 'It's fine, Jason, I'm unshockable.' She lights a cigarette and rolls down the car window.

'So I didn't sleep much last night. Or for the last few nights now that I think of it.'

'Why's that then?' I speed through a deserted roundabout at the junction of Broad Road.

'These days I actually prefer to sleep during the days. One way of avoiding the news,' he mutters.

'I try to avoid the news too,' I say.

'Anyway, I've rewritten chapter seven,' he goes on, 'with more to add.'

Curious now, I wait.

'It's hard to re-do the bits that aren't, strictly speaking, imagined, but which could be, if you get my drift. And the imagined bits that could be what we call real.'

'That's your job. Our job. The shaping of experience into form.'

'When was your last book?'

'2016.'

'I forgot. Sorry. That was. . .that was?'

'*What the Eye Sees.*'

'I remember. I haven't read it.'

'You should be ashamed,' I tease, half joking, wholly in earnest.

'It did well?'

'It did okay. It was optioned by a film maker.'

'Which one?'

'I'm not saying.'

'You writing the screenplay?'

'No. I took the money and ran. I hope you'll come to the opening if the film ever gets made.'

Jason snorts. 'You bet I will. Can you imagine it?'

Now Tess chimes in. 'I'll be there too, Jason. Can't wait!' And they laugh.

I pull up at Rossmore Park and wonder if the frozen cod at the bottom of my shopping bag will thaw out if I delay. Jason has something to tell me. The question is, how he will tell me. I remember thinking on my thirtieth birthday, when I was feeling adult and wise and a little independent, that I'd listened to all the nut-cases, energy-suckers, and useless human creatures I ever would listen to, and that it had finally dawned on me that I could do no more except step away, turn two blind eyes, not listen or nod as if I was interested.

Tess steps out of the car and wanders over to a picnic bench beneath a row of freshly-budding poplars. I admit to having often imagined a film premier, then put those imaginings to bed and simply got on with life. I dream of Lars Van Triers handling my work. He would be just right for my dark writing. I imagine Scandinavian audiences, and of showings at Cannes, Venice, Tribeca and Sundance.

'So you're not sleeping. Poor Jason,' I say.

'I walk a lot. At night, I mean.'

'That's one way of tiring yourself out. Tell me more. Is it something you can use in the novel?'

He sniggers. 'You're such a predator Frankie.'

'Like you. Leave no stone of autobiography unturned. It will offer a story.'

Car engine switched off, I scrutinise his phone face.

'You're sure you don't have symptoms of the virus?'

'I got myself tested. . .' Then he breaks off and stares at me closely. 'You're amazing, you know that? A beautiful, amazing kind of woman, I hold you in the highest esteem. You help me greatly, and I need to say this.'

Chin up Frankie, don't be flattered you pathetic slice of ageing womanhood, with your softening breasts and crinkling belly-skin. At the same time, I'm keeping an eye on Tess, because laid back as she is I'm not sure I'd want her to overhear this spiel. But she's still sitting on the park bench, smoking, talking into her phone.

'Okay. Well, thanks.' I clear my throat.

He says no more and just watches me from the rectangle of phone. Behind him are shelves of books, heaped chaotically, and the remains of a dead Spiderwort plant that trails over what looks like his poetry section, because I can spot the spines of Pablo Neruda's *Twenty Love Poems and a Song of Despair,* as well as *Luck is the Hook* by Imtiaz Dharker.

'Get yourself checked out again. Maybe yesterday's result was a false negative?'

'You think I should?'

'I do.'

There is something rather helpless about him. I might embrace him if he were here, or I might wallop him. I am neither his lover nor his mother, I have no rights. All I can do is make him write better, release his voice. Nudge him towards and beyond the possible, into the impossible, and convince me.

'I'd like to see you,' he says suddenly, just as Tess opens the car door and sits back in.

Her eyes are full of question-marks.

Sounds like one of those declarations men used to make when they wanted to pursue. Does that still happen? The old statement that is — was — exciting and desire-filled?

'Well you can't. And my sister's back in the car too.'

He ignores the last remark. 'But if my test proves negative again?'

'I don't know where I'll be. I may be gone back to Tipperary by tomorrow.'

'Will you or won't you be gone? Don't you know?'

Good question. The thing is, I don't know. I haven't decided. Ironically, now that Tess is here I don't want to leave. I sigh, thinking ahead to breaking this news to Christoph.

'Let's stay in touch,' he says. 'I might visit.'

'You haven't been invited.' The cheek of this guy.

'Invite me then.'

'You can't come.'

'If your sister can travel, so can I.'

'Now you're being pushy.'

'Yes, fucking pushy!' Tess throws in.

'I *am* pushy. Sorry, but I really need to see your sister. Professionally.'

I end the call. Now he has me thinking of how timid I was when I was his age. I didn't push myself, I hardly knew how, truth be told. But Jason is of his generation, and their fears are different, their anxieties nestle elsewhere, and they have no compunction about asking for help. Not a bad thing. Neither of us speaks for a while as the car passes by the houses on the edge of the town, the Baptist house with its foreboding sign of repentance, the big postmodern house which looks like a grey incarceration facility, and the quieter homes with new extensions, gable roofs, redesigned gardens, all the way to the first roundabout near the convent school.

'That went well?' Tess asks. 'He seems quite familiar with my name too.'

I give a grunt. Tess knows well I've been sounding off to Jason. She realises too that she has overheard what sounds like something less to do with writing and more to do with something complicated. Personal.

By the time we return to the house the sun is blistering light on everything, though it's not actually warm, turning the tops of the beech-trees Elma planted after Paddy's death eighteen years earlier into a frieze of limey green. Elma would be pleased if she could see them, if she could be persuaded to get into the car and be driven down the avenue. I've offered to take her, but she declines, and I wonder if she's afraid, or has become agoraphobic from being in the house so long. The daffodils are wilted and dead. First flower deaths of the year after the snowdrop, so it will continue from month to month, bud-bloom-fade, bud-bloom-fade. Nature has always told how it should be. Nature is the most obvious exemplar of all.

In the house I call upstairs. 'You okay up there?' No answer. 'Hello? Everything okay in Bedroom Land?'

'That you Frankie?'

'Do you need anything?'

'No thank you.'

'I did the shopping.'

'Good girl.'

As well as thinking that I have grown taller, Elma forgets that I am of pension age. Tess unpacks the groceries while I feed the dog and squeeze a sachet of jellied fish-smelling food into the cat's dish.

My phone pings. Occupied loading a four-kilo bag of dog-nuts into a metal bin, I ignore it. It pings again. Then a third time and still I ignore it. Tess is taking a Zoom call from the New York clinic and so I decide to take a shower.

Four years ago Elma agreed to the installation of a super-spacious shower, large enough to take a safety chair, with bars and rails. This luxury, thermostatic ten-inch rainfall showerhead in brushed gold, including hand shower, has been used by her at most twelve times, I estimate, such is the difficulty in persuading Elma to allow running water to touch her skin. At five o'clock in the afternoon, I feel a sense of luxury as I undress and survey my body in the long bathroom mirror. Narrowish shoulders and torso, slim hips, large breasts which have dropped over the years, wobbling belly but firm thighs and calf muscles because I'm a walker, and feet with bunions and hammer toes. I have no real complaint about my body and think of it as the temple of my spirit, a notion I wouldn't share with anyone. What seems most real to me is the absence of division between my head and everything below, that my brain is in my belly as much as in my head, or in my heart as much as in my head, that my blood, which runs throughout the strategic physical body, ferries information to be analysed in secret within operations as covert and knowing as MI6.

I tilt my head slightly up beneath the rainfall showerhead. I think I may be avoiding returning to Christoph. Something about Kilnavarn has claimed me, as it always does, and something about Elma. Not forgetting Tess. And now, Jason too.

I soap myself with Le Fragonard shower gel. Luxuriate in the scent of violet flower that now glides down my limbs, into the crack of my bottom, then beneath into one of my body's most unassuming areas. Christoph likes sex, and I still occasionally enjoy wrapping my legs around him, but now, it's more about intimacy than actual pleasure. My erotic focus is blurred. I wonder about younger women and their intense focus on fulfilment and orgasm, the automatic assumptions about the necessity of both. I was once like that, a bandstand leader in the matter of fulfilment. Now the point of fulfilment eludes me, a little like the point of closure that so many people talk about. But this is how nature works. It's not that I am right, or was right, or that younger women are right either. It's not a question of being right, but of recognising the body, and how nature whispers all the time, egging us on to do or not do, this or that, depending on where we are in the cycle of life.

Afterwards, I take my time and groom myself. Trim the longer trails of what remains of my still brown pubic hair, cut my toenails and file them, then open my toilet-bag and remove a jar of French Lime Blossom body cream. How good is that, I sigh, amazed at the accuracy of the scent. Back in the bedroom,

I change into a tracksuit, an upmarket, highly patterned get-up in greens and blues picked up when I travelled through Vienna airport a few years beforehand, but which fits me quite well. I shop like a huntress as I pass through the world's airports.

I consult Elma and Tess about dinner. Both agree that prawns and pasta would be lovely. Elma thanks me for cooking the meal. As ever, she says that anyone who serves anything up to someone should always be thanked. I smile at Elma's moments of good behaviour, which are genuine, sweet, and well-felt. I'll cut the pasta very finely so that she can manage with spoon and fork. Prawns with lemon-juice, white wine, garlic, chilli peppers, a little Roquefort cheese and cream, all tossed in pasta and served with a sprinkling of Parmesan. It should not upset Elma's stomach. The only thing that upsets her stomach is rhubarb, which is a no-go, Krakatoa volcano area as far as I'm concerned. As I'm chopping the garlic I start to mess like those television chefs who can chop at the speed of light. I misjudge where the knife is falling and nick the knuckle of my left hand. At first it doesn't bleed up, then it wells steadily and I run it under the sink, then scramble for a plaster in the cupboard above the cooker. I know I keep them there, along with the spices and salt, because I anticipate minor emergencies of this nature.

Only later, when we've brought Elma downstairs, when dinner is over and the cleaning up complete, do I glance again at my phone. One text from Christoph, *Will you be home tomorrow?* Five texts from Jason, *thinking I might travel to your town. Would that be okay? Did u get that text? Perhaps you're too busy? Frankie, are you there, hope it's okay that I'm thinking of coming to see you, Jason.*

Blood seeps from beneath the plaster on my finger.

15

In the evening, Tess brings Lottie with her down to the lake. She wants to pick wild onion and nettle leaves for a soup which, in the spirit of discovering native cuisine, she intends to make tomorrow. Much as I admire this romantic idea, I doubt it will happen. I call Christoph. As so often lately when on the phone to him, a sense of intimacy eludes us. We don't row as much as we did years ago. It amazes me that we never divorced, because despite the romance of the Rhineland engagement, for years we argued often and bitterly about everything. He likes to be right, of course, a hangover from the early years with me when he mostly was right, because I knew a lot less than I imagined but also believed myself in the wrong about many things. Despite that, and despite two affairs on my part, which he knows about, and one of his which he thinks I don't know about, we held together. That is neither good nor bad. We held together. No triumph and no shame. We appear to be necessary to one another.

On the phone now, he has no news and neither have I.

Everybody is at home. Nobody is missing anything except ordinary life. All the young people are going crazy without one another. I make a stab at conversation but I'm careful not to start venting about Elma. He's heard it so often and pretends to take my venting in his stride, but I know in fact he dislikes these outbursts. And I can't help it if, like many men, he appears to prefer a perpetually calm wife, a twenty-first century version of the wife in The Little House on the Prairie or the Waltons. I enjoy embellishing conversation with the right words, the shock words, the amusing words, to litter in private, to fling and throw, be irreverent and funny. This makes him nervous.

All he wants to know is when I will return. He's missing me. So is our little Pug, Silka. I miss Silka too, sensitive puggie Silka. Soon, I assure him. Yes, he misses my presence in the bed, my presence around the house, because despite all, I am his Aladdin's Lamp to stroke in the dark after he returns from the bathroom at night, yet this harmless and utterly affectionate reaching out to stroke my thigh sometimes irritates me. I am not a talismanic stone. Like an overworn garment, my body is now threadbare. Men don't realise how badly women of a certain age want not to be touched, pulled at, fondled. They interpret the gentle pushing away of an exploring hand as rejection, never seeing themselves as how they sometimes seem: needy.

'I'll be home very soon,' I reassure him. 'Can't wait actually.' This is not quite true, but I say the words because they are part of a ritual and in case it might be true and I can whip up genuine anticipation.

'When exactly?' he pushes.

I hesitate. 'I'm not sure. I want to spend some time with Tess now that she's here.'

'It's like waiting for Godot.'

'Unlike Godot, she came.'

'I meant you, not Tess,' he remarks coolly. 'Anyway, I didn't think Tess would come. You're too tolerant of her. Do you think she ever lies awake worrying about you?'

'I've never thought about it.'

This is a lie, and I wish Christoph weren't raising unpleasant ideas in my head which I have actually considered. Often. In the background, I can hear our dog yapping frantically.

'Someone must be coming, Silka's barking. You'd better go to her. I'll call tomorrow, okay?'

'How about you just come home? Frankie?'

I do miss certain aspects of my own home. The silent, frizzy-haired neighbour from further along our country road who walks with bowed head, four furry dogs prancing along beside her, the gentle American Mennonite family who run a collective and deliver seasonal vegetables throughout the year, the English couple who keep rescued donkeys in their paddock, and two different gay couples, men full of vitality who used to travel a lot, climbing Annapurna, canoeing in Canada, and sometimes, like Christoph and me, simply being at home by a log fire, entranced by the long evening view across to the foothills of the Galtees. That too, is my life, and I have neglected it, its richness. I have practically abdicated from it, a queen in self-imposed exile.

The conversation rattles on awkwardly. We discuss Jason.

'I don't trust Jason,' he grumbles.

'Oh for heaven's sake Christoph!'

'I don't trust many scribblers, you know that already, *Liebchen*.'

Christoph believes literary men to be unreliable, *Sie können Ihnen keine Brötchen verdienen,* he might say, meaning that such people can't put bread on the table. Christoph has always believed in putting bread on the table, in having enough, of assuming responsibility. The scribbling crowd, as he insists on calling them, talk about anything and everything but their actual work, each knowing they all lead an inner life, quite mysterious and circumscribed from the rest of the world. Christoph, though, is knowable, and wants to be known by me. He has rebuilt his library in the house and added on a garden studio where he heads most mornings after breakfast. It's sound-proofed. Sometimes he records his own translations of German language poets, among them Ingeborg Bachmann, which he then posts to his YouTube channel.

'I'll be recording with the Berlin studio on Wednesday morning,' he tells me.

As a commentator on Deutschlandfunk Kultur he has to read some of the latest books, including work from young women writers. One or two of these women have very sharp elbows. They carry centuries of grievance, he adds forgivingly. This is not news to me, but I'll be interested in his participation in an online discussion on the new wave of female authors being translated to German, often described as brave, courageous, amazing and dazzling. I wonder how these commentators can actually see the words on the page, they are so bedazzled.

'They should probably use someone younger than me,' he muses, 'someone who might believe the hype.'

'They absolutely should not.'

We are of one mind when it comes to cultural discourse. We share a mutual suspicion of the *Zeitgeist.* He gives a little growl of laughter and the tension between us dissolves.

'Seriously Fran, I'm expected to glow like hot plutonium on this. If I try to have an actual conversation about the quality of the work instead of gushing about themes, *ich werde kastriert!*'

'You're an old dog now. Find a way to ask questions. You

can do it.'

'Oh, you *cynic,*' he lowers his voice, then laughs.

*

By eight o'clock the following morning, Tess is already up and moving around.

'Can I borrow Mammy's car?' she asks, towelling her hair dry after emerging onto the landing from the bathroom. She's naked. Only then do I really see the network of tattoos along her torso and back, some of them floral, others showing arcane phrases and symbols that emerge above her shaved bush. I wonder vaguely if I should be shaving mine, but to what end I am not sure. I don't want to look like a child.

I hesitate before saying yes. It's unlikely Tess will be stopped while driving. Even so, there could be an accident, and she hasn't driven on the left for years.

'If you feel safe about it. I mean, if you have an accident I'm not covered, and you're not covered either.'

'I'm not going far. I drive slowly. I want to drive up the mountains to Bragan, take a few pics.'

'Cool. I won't go this time. But the heather's in bloom.' She checks herself in the landing mirror. 'You know there's a few IRA victims' bodies buried up there?'

'And?'

'Well, the Disappeared. It's a strange part of the world.'

I shrug. This is not news. 'Anyway, see you later. I've some work to do on Jason's script.'

As she turns away I call out. 'Hey, are you making up that soup today?'

She hesitates. 'Right. Well, maybe tonight?'

'The leaves will wilt if you don't use them soon.'

She turns on her heel and moves away into her bedroom. 'Whatever. It was only an idea.'

*

For a change there's no text from Jason. I call him. He picks up and immediately I switch to video. His image judders and shakes, he is obviously on public transport.

'You're on a bus?'

'Caught the last bus outta town, heading for your little hamlet.'

He still looks unwell. 'You shouldn't come here,' I say bluntly.

'I'm not sick or anything. I've printed out a new version of the manuscript and I'm bringing it to you, in person.'

'Don't be selfish.'

'Selfish?'

'I don't have time to spend with you and you can't stay here. There's an old person in the house.' I probably sound quite stuffy.

'I don't want to stay. I'll blag my way into some hostelry or other for the night.'

'In case you haven't noticed, the hostelries, as you call them, are all closed up. What fucking planet are you living on?'

Occasionally the image distorts and his jawline twists and elongates, making him spectral. He is wearing a black t-shirt, a battered leather jacket visible beneath a dark green parka. A diamond earring glistens in his left ear.

'You should take the bus right back to Dublin,' I say more softly. 'Get off at Ardee and wait for the next express. Or call your girlfriend. Tell her where you are.'

A profounder silence now. 'There's no girlfriend. She's gone.'

'When?'

'Two days ago.'

'Why?'

'Look, she'd had enough of me and my. . .*weirdness*, the word I believe she used.'

'I see.'

'And I'd had enough of her if I'm honest. She liked to monitor my proclivities, as she called them.'

'I see.'

He's pale and dissipated looking. Lips quite pink. Shadows beneath the eyes. And that hair, a tousled white straw on his pate. Have mercy, I think. Mercy as a quality. Not strained. It droppeth as the gentle rain, as Portia said to Shylock. Two people are thus blessed, both the merciful and the mercy-recipient. So I never was one for adhering to the rules, despite appearances.

'I don't have the car right now. You'll have to walk from town.'

I'll meet him and bring a snack. There are plenty of left-overs from yesterday evening's dinner. Elma has only eaten a small portion of prawns and pasta, and took rice pudding from a tin rather than the raspberry roulade I bought. There's plenty of food. The sun is shining and we can picnic beside the lake.

'See you later then.'

The signal drops and my screen goes blank.

No point now in continuing to read his previous manuscript, I go to the kitchen and have some cheese, crackers and a cup of tea. Elma won't eat and wants to be left to sleep. I watch over her momentarily, the small body in the large bed, half turned, eyes closed. Fragile, I think, quite fragile and weakened now, no matter what. Every so often I want to enfold her in my arms, to hold her in the way I'm sure she was not held as a child. But I leave her be. Before I leave the house to go down to the lake, I check in again, watch closely to see if her chest is still rising and falling, or if it has stilled and emptied of air.

I wait by the lake. My hair is clipped up and I've drawn a few strands down to create a casual look, then pull at the rest of it a bit. It irks me that I give any consideration whatsoever to what anyone thinks. I've also put on some lipstick and a smear of scented body lotion. While it's okay to be older, there's no need to play Central Casting's Hag of Beare either.

Finally he's in my sights, striding along the road on the far side of the lake. It's an even, energetic stride, and from a distance I can see it's lop-sided from the weight of his rucksack. He makes his way as far as the gates, then turns directly away from the avenue and into the lake field. He's spotted me. He walks with determination, like a man who knows where he's going. The parka is slung open, the furry hood drooping along his shoulders. As he nears, he reminds me of one of those rare white corvids, with his hooked nose, and wide beakish mouth. Oh, white raven sent by Apollo, I think, to spy on his lover Coronis. But I have no lover, and this is a man, not a raven. When he throws himself on the rush-tufted grass near the lake edge, he shakes off the parka.

'Nice jacket,' I remark.

'Another ex's Christmas pressie,' he replies. 'She liked that look.'

He pulls a pair of sun-glasses from his jeans pocket, puts them on, then turns to me. 'I know you're wondering why I'm here. It's not what you wanted and maybe I shouldn't have come.'

'Men never listen.'

'Oh come *on*!'

I've brought a cotton shopper imprinted with elephants' heads and trunks — it strikes me that Tess would like it — and I unpack some buttered rolls filled with left-over prawns slathered in garlic mayo. Two bottles of beer, still cold from the fridge. No bottle opener. He reaches out for them.

'Wash your hands first. In the lake.' He does this, carefully, taking his time. I watch as his boots sink slightly in the soaked shallows. He dries his fingers on his coat, then moves up the field a little, to sit closer to where I'm perched, on a piece of weathered sandstone. I hand him sanitiser.

'Here,' he says, finally taking the beer bottles, striking them lightly against the thin edge of the sandstone rock to open them.

'Thanks.'

'I never expected a picnic,' and bites into one of the prawn rolls.

'You hungry?'

'Not really. Thirsty, though.'

'So how are you feeling?'

He doesn't look at me. 'A bit better, away from the city. My head was done in, between one thing and another.'

I assume him to be a heavy drinker. The jaded pallor, the rangy body, the way he picks at his food.

'Were you drinking last night?'

'I wasn't hammered. I had a few, that's all.'

'No need to be defensive. I just assumed.'

'Well don't assume. You don't know.'

An irritating exchange. I've almost finished working with him, bizarre as it is that he's travelled to Kilnavarn. He changes position, moving the backpack so that he can lie down and rest his head, the parka jacket beneath his body. He takes a cigarette from an almost empty pack and lights up.

'No objection?' he asks, quieter now, as he exhales the first long breath.

'None whatsoever. Can I have one too?'

'There was I thinking you had no bad habits or addictions.'

'That's such an unoriginal comment.'

'Oops, so I failed the originality test,' he retorts, but I ignore him.

There is something soothing about smoking. Irreplaceable, beautiful, and a thing that sometimes makes thought and reflection possible. I tried hard to smoke when younger, but mild asthma made it difficult, so I mostly quit. Cigarette in hand, posing, made one approachable in those brittle days of discovery. I mentally pull up an image of myself, Munich, 1975. A wicker chair outside the Erlkönig bar in Munich, a boyfriend from Augsburg, both of us smoking Gauloises Disque Bleues, sipping Pilsener beer, the night air cooling, light dimming and young couples everywhere, like colourful moths around fat, yellow candles. I sit now, arms wrapped around knees, smoking peacefully.

'I never became hooked on cigarettes,' I announce, 'I don't think I have an addictive personality.'

'We all have our addictions,' Jason answers dreamily, staring at the clear sky.

Somewhere above, the *cep-cep-cep-cep* sound of a skylark pricks the air, and on the far side of the lake the bubbling trill of a curlew. The skylark makes me feel happy, the curlew has a more mystical effect, but regardless, I love them and associate the curlew with silent winters above the lake, the noise and hustle of the town barely audible from over the hills.

'So what's yours?' I ask him.

He turns and looks at me. The silence builds, then two grey crows scrawk overhead, flying rapidly up the hill towards the rookery.

'Oh I'm really unfashionable. I believe in love. Passion. Finding the one person, the forever person, y'know?'

I smile, gratified at this confession. 'Sounds quaint,' I say softly. He doesn't need to tell me where he's coming from. 'But no harm either. I wouldn't be announcing it to many of my contemporaries though. Or on Tinder. Or Bumble, or whatever your favourite platform is.'

He shakes his head, almost in disgust. 'I don't use those. Not for me.'

'So how do you meet someone nowadays?' I'm curious now.

'I believe in taking my chances. Sometimes I bump into a girl, a woman, but mostly I just drift.'

Much of the time he enjoys his own company, he says, even before his girlfriend dumped him. They'd only been in the house together for six weeks, he adds. He's happy to earn enough to get by on, but too many women bore him. No surprises there. As I recall, too many men bored me too. Still do. Social performance brings out the worst in us.

'Like, I meet a girl and I'm attracted to her, right?' He goes on. 'But then I have to get around this absolute shite about appearances and being seen to have a good time? Some of them drink enough to sink the Titanic. Does my head in.'

'But you drink too,' I interject.

'That's different. I can hold it. I hate the sight of a drunk woman, if I'm honest. I start to feel sorry for them when they get into that state.'

I say nothing for a moment. 'Bit of a double standard though, isn't it? You, I mean, appear to allow one behaviour for yourself but dislike it in women? *Seriously*?'

'It's the way I am.'

'That's not an excuse.'

'Maybe I can't offer one, Frankie? What I feel like doing when I see a girl so fucking stupefied, I mean *staggering*, is to protect her.'

'From?'

'From herself. And rape culture. Let's face it.' Before I can respond he changes tack. 'And I definitely don't want to meet the sister or brother of someone I've been seeing only a few times, and definitely not her parents. I'm not marriage material. Once I get that across to the girls my age, they drift off.'

'That probably suits you,' I remark.

'Too right it does. But I am interested in women. Not that there's a huge demand for snowy blond men, I've observed. Most women like em dark.'

I'm glad I'm not on the market. I'm glad that part of my life is over, at least as it was once conducted.

'I guess I was a bit like you,' I tell him. 'Except I'd no confidence, but I had this huge romantic belief in love as an ideal. Hard to get anywhere back then with that in a society that offered religious pigswill and repression.'

'Was it really bad? Pigswill?'

'It was. Believe me, it was. Most of us didn't realise just how bad it was. We grumbled, we bought the liberal Brit mags like Cosmopolitan, we read Germaine Greer and knew what oral sex was, but we still didn't understand. Not completely.'

The conversation fizzles out and we finish off the prawn rolls, which Jason appears to have an appetite for now. Afterwards, we smoke peacefully. I am thinking that if I were young I might, in a manner of speaking, pass the time very pleasantly with Jason. His words are the kind of words I'd have loved to hear spoken to me when I was a girl, words that offered a version of freedom, the version that most young people need but often don't get. A light breeze whips the smoke away behind our heads. The air current is westerly.

'It's lovely here,' he says.

Our gaze follows a train of ten cyclists on the far side of the lake. Their voices are deep and happy with being outdoors and active. They're all geared up as if preparing for La Vuelta when in fact they're probably breaking the distance curfew by a stretch.

'You don't get that dressed up for a 5k cycle,' Jason drawls with a snigger, as if reading my thoughts. Then the cyclists move on down the road, disappearing round a bend, and complete silence washes back over us. It's eerie yet beautiful. I could sit here forever with Jason beside me. For no particular reason, I feel consoled and even relaxed.

'You can bed down here for the night,' I tell him decisively, 'or for as long as you like. Take the room beside Tess's. Elma won't mind. You'll be a distraction. And she likes men.'

He follows up the field and on to the avenue. A thin fleece of pale cloud has spread from the west, although no rain is expected. I think of the times I have led young men up to the house, in all weathers and none. One, after Christmas, sheltering me beneath his coat as we stumbled through deep snow up the garden, up the steps, finally reaching the house and the urns with their frozen plant shape-shifter remains. A beautiful winter, when I decided not to marry this man, who lived with horses and dogs on a small country farm, but also with his mother, a situation I did not trust. I was already seeing Christoph, having more or less decided to choose him, even if he did not propose until months later, not until the following summer in Germany. And before all that, there was a young man who tried to rape me in his car, when we pulled in on the avenue for privacy. How casually I consider it now. It was not traumatic, and I did not feel injured, either then or since. I was stronger than him, or at least, strong enough, able to hold myself very hard and push back against him. Maybe he decided it was too much trouble, who knows what way a rapist's mind works with a woman beneath him. And there was the one from Kerry, a very innocent young Garda — virgin to the core — dispatched up to the border region. I went out with him because I felt sorry for him. He arrived at the house with a box of chocolates for me. He was polite and good-looking, but I knew instinctively that he would not do. He extolled Banna Strand in Co Kerry and how it was the most beautiful place in the whole world. He was aching with homesickness, anyone could see that. He'd been transferred to a harsh and sharp-tongued terrain where nothing was as it seemed and everything and everyone was suspect as long as the Troubles prevailed in the North.

Looking back, I had given each one instinctive consideration in my head as a possible partner, and the Kerryman would not do. It was snobbery on my part. I didn't see myself paired off with a keeper of the law, with someone trained in rules and regulations and codes of public behaviour, no matter how handsome. Mostly though, I knew he wouldn't have been educated enough for me and my aspirations. Living with him would have been like kicking a puppy.

16

Before we enter the house through the back door, Jason pauses and looks up at the roof, then down again, his eyes scanning the different upstairs windows. The window at my end of the house is open and one of the pink drapes has been sucked out into the breeze, where it flaps gently beyond the sill. I pause and listen, and although I can hear nothing I sense that the air in my bedroom is active, that the lampshade may be swinging and not just in the draught.

We're no sooner in the house than we are greeted by the whirr and drone of Elma's chairlift.

'Venus, descending from the clouds,' I remark.

'Aren't you lucky to live in a land of gods and goddesses?' says Jason, looking towards the hallway as I gaze, startled, up the stairs.

The chair comes to a halt, then spins around. I wait for her to appear around the corner of the hall. Then Jason raises his eyebrows as walking aid and Elma gradually appear. Somehow, she has managed to get herself up, has staggered to her clothes chair in the bedroom and pulled on a few garments. I step forward quickly to conceal her from him but really to spare her dignity. Even if she is not aware of it, I am, and of her fading. My mother wears a pink, slightly stained blouse, which hangs unbuttoned at the front, revealing her bra, with one breast in and one breast half out. Her trousers are pulled up but unzipped, and her tummy protrudes slightly. On her feet her sandals are unbuckled, her twisted toes peeping out the front. *God help you,* I'm thinking as I set to popping her left breast into its cup, at the same time, a quiet stream of *Damn! Damn! Damn!* issues from Elma's mouth.

'Someone I'd like you to meet,' I say, buttoning her blouse.

Elma's eyes are full of curiosity as she stands still and stares at Jason. Her breath is coming in short little puffs.

'This is a writer friend of mine. Jason. You remember I told you I was working on his novel?'

Elma does not remember anything about the novel, but she is good at camouflaging.

'You told me. Welcome to Kilnavarn, Jason.' Her most gracious tone. Despite her appearance, she is in full lady-of-the-manor mode.

'How are you Mrs Esmond?'

'I'm very well thank you. And you?' Polite. A cool breeze.

'All the better for seeing you, Mrs Esmond. Frankie has told me so much about you.'

I glance at him. I had no idea he could turn on the charm like this.

'You'll join us for dinner here in the big kitchen, I hope?' she says grandly. She is staring hard at him from her one good eye, taking him in, still undecided as to whether or not she likes him. 'You've travelled far?'

'From the city. Things are bad there.'

'Ah, things are bad there. The world has always been so. But things will improve in the course of time, as you know. It's like the pendulum on a clock. The economy will get better and we shall triumph.'

For a moment I wonder at her civility to Jason, then realise that this is Elma's default attitude in the company of any half-decent-looking male. A man's woman to the core. Even at Paddy's funeral she set up a separate table for herself, away from me and Tess, and waited as it filled, first with her four remaining brothers, and then with other men, friends of Paddy's, but also one special friend of her own. She was 74, with a sense of her own majesty reflecting from the full facelift she'd had some years before. In grief and anxiety prior to Paddy's death, she shed a stone and a half in weight and presented to the mourning world a brand new svelte body enclosed in a tight-fitting, lacy black dress.

'I hope you are not Frankie's boyfriend,' Elma goes on, making her way slowly down the kitchen towards her own chair, pushing the walking aid, which creaks along the floor ahead of her. 'Frankie has had occasional boyfriends since she married. She thinks I don't know, but I do. I could always tell. Hers wasn't a marriage made in heaven. Too dull for her,' she gasps and takes a deep breath before continuing. 'I recognised the signs from the start. She was too timid and ran into the arms of the first nice man she met who would take her away from me and her father. But a very passionate girl. Not now, of course. Too old for that kind of thing.'

'He's not my boyfriend. I'm working with him on a project,' I attempt to keep my tone light and even.

The words strike like pokers. Truth in a quick jab, sometimes light-hearted, often satiric. Such well-chosen words, I marvel. *Boyfriend. Occasional. Marriage. Heaven. Signs. Dull. Passionate.*

Old. I'll mull over what Elma has just said, but later, when the bedroom light is out and I can stare into the dark. Or perhaps I won't bother. Perhaps I'm capable of moving beyond reacting too deeply to what is, after all, a kind of truth. Is there such a thing as a kind of truth? I believe so. Surely truth is not necessarily watertight or categorical?

Elma points to another chair and instructs Jason to sit down. He obeys. She has begun to ask him about the city, which she hasn't visited for several years, she says. She misses Dublin and the shops. She saw *Madam Butterfly* in the 3 Arena with Frankie, and it was wonderful, unforgettable. Jason responds knowledgeably. He heard Ermonela Jaho as Cio-Cio-San in the Royal Opera House two years before.

'I've never heard of her,' Elma admits. 'I'm of the generation that enjoyed Renata Tebaldi, Callas, Sutherland and the like. I lost interest after Cecilia Bartoli. The most adventurous voice of all.'

'You'd have loved Jaho, I swear.'

The little exchange sounds so normal. I breathe a sigh of relief, then hurry out the back door to the overgrown kitchen garden. I rip up a bunch of wild garlic and some dill. Fish, steamed, supermarket-bought fennel, and salad, I decide quickly, with mashed buttery potatoes and a dash of spicy horseradish, just as Elma and I have always enjoyed, though Tess and Paddy less so in the years we were all together.

'Not vegetarian, are you?'

He shakes his head and smiles at me.

'Just checking.'

'We're having a lovely conversation about opera,' Elma says. 'So good to be able to speak with a cultured person.'

During the meal, Elma tugs with trembling fingers at pieces of buttered hake, raises them to her mouth, then chews with concentration, every so often fixing her one-eyed stare on the dinner-plate as if to check what's actually there. The mashed potato she spoons up with a teaspoon, and the finely chopped salad she ignores. Jason is quiet.

'That's not your natural hair colour, is it?' Elma stirs suddenly.

Jason blinks and looks at her. 'Actually, it is. My father was Swedish and very blonde, though my mother was Irish.'

'Past tense? Dead? *Both* of them? To lose both looks like carelessness,' she cackles.

Jason laughs a little stiffly at this.

'Mother!'

Elma ignores me. 'So it's really your own colour?'

'Yes.'

'I once had a friend whose hair was that colour. Dyed of course. My dearest ever friend in life. Mrs O'Farrell was her name. We told one another everything. And I mean everything! But she abandoned me.'

Elma has been abandoned, Elma is always abandoned, I'm thinking.

'Oh, forget her, Mum. She wasn't a real friend anyway, you've often said as much.

'That's so true,' Elma says more thoughtfully, as if this was the first time in her life that she had realised this.

'Fair-weather friends,' Jason adds.

Elma turns and eyes him carefully, studies him. 'You never spoke a truer word,' she says in a low voice. She has accepted him. 'Fair-weather friends. Nothing worse. One thing I will say about both my daughters,' she nods towards me in a regal way, 'is that neither of them has ever been fair-weather friends to me. Either the love, or the —'

'*Mother*!'

'Nothing in between,' Elma says with finality.

I consider Elma's family yet again and wonder about their emotional abandonment. It was never a material, physical abandonment. It was more like a benign hauling up to adulthood. The house was roomy and comfortable, even if too many people lived there. I often think of the demented granny hammering at the locked bedroom door. No wonder Elma did badly at school. She was failed, I think. I have a dim memory of something she used to tell me that still seems so vivid I might as well have been present even though I was not alive. It's not my experience, yet I can see my mother as a fine-boned blonde girl pulling a pillow over her own head to try and block out the noise of the behatted grandmother ranting beside her in the middle of the night. I am busy stealing memories and running with them, it doesn't matter whether or not I myself have experienced them, they are the truckloads of fragmented collective knowledge passed on, then reconstructed, to be re-examined by each generation before it then attaches to consciousness where it is relived. Perhaps something of that abandonment made me see Tess differently. Tess, abandoned once. Then failed by Elma, although not physically abandoned. Because Tess made her relive her own pain? Perhaps. And Tess, ironically, as strong in her way, as Elma has always been in hers.

Just as Elma is regaling Jason with the story of her childhood, and how the piano teacher once locked her in the practice room to make her practise for an extra hour for not having learned the scale of E major, Tess arrives in the back door.

'I was an adventurous child,' Elma explains to Jason, ignoring Tess, 'but not everybody liked me.'

'Oh I'm sure they liked you well enough, Mum,' I remark.

Elma draws herself up, puts her spoon down on her plate.

'They did *not* always like me, Frankie, so don't try to sweeten the pill, for heaven's sake you're always moderating things. I was *not* a nice child.'

'Hey-ho, what's up?' Tess stands with a bunch of purple heather in her arms.

You weren't always a nice adult either, I think distractedly, even if I've been spared her violence and was never lifted by the head off the ground as Tess once was. Perversely, Elma has always stood singularly as one who would not bow beneath the harness of anything. It had nothing to do with feminism, so much as will. She believed in a certain type of marriage, desired it and achieved it, believing in the freedoms it gave her.

'Hi, I'm Tess, in the absence of being introduced,' Tess says to Jason.

'We've already met virtually, I believe,' he replies.

'Good to meet you in the flesh.'

'You wouldn't want to see me in the flesh,' Elma drawls, and we all laugh.

'Your dinner's in the oven,' I say.

'Ooh, yum. I'm not used to this.'

'We're just talking about that Mrs O'Farrell, remember her?'

'Vaguely. I think I'm too young.'

'Custom officer's wife?' I say, 'Blond and curvaceous as I recall. Had a horrible son called Aloysius who tried to push me out an upstairs window once until Mum intervened.'

We laugh again. Tess shakes her head. 'Nope. Before my time.'

'Well, returning to more pleasant times, Mrs O'Farrell didn't live to see you get on in life, Mother, that's all I mean. Her loss,' I say.

Jason reaches across the table and suddenly clasps Elma's hand. 'I think your daughter is right, Elma, may I call you Elma?'

Elma looks slightly shocked by this attentiveness, her mouth falling open as she allows her hand to rest beneath Jason's. 'She is quite correct because I too have had fair-weather friends. Bullshit artists if you'll pardon my French?'

'Me too,' Tess says.

'Me too,' I throw in.

'Oh of course *you* have, Frankie', Elma laughs gaily, 'but in your case it's because you listen to too many needy people. I mean, who was that looney so-called film director you brought around the place one time when you were in college? Anyone could see he was a nutcase and only for your dear father, God bless him, getting in touch with Detective Sergeant McCabe, he'd have fleeced you and anyone else he could fob off with his sob-stories.'

My mother can always disinter buried information guaranteed to maximise embarrassment. She passes herself off so well that half her nieces and nephews think I'm exaggerating when I say she has been diagnosed with a very mild form of dementia. But then, labels are useless. They mean nothing.

'And did I get on in life?' Elma asks suddenly.

'Whatever that means, but you probably did,' I say, gathering up the dinner-plates, irked and agitated by the whole conversation.

'Ah now,' Jason says agreeably.

'There's a good boy, no need for any of us to fall out,' Elma looks at him approvingly.

While I am cleaning up, Jason begins guiding Elma to the sitting-room. Tess is still hoovering up a second helping of dinner and not really talking to anybody, her mouth is so occupied. I can hear the to-and-fro conversation between Elma and Jason. They are discussing her life with Paddy. A wonderful man. So lucky to meet him. A Harris tweed jacket, smoked a pipe. Drove a cream-coloured Austin A 40. 'If you know what that is, you probably don't, your generation knows nothing about real motorcars,' she adds.

'I can look it up.'

'Of course you can, everyone looks everything up nowadays, Frankie's never off that phone either. You're all a crowd of know-alls who know nothing,' she grumbles, then laughs to take the sting out of it. 'Don't mind me. I say what I like.'

The voices fade as they move off into the hall. Tess and I rinse off the dinner plates in the scullery sink, then place them on the dishwasher rack. Tess shuts off the door that separates the scullery from the kitchen.

'Cool guy,' she says, dumping the cutlery into its basket, then packing in the saucepan, frying-pan, salad bowls and dessert dishes.

'Guess he is,' I reply. 'He's easy to work with. At least he can accept suggestions.'

I set the dishwasher on its economy cycle, wipe down the worktop, put Lottie and Jimmy outside and close the door. Now that Jason is here, it's possible Lottie, free and in the open air, will be forgotten for a short while.

'So what was it like in Bragan?' I ask Tess.

'It creeped me out, if I'm honest.'

'Told you, didn't I?'

'It's yonks since I was there. Once when I had the pony, I remember driving back from the North with the horse-box, me and the fellow I was with at the time. It was a blazing hot day and we went over the mountain, stopping off on the top. Took the pony out and the two of us rode him bareback up there.'

'Together?'

'No, we took turns.'

'Were you sober?'

Tess hesitates. 'I think so. It's very clear in my head. You'd never know what the place was to become.'

'A dumping ground for bodies. Right at that time when you were up there.'

We chat for a while about places haunted by the past, by sadness, by strands of terror that nobody has taken away for cleansing and healing, and after I carry a fluted turquoise vase of fresh anemones upstairs and check the bedroom beside Tess's, where Jason will sleep. The bed is already freshly made up, because Hilda used to sleep there sometimes and would always change it before she left in the morning. I set the anemones on the dark oak dressing-table in the room, in front of the mirror, where their reflection shimmers back at my face, my searching eyes. How I want to live.

17

I show Jason to his room, hand him two towels, pointing to the tiny, old-fashioned shower-room off a recess to the left of the bed. It smells of age, and old tiles, and perhaps a leaking pipe. Some of the tiles have loosened on the shower wall. The bedroom is panelled in deal, and the ceiling slopes down almost to behind the bed. There is a skylight window, and one long window which faces east. Tess's pet mice escaped into this when she was nine, and Paddy tracked them patiently on hands and knees as she sobbed about their loss.

'The shower controls are a bit pernickety. You might get a blast of sudden cold, but just tweak the dial a little and it should be okay.'

As I go to leave, we each hesitate. There is a definite tension between us. I feel I ought to hug him. On impulse, I move towards him and his arms enclose me. Nervously, I hold myself slightly away from him, cautious of contact with his abdomen and groin.

'Thanks Frankie. It's great to be with you. An honour, in

fact,' he smiles sheepishly.

'Ah sure. I'm glad you've come.'

'Really?'

'Stop looking for compliments. Really.'

He smells good, his body odour fresh, with none of the riper musk that occasionally trails Christoph. He flops on the bed and looks around approvingly, his eye taking everything in. As I watch, I see him in a haze of bluey purple evening light. The cream drape which drops over the long window is now blue, and the bed linen on which he will rest his head is tinged with blue. How beautiful he will look, head on pillows, blond hair flowing back on the linen. How I would love to lie there with him. How I would love to feel tense and urgent again, with desire I mean.

'Know something? It's lovely to be looked after,' he whispers, sitting up on one elbow.

'Looked after? How so?'

'Hospitality, I suppose. A lovely meal, a nice private room. Great company. I just wanted to say thanks.'

I throw him a wink. 'See you in the morning.' I step back onto the landing and leave quickly.

After seeing to Elma, after telling her again why she needs night-time sanitary wear, then helping her swivel herself onto her mattress with its blue protector, I'm in my own room. I read for a few moments from a celebrated memoir of mourning in which the Californian author's husband died right in front of her eyes one Christmas. The author, I conclude, although interesting, is a narcissist and it really is all about her and her precious Californian life. She is so removed from the rest of the world and its troubles that I think she's got to be joking. But the need to reflect on the way life can change so suddenly and forever is not strong enough to prevent sleep. Not even Roddy Boyd's scratching nib can prevent it. He's busy around me tonight, for sure. But I'm not worried. The more I *feel*, the more he responds with the quill. And he's not real, I try to convince myself. This is nothing more than a trace memory from an unsettled time. It hooks itself into my little emotional fish mouth and responds to the tossing flurries of my life. But for the first time, I feel peaceful. Less alone. Some kind of cavalry has arrived. I drift off.

The next morning Tess's case, her third piece of luggage, bursts open with a heavy clunk. More gifts tumble onto her bed. I'm standing in the doorway in a red and yellow silk chemise bought in Beijing many years before, which I rooted out of the back of my wardrobe. With Jason in the house, I feel the need to look good. I glimpse a tangle of coloured wrappings, clothing, a Sephora bag stuffed with make-up.

'This room was always warmer than mine,' I remark, looking around. Already, Tess's presence has changed it, and it is draped with her clothing and jackets, bags strewn on the rugs and floorboards.

'But yours was bigger. It was better, which I'm sure you know. Let's face it, you got daughter number one territory, I got the maid's room.'

'I adore Sephora cosmetics!' I'm not going to let her bother me with this kind of joke-serious-accusation.

With Tess now here, if I decide to, I really can leave in a day or two. On the other hand, Jason is also here. Although Christoph is waiting for me, the airs have changed at Kilnavarn. Or perhaps it's just the airs within me.

Gifts are unwrapped for a second time in Elma's bedroom. She fingers the slightly too large sweater, and the coral necklace which Tess gives her, then pushes them to one side on her bed, where Jimmy is curled, purring. Tess reminds me of one of the

Magi bearing gifts from the Orient, placing object after object, precious offerings, around Elma. 'Oh lovely, thank you,' she murmurs, and 'You shouldn't have brought me anything. You gave me that woolly thing yesterday, that's enough. Now, if you don't mind I'm going to have a little nap.'

Elma turns to one side, shuts her eyes, then opens one and looks hard at Tess. 'I must say you're looking well,' she says, and shuts it again.

'It's always like that now,' I tell her as we descend the stairs. 'She really doesn't want gifts.'

'She should make an effort and try to look pleased. It's not as if she sees me all that often.'

'Hardly her fault. I mean —'

'I guess you're right'

'Anyway, she can't help it now. And there's no need to keep piling gifts on her."

'Why are you letting her off the hook?'

'I'm not. It's cognitive stuff. Loss of inhibition and social niceties.'

'She lost those years ago,' Tess goes to fill the kettle.

'It's how she is. Have you forgotten how excited she used to get when there were gifts to be opened at Christmas or on her birthday? Like a child, ripping and tearing at paper, flinging it to the ground as she examined her latest toy or whatever it was Paddy had bought? The tape-recorder? The mink coat? The whopper diamond solitaire?'

'You're probably right. I'm still adjusting. Ignore me.' The kettle is boiling loudly, the washing-machine which I filled earlier is spinning, and the dish-washer is finishing its rinse cycle. Exciting times, I'm thinking with a twist of inner bitter lemon.

Tess has brought a hand-made Native American urn for me,

earthen-coloured, with wild brown and white horses racing across an imagined prairie. And a tennis shirt for Christoph.

'I take it Christoph still plays tennis?'

'More than ever.'

Since his retirement, Christoph has more than occasionally abandoned study and taken up tennis, even travelling to Spain every autumn with a group of guys who spend a lot of the time slagging one another off, but play robust doubles all day and dine well every evening.

'Nike,' she emphasises, 'a Breathe Slam model too.'

'He'll love that,' I say, though Christoph isn't interested in labels.

'So how you doing up here? Tell me honestly.'

I restrain myself from re-laundering my thoughts about feeling high, dry and deserted and that she could have come much sooner, that I've waited for her arrival for so long, and could she not have asked for special leave at the clinic? But I don't say that, because there would be no point.

'Mostly like shit,' I reply. 'I mean, I feel like shit a lot of the time. But not now. Since you've come. . .and since Jason has arrived, I'm a bit distracted.'

She regards me momentarily. I'm not actually expecting much by way of a response. Tess's default position is often one of non-committal silence. She asks if I want tea. I nod, and she then begins to talk about her own work before I can tell her anything else.

I ignore this and instead eyeball her. 'You asked how I was doing up here. Aren't you curious to hear more?'

'I do know what you do here, you know. I'm sorry I haven't come sooner. Getting time off work was difficult in the land of Live to Work. I'm catering mostly for kids in public schools. I end up spending my own money buying materials these schools can't provide. We're talking basic materials. Like, it's insane? Sometimes I want to go back to my old student job in Starbucks.'

Tess is sitting at the kitchen table, a round tin of biscuits and cakes open, selecting a Mr Kipling's French Fancy.

'So you've said,' I respond.

'I can see you're holding onto some anger,' she mumbles, teeth sinking into one half of the little confection. She chews steadily, then slugs her tea. I feel like smacking her face.

'Surprising, is it?' I'm pacing around the kitchen, mug in hand. 'I've been on my own, as you know.'

'I know all you've done here, I really do get it, you know. And I'm grateful, I'm *so* grateful.'

'*Grateful*? I don't want your gratitude unless you can translate it into action. Actions, you know? Louder than —'

'Blah-blah-blah, yeah, louder than words, that always was your fucking chant.'

'It's true!'

'You could have walked away.'

I stop dead, half a biscuit still unchewed in my mouth. 'Walk away? How could I do that?'

'Think about it. What do many other families do in a similar situation where the burden is falling on one person? No? You don't get it? Surely it's obvious. Put Elma into the nursing home.'

Perhaps I should have. But the fact was I couldn't. No matter what way I dressed it up or justified it, no matter what some people said about how content the old people were in such places, I never for one moment believed it.

'Are you mad? That wasn't her wish. She never wanted that. Feet first and in a coffin, she always said. And can you imagine? Afternoons of Bingo and flower-arranging for our mother? Cheery helpers talking to her as if she was some drooling half-wit? Awful trad music banging into her ears on Mondays, bingo on Tuesdays, some kind of scrawling that passes for art on Wednesdays? Not on my watch!'

'Well then, stop blaming me for the fact that you're on your own with her! You've got to stop dumping emotional shite on me. So I went away. My choice. I saw no point feeling compelled to drive up here every two weeks to hold Elma's hand after Paddy died. I had a good long think about that.'

'I bet you had,' I say quietly.

She throws me a look but ignores the comment. 'I knew it wasn't for me. Nothing I would have done would ever have satisfied her.'

'But did you never think about me?' I ask lightly, trying to calm myself, suddenly full of self-pity. 'Did you never think about what you were doing to me when you walked away?'

'I did.'

'And?'

'And *what*?'

'What did you think? Seems to me you were always able to walk away from uncomfortable situations. It wasn't so easy for me. Great for you that can see how it should be when you're over in New York.' Now I'm finding it difficult to keep my voice steady, to avoid the tremble that undoes my throat. To my surprise, Tess agrees.

'I know it wasn't easy. You're right.'

'I am?'

'I walked out and to be frank I didn't give a brass farthing. I felt a bit guilty, but on the whole, and once I was away, even that faded. I was able to sleep well.'

'Just as I thought!' I snap. 'Maybe Elma was always right. It's your nature! And you can't blame family for everything, not when you don't even know what you come from yourself!'

There's a long silence. We are both breathing heavily. The air is electric with disclosure and rage.

'Ouch. Ouch.' Tess eventually directs her gaze at the floor. 'All the old cliches, eh? Well, you know what? I still hold a grudge or two against you, even if you've taken the brunt of caring for her.'

'*What* fucking grudge? How many more times do I have to say sorry for something I didn't do? I was a child, in case you hadn't noticed! I was a *child*! It wasn't my fault she preferred me. The only reason she preferred me was because I was more compliant, what she called *good-natured, agreeable*, that kind of nonsense. I did the things she wanted! I was afraid not to!' I slam a tea-mug on kitchen draining-board so hard it cracks, then splits. We watch as the dregs of my tea splatter and drift, then drain into the sink.

'I said two things, and you only heard one of them. I said I hold a grudge or two and I also said you've taken the fucking brunt of it. Are you deaf?'

'It's time you gave up the grudge. Deal with what happened. As that stupid apron you brought me one time says, *Shit Happens!* You have your shit and I have mine. Get used to it. And by the way, I know more about what happened than you do. I saw things you don't even remember!' My voice steadies itself. 'Internalised experience? Dissociated memory? Repressed memory? Does that mean anything to you? Surely you're coming up against those terms in the clinic from time to time?'

'All I'm saying,' she takes up steadily, completely ignoring what I've just spewed out, 'is look after yourself. This isn't a competition.'

'Oh isn't it?' I reply bitterly.

I scarcely recognise this calm, professionalised version of my sister. 'Since when have you ever cared about how I look after myself? Don't make me fucking laugh,' I mutter. 'I couldn't put her into a home. It was her wish to stay at home. I tried to respect her wish.'

'So far so traditional. But really?'

'Would you have done it, if you were in my shoes? Could you have?'

Tess is quite cool. 'Yes. All things considered.'

'All things considered,' I repeat thoughtfully.

'It'd be my life or hers. You've let her ride roughshod over yours. She didn't mean to. I think. And by the way, I'd be surprised if you even recognise Christoph when you see him again.'

'Hey, back to fuck off!' My face is heating up.

'I'm just saying she's a taker. Remember that.'

'She isn't. She really isn't. Without realising it, she's a feeble old lady showing us how to be old ourselves when that time comes.'

For a moment, neither of us speaks. Then words slip out and I know they're unfair. 'Anyway, you know all about taking, don't you?'

She darts towards me, hand raised as if to strike, but I block her arm. 'Don't!' I warn, 'You'll regret it.' To my surprise, she heeds me, takes a few steps back from where I'm standing, and crosses her arms tightly.

Tess does not see anything beyond her own childhood injury. I can't blame her. And she can't even recall the half of it. Adulthood has not erased the pain.

'If you'd come home more often, it would have helped, you know, if you'd actually stayed for a couple of weeks here in the house, instead of touring the country like some dispossessed Russian aristocrat from the past.'

'Gee thanks. That's freakin' classy. Well maybe I am

dispossessed even if you can't see it that way and prefer to sound so smart, oh so smart with your literary comparisons! I thought about it a lot, I discussed it in therapy too. In the end I couldn't do it more than once every eighteen months or so. That was my deal with myself.'

'Oh, *therapy*? You discussed it in therapy. Nice.' I take a breath, and my voice is tight and almost squeaky. 'So was that the reason you stayed at the hotel in the town when you did show up, instead of coming here to the house? Instead of being here at night with her when you might be most needed?' I have to swallow hard.

Tess glances at me, then looks away. 'I had to protect myself. In fact, I'll always protect myself.'

'Protect? Always?'

I'm still turning the word over when Jason enters the kitchen, rubbing his hands together awkwardly, as if unsure of what to do. He senses an atmosphere.

'Kettle's boiled,' Tess says, making a quick recovery, smiling up at him so angelically you'd swear we'd just been talking about our favourite movies, Sephora cosmetics, or World Peace.

'Thanks,' he replies, taking a chair. Hair messy, eyes sleep-heavy. He sits a moment, clearing his throat, then helps himself to a slice of rye.

'We're talking about Mother. About Elma,' I explain although my hands are shaking.

'And we're talking about Frankie too,' Tess adds in a slightly dialled down tone of spite.

Quickly, I leave the kitchen and head to the bathroom, where I shut myself in. For the first time in years tears are flowing from my eyes till I'm like a crying clown. Tess has a different capacity from me, follows the garbled version of memory rather than the one I saw unfold, can inflict her own brand of punishment without a second thought. I wait for a few moments until the tears stop, aghast at myself and my suddenly thinner than paper skin, that such realisations should have burst out of me now. I rinse my face in cold water, inspect myself in the small overhead mirror. My hands are trembling, but I look okay. Not too blotchy. Eyes a little pink-rimmed. I wait a few minutes and let the tap run while I take deep breaths. In for seven. Hold for four. Exhale slowly for five. It's all in the breathing, they say. I am never going to confront Tess again about any of this. It's too late now and it would make no difference. Whatever she is, she is not my enemy.

In the kitchen, the conversation has rolled on to the presence of the zoonotic emanation that has apparently leapfrogged from some random animal or bat in Wuhan. I glance towards Tess, but she's looking calm and focussed on Jason, a fresh mug of coffee in her hands. I feel inexplicably lighter. I've probably said everything and so too has Tess. I tell myself I've stopped caring about her feelings. She asks Jason about his life as a writer, which is more than she ever does to me, I note pettishly. Where he lives. Where he was schooled. How he found his way into writing. They find a friend in common in Dublin, then begin to overtly criticise the friend, and bend over with stomach laughter.

Tess is talking about the attic, which she hasn't visited since she was a teenager. It was a great hideout, she tells Jason, sipping her coffee, munching on a Fox's chocolate covered biscuit. Like me, she could escape up there and be alone. Sometimes she played with old dolls and a moth-eaten teddy left by the previous owners. Nobody knew where she was. But I also used to escape up there. There was a freedom to it.

'Maybe we'll go up later,' she says to nobody in particular.

'After dinner?' The idea of an excursion up the stairway and around the corner that leads to the attic door appeals to me.

'What's in it?' Jason enquires. 'It's quite a big house. You must have loads of stuff up there. And didn't you used to get scared during the winter out here?'

'No,' we reply in unison, then laugh, even though I'm certain we have not forgiven one another for the earlier conversation. But that's our private selves. We can both perform outside the parameters of the private. We're used to it. We don't add that the problem wasn't the house, which has always been benign. We love the house, a tender place in the earth, on its hill, with another hill and wood rising up behind the house with its turret and oculus window.

'It was a safe house,' Tess says, 'even if I couldn't wait to get away from it.'

'The house itself was very safe,' I echo, 'We always had this feeling of being connected to the ones who were here before us, like Roddy Boyd. Dad found papers in the attic, discards from way back in the mid 1860s, beautiful hand-written documents with lists of names.'

'Well,' Tess qualifies, 'it was safe to a point.'

We stare at one another for more than a few seconds, our eyes meeting in a brief moment of understanding.

'And there was a tiger?' Jason asks in an incredulous voice.

'Well yeah, it had an indoor cage. In the dining-room in a little annex Boyd built especially extended out the north side of the house to accommodate him.'

Tess interrupts with a scoff. 'Don't tell me you're going to start banging on about Boyd and the fucking tiger again Frankie! Do you actually believe all that?'

'Totally! The traces are everywhere. Even the smell. Can't you get the smell sometimes, Jason?'

'As in?'

'As in C-A-T.'

We describe the evenings we imagine, when a fire blazed in the hearth and, according to papers held in the local heritage centre, how Roddy Boyd surrounded himself with other men, skilled poker-players like himself. Tom Macklin, his right-hand man in all undertakings, ferried drinks into the long dining-room, stoking the fire when it threatened to die.

'That's what was said around here,' Tess says, 'though I don't believe the half of it.'

'But sometimes, you need to imagine,' I add.

Tess smiles and her right hand caresses a cigarette. She has unloosened her hair and it coils on her shoulders. Silence descends and we each make our excuses and leave the kitchen. Tess returns to bed for the morning. Jason is in his room. Elma is washed and asleep. There is nothing else to be done. I read in Paddy's study, which was really his drinking room and where he stored rows of specialty whiskeys. Haig Dimple. Mackenzie Blended. Middleton. Red Breast. Powers. Bell's 12-Year-Old Blended. He would retreat there after a particularly hard day in theatre, or after a protracted hospital board meeting. It's where he went the night after he beat Tess to please Elma. Now, it's peaceful, the new green of ivy reflecting on the pale limed walls where the sun strikes it.

At four o'clock Tess reappears, freshly made-up and changed into a new outfit just as Jason talks about walking out to clear his head. I point out for him the quickest route down to the other side of the lake, to the fields Elma has rented out ever since Paddy died. She has never raised the rent. The tenant puts his sheep to graze there. Occasionally, a small herd of Hereford cattle are put into the next two fields, which the tenant sublets although he thinks we don't know about this. He's a dour man, empty of words, full of thrift. He has maintained the fields, never trimmed the hedges or interfered with the ancient oaks. It's a place of grazing, of stillness created by the patience of beasts, the air sweet with their cud, and in summer the ping of flies whizzing through shadow-flindered meadows.

'So what's the story with Jason?' Tess asks as soon as he has left. 'The real story, I mean?'

I describe my impressions in as detached a way as possible as I chop onions for the evening meal, spaghetti bolognese, with small pasta helmets to help Elma scoop them onto a spoon. I try to forget our earlier conversation, the tails of the past that still flail at us both.

'It's a work thing, right?'

'Definitely,' I reply with an eye roll behind her back.

'I did wonder. I was surprised to find someone else here. Young, isn't he?'

I'm non-committal. 'He took some notion to come here. I've been mentoring him on his novel.'

'Hmmm. I know your history of questionable taste in men. Apart from Christoph, that is.'

'This is definitely work. Growing friendship perhaps?'

'Yeah, right.'

'I mean it!' Despite my protest, I blush.

Tess says nothing.

18

Elma is calling. It is not her usual call, more of a weak wail.

'Frankie? Frankie, can you hear me?' Then, 'Are you there, Frankie?'

'I'll go,' Tess says, leaving and running upstairs.

There is silence for some moments. Then Tess's voice, urgent. 'Frankie! *Frankie*?'

'What?'

'I need you.'

'In a tick, just let me finish this.'

'Mum has fallen.'

I switch off the gas hob, leave the onions and beef sizzling, and take the stairs in twos. I'm not expecting any disasters. Elma has fallen frequently and not yet broken anything beyond a bone in her small toe. The problem is getting her lifted and into bed again.

'So you've fallen,' I announce as I stride into the bedroom.

Tess sounds more sympathetic. 'Oh poor Mum,' she soothes,

'what happened? How did you fall?'

'I have not fallen. I was doing a few floor exercises. Yoga. That dumpy little physiotherapist Frankie brought in is always saying yoga is good for flexibility and balance.'

Tess and I exchange a smile.

'This might be tricky,' I whisper, looking at my mother sprawled beside her bed, nightdress up to her waist.

'Stop making a fuss Frankie,' Elma snaps. 'And stop whispering.'

'Don't worry, we'll get you up,' Tess says, touching Elma's forehead. The tenderness of it takes me by surprise, and Elma relents.

I remind myself that Tess is a health professional, accustomed to caring for stroke victims, stammerers, stutterers, and all kinds of people whose tongues and mouths have been wrecked either by birth or life. Perhaps, after all, she's capable of caring for someone she knows personally, perhaps despite everything she's capable of showing real concern for Elma. We calculate how to go about the lifting. Elma lies on the flat of her back, walking aid capsized on the patterned rug Paddy once lugged back from Abu Dhabi. Together we approach her, talking aloud to ourselves through each move, a hand each beneath her shoulders, another under each arm, as we attempt to hoist her forward.

'Holy fuck, what weight is she?' Tess's teeth are clenched.

'If you don't mind,' Elma interjects, 'I'm about nine stone.'

'That's over a hundredweight,' I remark drily, 'and you're going to have to help us. Push with your legs. It might hurt a bit, but try to push.'

'Yes, Nurse Ratched,' replies Elma.

Tess's face breaks into a smile. I try to smile.

'No need to pull that face, Frankie.'

With great difficulty, we heft the old woman onto shaky, swollen and purplish feet which can scarcely gain purchase on the floor, her thighs giving way, but we hold her firmly, then lower her to the side of the bed. She is panting with the effort. This shortness of breath I attribute to gradual heart failure. I have not done anything about it, as she's already on heart tablets. Besides, it's difficult to get the doctor to do a house call unless you've fallen into a combine harvester or drunk weed killer and tonic by mistake. It has to be a proper emergency, and by health system standards the failing heart of a very elderly woman does not constitute an emergency.

Elma squints at Tess, examining her hair. 'I don't like that hair colour, if you don't mind my saying so.'

'So you keep saying.'

'I'm only saying what I think. Why can't you keep it more like Frankie's? It would be softer, especially at your age.'

I leave Tess with Elma, who has decided that she will stay in bed and have dinner in her room. Regal but humorous now, she requests her wig as she doesn't want to frighten the nice young man if he happens to pop in to see her. Does he have a girlfriend? I hear Tess ask if she'd like to use the commode, and laugh to myself. Then I stop. I hear Elma's voice in the distance. Yes, she might take a few moments to herself on her throne, if Tess wouldn't mind?

The endless comparisons must have been hard for Tess to hear, I, the piece of grit whose presence unwittingly ground my sister down, a millwheel of frequent comparisons from Elma about her hair (too fine), height (too small), manners (none), clothing (peculiar, looking for attention), achievement (none), qualifications (none). No wonder Tess absconded. In her shoes, I'd have done the same. Tess had brains to burn, but brains became her weapon of resistance, ensuring she would never, ever please Elma.

'Couldn't you have tried to pass that exam, if only for your father's sake?' Elma once ranted after Tess failed first year anthropology at university.

Tess shrugged. 'I guess that course wasn't for me,' she'd murmured guiltily.

'It all cost money, you know Tess, fail it again and that's it, you're on your own!' Elma responded before going on to blame Paddy for never saying a word one way or the other about her performance.

Another year passed and Tess failed again, then failed better as Beckett once exhorted, except that nobody back then would have seen the genius of failure in the way that Beckett did. Certainly not Elma, who herself had never studied but regretted it, and knew how study could make a girl independent. Nor did she see, as both Tess and I do, how alienation is the magic of artistry and art. That being alienated, Tess especially was bound to fail but then recover in brilliance, that being alienated I would never have followed any of the professions Elma imagined: modern language teacher, music teacher, doctor, scientist. Instead, I am a writer, to my core, because I need to discover what my thoughts are, I am a writer, as well as a walking wound of protest.

I wish I hadn't witnessed so much. I wish that, even as a child, I could have spoken. I wish I had not grown as a result to be an over-serious, slightly repressed woman. If I were to encounter Paddy in some dream hospital corridor, I'd tell him of his failure, of his inability to stand up to Elma. He too is to blame. They both failed. Then they failed better in the rearing of their daughters. My head is pumping with anxiety now, I'm sure my blood pressure is rising.

But defilement comes in many guises. A child's dreamtime can be raped by voice, or slaps, or beatings. A child's dreamtime is commonly ripped into, something I will never reveal to Tess, who cannot remember it, which Elma confided to me after Paddy's death, and which I now describe in a distant voice of neither ornamentation nor drama. An adult, depending on the day and the mood, the sunshine or the rain, on whether she was tired or bored or neither, on whether she felt like getting up out of bed or going shopping, used to sometimes pinch the baby's flesh to make the baby cry, then slapped that baby hard for crying in response to being pinched. The cunning miracle, that baby was never murdered; the tragedy, that the woman had no one to talk to. Right now Tess is upstairs with Elma and I haven't the slightest clue of their conversation. It is unlikely to be confrontational. The hinted-at recriminations at Tess's failure to stay married, at Tess getting pregnant within five months of arriving in America and marrying after Allegra was born have mostly disappeared. Now, when she remembers, Elma admires Tess's career as a speech and language pathologist in so far as she understands what Tess actually does. She tells Tess that she has made her, and her late father, God-bless-him, proud at last. The only failure now is that her husband, a Brooklyn lawyer, was not a keeper. At least Tess did not wish to keep him, once she discovered his cocaine habit. She knew the cocaine would be like a white storm blowing its way up his nostrils and through their marriage.

Tess comes into the kitchen carrying a plastic bag from Elma's room.

'Where do I put this?' she scowls, holding it at arm's length.

'Out the back. In the black bin.'

The work of sanitation. Tess is not pleased. I gloat a little.

Jason returns from his walk, hands in pockets. He has met someone on the avenue, he tells me. A woman who says she is Elma's carer.

'Oh. That's Hilda. What'd she want?' I ask, still pissed off by her withdrawal.

'She said she was uneasy about coming to Kilnavarn. She said she and Elma get on the best. But she's afraid.'

I snort. 'So, what was she doing on the avenue? Picking cherry-blossom? Spare me.'

Jason smiles. 'Eh no. I'd say she was testing the waters, like she wanted to come up but is afraid of bringing infection into the house? She seems very attached to you all.'

'I'd say she's afraid for herself. But yeah, she's attached to us. Has she gone?'

'I'd imagine so. She was turning to go back as if she'd changed her mind.' Jason shrugs his shoulders and asks if he can help me.

'You can maybe set the table? Everything's in the dresser.' He moves quietly, deftly, lifting delph, finding cutlery in the drawers, removing glasses from an open shelf beside the dresser. It's as if he has a feel for a kitchen and a place and is no stranger. Tess has no clue or memory of where anything is stored and moves around the kitchen fingering drawers and cupboards like someone with very compromised eyesight.

'I'm sorry you've had to hear so much of our shit,' I say to him. 'You must think we're crazy.'

'Nope.' He is laying cutlery on the long table, placing glasses, setting a jug of water, finds ice-cubes in the freezer. He's handy, I note. 'I'm used to all kinds.'

'But you were raised by your Mum's parents?'

'They adored me.'

I marvel at his certainty of being adored. 'Were they modern grandparents then?'

'They'd been around, done a lot of the things they'd wanted to do. I think they were actually part of some crowd known as the Screamers, back in the 70s. They were and still are Reichian theorists. Of course, they're still living and in their eighties, he adds.

'Sounds as if you were what I'd call gently reared,' I remark.

'That's a neat way of putting it. I guess I was.'

'How are you feeling today, how's the pain?'

'I'm okay. It's easing off a little, even though I think I might be developing arthritis or something like that.'

'You're a bit young. A blood test will tell a lot,' I say.

Tess interrupts and parades past with a bundle of sunny yellow forsythia stems in her arms. She looks tense. 'I see the bats are back.'

'Oh. Yeah, I think so. But they're not in the house, they're in the stable roof.'

'Hate them critters,' she remarks with a shiver. 'They're out there swirling around already.' She locates a tall jug on the dresser, fills it with water, arranges the forsythia.

'It's their time,' Jason says quietly. 'They enjoy the early evening. When I was in Romania I used to see zillions of them by seven o'clock on warm evenings.'

'Are they different from Irish bats?' I ask.

'Probably. Incredible little creatures really.'

'Spreaders of disease,' Tess counters, setting the forsythia on the table.

Jason glances at me, gauging my response, but I pretend not to notice.

'They're fascinating,' I continue, 'and we've had our share of them over the years. Remember the one in the window-shutter?'

Tess gives a shiver. 'I hate them.'

'You can expect to see some old guano if we go to the attic later,' I tell her.

'Then I'm wearing my boots.'

While Tess carries a tray upstairs to Elma's room, Jason moves closer to me. 'I need to tell you something,' he says.

There is an intimacy to that sentence. I turn to him. 'What is it?'

But Tess has pushed in the kitchen door. 'Orange juice, she wants orange juice. Sorry. I sense I've barged in,' she says with a smirk.

'It's okay. You haven't missed anything,' he answers with a shrug.

Later, Jason and I get drunk. We've finished two bottles of wine. Tess has downed a litre of Diet Coke and a full tube of Pringles and is chewing thoughtfully. We appear to have reached a plateau, Tess and I, despite fighting earlier. Elma, upstairs, is dozing. Tess sat up with her for a while, and they chatted about the usual things of interest: fashion, hair, music and New York, but Elma is tired. Tess thinks the tumble has shaken her.

'She'll be fine,' I insist. 'She's fallen umpteen times before, my God she must be made of rubber.'

Tess's eyes swivel towards me, she looks slightly surprised. 'There's always one last time.'

*

It's time for bed. I take my time preparing. There's an April full moon and for the first time in weeks, temperatures have lifted. I raise the peeling window sash and the night air flows in. The birds are still singing, unstoppable. I've taken a shower, moisturised my skin and dabbed the slightest touch of Guerlain between my breasts. At times such as this, I feel visionary, odd as it sounds. I can see behind me and around me and before me into the immediate future with a certainty that ignores everything and everyone around me. Perhaps, in more respects than I have admitted, Tess and I share a capacity to ignore what we don't want to deal with. Except that for now, everything is — briefly — under my control.

Around one a.m., the lightest knock on my door. The steep black roof above me has closed its wings and the house is in its first dreaming. Jason pads into the room, he's in shorts and a white T-shirt. It's as if everything is prearranged, which it isn't. He touches me lightly as we sit on the side of the bed, then he pushes the hair back from my face, his fingers exploring my hairline.

But there we stop. I grip his wrist and pull his hand down and clasp it. We lie back on the bed, a goose-down duvet cushioning us. I tell myself I'm too old for any of this. No amount of post-menopausal self-help will ever convince me otherwise. Despite my current state of semi-arousal, I fill with shame, shame for my own gradual wrinkling up, my drying out, yes I'm an ageing woman whose private body is pale pink and thin, fragile as a crush of beached shells, my arms have lost muscle tone and my bottom has begun to sag, my breasts are looser than they used to be. Like most older women today I disguise myself as younger, the two true elements of my femaleness hidden inside me — my decommissioned womb, and my brain — and surely he must recognise such disguise.

His hand slips beneath my loose t-shirt to touch my left breast. Very gently. Then the right, then back again to the left as if he can't decide where to place his hands. He pauses to check how I'm taking this, reaches down to squeeze my hand. Noticing the plaster on my finger, he loosens his grip, raises my hand in front of his face and examines it.

'What happened?' he asks.

'I was chopping garlic.'

Then, childlike, 'Can I see?'

Slowly, staring him in the eyes, I carefully unpeel the plaster, which is drenched through with dried blood. He holds this part of me so gently, a hand that has lifted and cleaned, that has balanced vegetables on a chopping board and has balanced Elma so that she will not fall, a hand that has washed and fixed, a hand that has held Christoph's body, that has turned pages, has typed a zillion words on five different laptop keyboards in the past twenty-five years. He is holding this hand so kindly, like a precious object. He hasn't even noticed that above his head the bedroom light has begun to swing back and forth. He begins to suck slowly, runs the tip of his tongue along my finger from nail to knuckle, pausing to gently lick the wound, which is small, clean and healing.

I take a deep breath and hold it. The sensation of his tongue. The heat of flesh. 'Would you just lie here? Beside me?'

He turns on his side and looks into my face. 'Sure,' he whispers. 'We don't have to do anything at all. I'm just happy to be here. With you.'

It's so ordinary, so easy, unlike anything I have experienced with any other man, including Christoph. No other man was content to simply lie with me, to rest with me physically, and not need to enter me like a knight breaking into the citadel. I'm thinking there must be a new breed of male around the place, and wonder if there are others like Jason. I pull up the duvet. I feel safe. I have asked nothing other than to be let be, to be accepted in my body and in myself as I wish to be. After a while, Jason's soft breaths fill the night and I switch off the bedside light, ignoring the motion above me from the centre light, which is spinning quietly. I think guiltily about my betrayal of Christoph, then doze off.

Around four a.m. I nudge Jason, try to push him gently away. It's too hot. He should return to his own room. Beside me though, he's shivering.

'Holy fuck I'm freezing,' he whispers.

'I'm overheated,' I complain, reaching to touch his arm. It feels cold.

'I've been lying here trying to warm up for the past half hour but I didn't want to disturb you. This sounds nuts, but something happened to my body. You were asleep. I couldn't move until you touched me, I tried to speak but couldn't get the words out. It's like I was being watched?'

'How do you mean, watched?'

'Sleep paralysis or something? I swear it felt as if someone was staring at me on the left side of the bed, eyes boring into me and not in a friendly way, practically looming over me. I'm fucking spooked.'

The room is perfectly peaceful in the dark. I take Jason's hand and for a moment, say nothing. I switch on the lamp and look up. The ceiling lights are still spinning and swaying, as if bashed strongly by an unseen hand. I hear him swear, feel him tremble. A glass of water I'd placed on the surface of a box of books beside the bed is now on the dressing-table, the liquid within shivering as if the glass had been set down roughly.

'Look. . .' I start to explain.

To me, there's something a little comical about it, though Jason won't see it that way. This is my secret after all, my room, space, history with the memory of Roddy Boyd. What can I say? Can I make light of it?

I open my mouth again. 'We have a slight poltergeist problem in the house, in this room if I'm honest. . .' My voice trails away.

Jason is staring at me. I pull him closer, stroke his back.

'You're having a laugh,' he says, not amused.

'It's true.' I watch for a reaction. 'This room's different from the others. Haunted, I suppose, if you believe in that kind of thing.'

He says nothing, scans the walls carefully as I continue to hold him, massaging his back and neck gently.

'Are you warming up?'

'Just about.'

'It's not really a problem.'

'No? A *slight* poltergeist problem, you call it?'

'I had no idea this was going to happen. I know something did happen, I don't doubt you. It's just that. . .'

'What?'

'It's never happened like this before.'

'So how has it happened?'

I explain what I can. He senses my reluctance to elaborate and doesn't press me for information. In the end, he lies quite still against me. Now that his body has warmed up, I want him to return to his own room. I feel his erection against me and pull back. He kisses me once, against my ear, then touches my face with his fingers.

'I'll never, ever, forget this night,' he says in a low voice.

'Oh you will, you will,' I assure him.

'I won't, you know.'

'Literary mentoring with a difference,' I say, and he manages to smile.

As the door shuts behind him I follow the sound of his footstep as he makes his way along the landing to his own room. Above me, nothing stirs. The light fitting is completely still. I sleep deeply.

19

The first hours of the day are peaceful. Tess isn't up. After washing Elma, I bring her breakfast upstairs, then return to the kitchen.

'You're not sorry, are you?' I ask, turning to Jason.

He shakes his head. 'I'm not sorry. Even if the night was beyond weird. It was tender too.'

'Just one thing though. Don't mention any of this to Tess, and certainly not the poltergeist thing.'

'Why?'

I'm not sure why I am more concerned about Tess hearing Jason talk about the poltergeist thing rather than the fact he was in my bed.

'Some things don't need to be explained. And she can be...'

'What can she be?'

'Freaked. Nervy.'

He pulls me towards him. 'Not a tough old boot like you, eh?' he teases.

I push him away but say nothing, a little annoyed by

this description.

This is a once-off, I repeat in my head. A once off, and I want him to know that. There'll be no moaning, weeping, gnashing of teeth or being lovelorn. It was what it should be. I have no time to spare for longings about things that are impossible. My future is short. I have no time, no time, no time.

'So you know it's over as soon as it's begun, right?' I say.

'That's like a line from some bad 1980s song'. His eyes are so bright, the smile that lights him pours into me. 'And you're a legend,' he adds.

I shrug the compliment away. 'Dunno about that. But it's better this way. For you too.'

'How do you know what's better for me?' he sticks his neck out indignantly.

'I don't. But it's better for me. Just think about it? At my age? It's not going anywhere.'

'I suppose so,' he relents.

'You'll be glad in the end. Trust me.'

We eat our breakfast. The coffee is strong and hot, the toast crisp, the lime marmalade sublimely tart on my tongue. The day proceeds. Tess appears around noon, dressed but incommunicative. Vaguely, I wonder if she'll ever actually cook a meal, smiling to myself at how anyone can reach her age with such a determined attitude to not cooking.

As the morning stretches out, I return to Jason's manuscript. He is sitting in Paddy's study on his own laptop, communicating with someone he met while travelling in Romania. It strikes me eventually that Elma is remarkably quiet above. She sleeps as the sun moves around the house, as the branches of the spring trees creak into life and the jackdaws are clucking and chittering in the chimney-pots. She sleeps more and more, unwilling to be disturbed.

By late afternoon, the intensity between Jason and me has eased and things have returned to superficial normality. We are sitting in the kitchen with Tess and his curiosity about the attic is effervescent. He is murmuring like a persistent, nagging child, asking to see the oculus.

'I haven't been up there for yonks, but I'm assuming it's the kind of thing you'll love,' Tess says pointedly, settling herself in front of a large bowl of breakfast cereal although dinner is not long over. She stares absently into the blue and white striped bowl brimming with milk. She doesn't seem to notice anything different between Jason and me.

It's been a long time since I ventured into the attic. In recent years I've remained within certain domestic boundaries, confining myself to my bedroom, Elma's bedroom, the bathroom with its wide shower, shower-chair and the many supporting handles and rails installed by Christoph, and the kitchen. Heart of the house.

A spirit of adventure fizzes. 'Will we go up there?' Tess asks, finally pushing the empty bowl of cereal aside and standing up.

I sense her politely ignoring me. Perhaps yesterday's row has only now caught up with her, and she's truly pissed with me.

Jason looks at her. 'We should do.'

I'm being drawn along although I'm wary. There are so many journeys and explorations in our lives, yet this attic is what attracts us the most. We move quietly so as not to disturb Elma. But as ever, the tenth step creaks as we step on it in turn, and she calls out.

'That you Frankie?'

'It's all of us,' I answer.

'C'mere.'

Her television is on. *Coronation Street* has just ended. Next thing the vigorous Ulster Television announcer hands us over to the ITN News. The news is as usual. Statistics and comparisons. Italy and Spain. Comparisons between Northern Ireland and the Republic as if it was a competition. Then between the Republic and the UK. The British PM is back in Number 10 Downing Street looking like a dishevelled ghost.

'That'll straighten his hump,' I say, remembering his insistence on hand-shaking.

'Why? The poor man fell ill, God help him,' Elma protests.

Tess explains again what is happening. It isn't an ordinary flu. It can kill everybody, that's why they're being so careful to keep us apart.

'So why are *you* here? And that blondie fellow there, whatsisname, something from the legends?'

'Jason!'

He's cracking up at this.

I tell Elma we're heading up to the attic for a while.

ww

'Of course not, son! You go right ahead up. In fact, in fact, I might join you. I need to stretch these legs, heaven knows Frankie's forever nagging me to get out of the bed and walk up and down for exercise.'

There's an awkward silence.

'It might be tricky,' Tess cautions.

'Why shouldn't I?'

'You won't be able for the climb. There are too many steps,' I add.

'That's what you think! I used to trot up and down the stairs four or five times a day years ago. And in stilettos!'

'That was then, Mum. For fuck's sake, you can't even stand now.'

I leave the bedroom to try and calm myself, then lean on the banister at the top of the stairs. Below, light is spilling across the wooden floor, across the worn rug, angling against the carved escritoire on which, earlier that day, I placed a green glass vase loaded with anemones and still dewy, dip-headed daffodils. That peculiar ache of loss has again settled on me, setting small, anxious claws at work in my belly. I have oscillated from thinking how I cannot wait to be rid of Kilnavarn and its land, back to a longing to place it safely in its casket of beauty and hold it close for as long as I live. Would Christoph want to live here? Probably not. In the end, we'd miss our own place. Would Tess, in the event of returning to Ireland? Her presence, no matter how occasional, would change the spirit of the house. That awkward, beautiful, haunted spirit of over a hundred and seventy years which I have loved for so long. But that might be okay too. She would change Kilnavarn, because despite all her cool chic and for her own reasons, she doesn't trust the house the way I do. But that will probably not occur. Each of us has a separate destiny that doesn't include a life at Kilnavarn. We will let go. Will have to let go. And then move on. What moves cannot freeze.

Tess and Jason emerge from Elma's bedroom. Jason is grinning.

'Your mother is gas,' he says, 'a complete devil of a woman.'

'Glad you think so,' Tess drawls.

It's good that he's so charmed, I muse. Goodness should travel where most needed. But Elma has not resigned herself to staying in bed and wants to be hoisted up the narrow staircase. She has persuaded Jason that he'll have no trouble at all getting her up there. I open my mouth to object, then rationalise. Someone is on hand — Jason — someone is bearing responsibility, even if it's going to be complicated. I don't think it has dawned on him that Elma as a dead weight feels like a baby elephant. Briefly,

I think my eyes are going to well up. Tears. Again? The woman who can't cry? I follow Tess and Jason back into the bedroom, not entirely certain what I'm on the brink of crying about.

'I hope this isn't too much,' I whisper, wiping my eyes quickly. Even in bed, Elma's breath is shallow and a little laboured.

'It is, probably. But let her do it,' Tess replies with a shrug.

'It's not too much for me,' says Elma. 'And I'm not deaf.'

Between them, Tess and Jason lift her forward. I fetch her dressing-gown and draw it on, tying it in a double-knot at the waist. Then I put on the pair of black Sketchers which give her a little grip and support, and draw the Velcro tabs firmly down.

'Lift me,' Elma commands.

Jason lifts her, and despite her protests, swings her towards her unused wheelchair. She objects, holding stiff arms in front of her face in an act of resistance.

'Trust me, Mrs Esmond, this makes it all a little bit quicker, so we can just whoosh you across the bedroom and out to the landing.'

I notice how less fussy Jason is than Christoph, but then Christoph wasn't always as fussy as he is now. Long ago, he found everything easy too. I tell myself to stop making comparisons. After all, I'm not in love, and I will never ever be in love again the way I was in my thirties and forties. I'm just distracted and a little opportunistic.

At the bottom of the attic stairs, Jason puts the brake on the wheelchair. We scrutinise the red doorway, and glance back at Elma. The stairs are just wide enough. Jason will be able to support her with one arm while his other grips the banister. Tess and I can push from behind. The medics and carers would freak out if they got wind of our activities.

'This won't work. It can't,' says Tess.

Jason ignores her. He seems confident about his own strength.

'Mrs. E, nothing for it but to half lift you up the stairs. You can lean on me and I'll hold you. Is that alright?'

Elma looks at him as if he's insane. 'Don't be ridiculous, you can't carry me! Sure I can walk, can't I? I've always walked, I used to walk miles in. . .' Then her voice fades a little and she lies back in the wheelchair and squints through her good eye up at the attic door. She looks doubtful.

'Still sure you want to go up?' I ask. She regards me as if that's the most idiotic question she's ever heard.

I slither ahead of Jason up the stairs and pull at the bolt. My fingers feel suddenly feeble, and at first it doesn't yield. I curse, then try again, feel my heart pounding. It misses a beat and for a moment I am light-headed, dizzying, I may fall. What we are doing seems to be — is — excessive in a way I can't define. My fingers grip the bolt tightly, and my heart steadies again. Breathe in, breathe out, breathe in, breathe out, the simplest of instructions, the simplest of self-regulating mechanisms. Finally, I concentrate on the bolt, give one more pull and, dust-encrusted, it releases back sharply. I switch on the attic light with some trepidation, surprised that it's actually working.

Here we are, an old woman leaning on a strong young man. With one arm wrapped around his neck, practically choking him, with Tess behind, supporting her, Elma's other hand grips the banister as Jason takes the weight from her crippled legs. He slowly begins to take the steps. She is like a huge ragdoll, her right arm grips the banister on her side of the stairs so strongly that I can see her determined white knuckle-bones. She calls out fearfully every so often, *don't drop me! I'll fall! Oh God, please don't let me fall!* Despite fear, she is resolute. She is helping Jason, step by step, her hold on the banister and on her own body is fierce and decisive. Nothing and nobody will prevent this ascent.

Each step on the way up is worn by the footsteps of over a century and a half. Each one creaks as each foot presses down, then sighs and squeaks on release until finally they arrive next to me at the worn, red-painted door which might once have been a fire engine shade but is now more fading autumn rose. Sweat has broken out on Jason's forehead, his veins are bulging and I'm afraid he might collapse if we don't get into the attic promptly. He grips Elma's hands while Tess bears up from below.

But down on the other floor, something stirs. I feel it. I hold my breath and listen as the door to my empty bedroom creaks open, releasing a powerful draught of air that courses along the landing and up to the attic.

'What's going on? What are you doing?' Elma cries out. I have begun to whimper in short, harsh gasps. I hear Elma's words, *what's going on, what's going on,* but cannot answer her.

'What the fuck is that?' Jason grunts, his hair sheering to one side in the strength of the draught, 'Holy *fuck*. I can't hang on much longer. What's going on, Frankie?'

In the half-light I see accusation in his eyes, but he hoists Elma a little higher. I get the impression he is not fully aware of the draught pushing upwards and around us. But Tess is. We daughters of the house can sense something mercurial, both hot and cold. She turns towards me. She is blinking rapidly, arms tightly crossed before she releases them, then grips them again as if in self-protection. There are goosepimples on her neck, yet she is perspiring. I catch the whiff of her musky body odour, of hot underarms and a damp back.

'Did you forget to switch on the central heating this evening?' she demands, 'I'm frozen and sweating and what the hell is going on in this fuckshit crazy house?'

Then comes the audible creaking of the lightshades in my

room, violently back and forth. The house is alive, stirred in its deepest self. This phenomenon is new to me. Perhaps everything in the web of existence, not alone us, is deeply aware when something is at an end. That's the nub of it. But we repress such realisations. Instead, the elemental things, the liminal and sometimes inexplicable, move forward and speak to us, enunciating in non-speech through the language of physical movement, of the elemental winds and fires, the unseen made manifest.

I try to soothe Elma, the palms of my hands drenched with perspiration, I am suffused with primal fear. The hurling passage of air from below continues to rise and rip, curls around us.

'You're safe!' I insist to Elma above the sound.

'Be careful, she says, peering from behind Jason's head, 'those boards might be loose. I don't want to fall through them.'

'It's fine, honestly. And I'm in!' I call back, coughing in the dusty air, my hand breaking cobwebs as I rush on through, Tess following rapidly, abandoning Jason to haul Elma over one final step. I want to get in there quickly, for us all to be safely sealed behind the attic door while below, the house, the room, seems to be having a tantrum.

'Oh my God, what's that smell?' Tess slaps one hand over nose and mouth, then clutches my shoulder.

I recognise once again the faint odour of spices, of dried herbs, and perhaps cumin. I recognise also the funk of cat. 'It's almost like being in the souk,' I remark quietly, body trembling as I pat Tess's hand. I can't possibly explain to her, or anyone, how this is Roddy Boyd's work. Through me, his residue is real. He has watched me grow from girl to woman. Observed my reading, my yearnings, my romantic unspooling in its awkward way. He fears losing me. I know also that he won't harm me.

I look again at Tess, whose face has drained of colour. She trembles, eyes wide, then loses her balance, knees buckling. I move quickly, catch her in my arms, feel the unexpected weight of her body as she tilts against me and we both stumble back against the attic wall.

'You won't fall. I won't let you fall,' I say softly as I straighten up again. Hand placed on her arm, I hum the soothing tunes I've hummed so often with Elma when I need to anchor her, the only soothing words I know, emerging effortlessly now, about an old woman sweeping cobwebs off the sky. *Old woman! Old woman! Old woman! Quoth I. . .*

Tess looks towards Elma. 'Mammy!' she calls hoarsely, frantic, but Elma is too distracted with her own welfare as Jason holds her secure.

I embrace Tess and press a kiss to her cheek. 'You're all right,' I murmur, 'you'll be fine. Nothing bad is going to happen. I won't let it.'

And I'll be with you again, by and by.'

'Promise?' she shudders in my arms.

'I promise. Now take a few deep breaths. I'm sure you've often said that to your clients, eh? Tess? A few breaths, just a few breaths.'

Never before have I wanted so much to be her sister. I hold onto her for a while, feel her hair against my cheek as we rest against one another's shoulders, arms around one another's backs. It's an easy fit. We have found a shape for one another. Finally, her strength returns. There's even a hint of softness in her eyes as she regards me as if in genuine surprise. In that moment, I know I will defend Tess for the rest of my life, Tess who called spontaneously out of fear, for her Mammy, some Mammy, any Mammy.

Gradually, Jason drags himself and Elma through the doorway, muttering about the smell as it invades his nostrils too, his eye scanning for someplace to put Elma down. He has become quite the man in control of the situation. I check that Tess is able to stand without fainting, her face is still pale, then pull the attic door shut and bolt it from within. There's an old bamboo rocking-chair to my left and I move it forward, testing it with both hands. Jason begins to lower Elma so that her feet will touch the floor. Tess has recovered enough to anchor her by the hips, and I catch her arms. Together we swing her around and down. She cries out but we ignore this. The question of how to get her down out of the attic has only just crossed my mind, but I say nothing. Instinctively, Tess and I move towards one another, then towards Elma. I grasp Tess's hand and she grasps Elma's. Tension and tremble radiate from Tess's arms to mine, down into our hands and fingertips. We hang on to one another as if for dear life. I take Elma's other hand in mine and we remain quite still, a small circle listening to the restive house below, as it feels itself on the brink of desertion. She is leaving, it announces sadly. She is leaving. *She is leaving*, it howls.

Elma's hand doesn't tremble, but is steady in mine. It is firm in this moment while my own body melts and shivers. Tess scans the walls and rafters uneasily, still gripping Elma's steady hand. Jason watches as he rubs the back of his neck, easing his muscles, shaking his head. He speaks quietly, his voice ironic. 'I think I underestimated this place.'

The air quietens, like a body relaxing after an allergic reaction. My own fear is dissipating. Although the temperature in the attic has soared, the pungency is definitely in retreat. Elma is sitting quite comfortably in the rocking chair. I release her and move to the oculus window, where I push at the mortice fastener.

It is encrusted and stiff, but I wedge my thumb beneath and eventually it releases. Garden air rolls in. An uneasy peace settles.

'You okay?' I call back to Tess.

She nods.

Elma looks around. Her blue eyes are filled with wonder, her good eye taking everything in as she settles herself in the old rocker, the pupil of her blind eye edging more into the blue. She tilts the chair back slightly to get a better look at the ceiling, draped with web, but dry and firm, the old wooden beams still solid. To her right, the oculus window looms.

'It's a loftier space than it looks from outside,' Jason, still nervous, looks around, hands on hips. 'Impressive though. Look at that view,' he says quietly, and I follow his gaze, out and down over the hurtling roof, towards the lawn.

Tess also crosses to the well of the oculus. The twelve glass panes enclose her on all sides. She lifts one of the other mortices and pushes it open to the air. She seems calmer, though she clenches her arms every so often, breathes in deeply, holds her breath, then exhales. Every second pane is clear, the rest are opaque, the glass striated with hints of pink. The attic shimmers in the evening heat, and we look steadily at one another from opposite sides of the window glass as if in slight surprise. It feels like summer, although it's not. Elma is murmuring to herself, not listening to us or watching us in particular, yet wide-eyed and interested.

'Quite some space,' Jason murmurs.

'Why are you whispering? You're not in a church,' Elma says.

He shakes his head at her. 'Dunno. Must be the atmosphere. It's kinda holy, isn't it? Don't you think there are places which give off a certain feeling?'

'As in sacred feeling?' I ask.

He nods.

'Ah, come on now,' Tess says with an eye-roll.

'Sacred places do exist, you know?' I reply in a tentative half question, knowing Tess's position. 'Has it ever struck you that this house, or part of it, has its special. . .no, solemn and sacred needs and moods?'

'I suppose. . .at a push,' she responds, her hairline damp with sweat. 'I guess anything is possible. Yeah, anything.'

20

The house has retreated back to ordinary stillness. We move and shuffle our way around the attic, still cautious, still listening. The leavings and forgettings of the decades are strewn and piled carelessly, including Tess's embossed leather boarding school trunk and my more rudimentary wooden version. Alongside them in lopsided clusters, books and more books, old lampshades, a three-legged coffee-table, six French colonial sconces, each with its own cherub, from the long dining-room, removed by Elma when she was modernising four decades earlier. I cross from one gable end to the other. At the far end lies a stacked pile of cardboard boxes. I drag one out, the largest of four. Elma tells me to leave everything alone, that Paddy put everything in order and things must not be touched. I naturally ignore her. The box is taped shut. I prise it apart. Within lies a stack of tattered, faded photograph albums. I raise them towards the light. There is one large album, but instinct makes me select a smaller one. Small sometimes indicates preciousness, and what is precious is of interest to me. I open it and flick through the charcoal-coloured pages, most of which show Paddy and Elma's foreign holidays. Beach scenes in which each takes a snap of the other because it's just the two of them. Paddy stretched in a lordly way in turquoise swimming trunks, smoking a cigar beneath a sunshade. Elma posed so that her thighs are not revealed but her cleavage is. How pretty she looks in her cinnabar coloured turban, a gold necklace shimmering delicately at her throat.

Most of the photos in the other albums have come loose. One collection, with many snapshots of nuns, must have belonged to Paddy's sister, Auntie Clara. Nuns alone or nuns in smiling groups. Nuns crocheting or nuns paddling in the sea. Paddy and Clara's sister, Auntie Nora became a nun. Her religious name was Mercedes. So, Sister Mercedes on a day out at Bray Head, 1959. There she is, industrious fingers knitting away beneath a white wimple that enclosed head, throat and neck, and a huge and awkward coif, which shades her knitting from the sun. Auntie Clara almost became a nun, but decided not to at the last minute. According to Elma, she didn't like taking orders, an observation which always amused me. I turn more pages. Nuns and yet more nuns.

I stop turning pages. 'Tess, come here,' I call.

Tess picks her way along the central planks, carefully stepping over the guano, and crouches down beside me. I hand her a black and white photo, which has somehow got mixed in with all the nun pictures, and she holds it out and scrutinises the image.

'They look so happy.'

'Nothing phoney about that, is there?' I whisper.

Elma cannot hear us, we are at the far end of the attic and she is quiet, staring, transfixed, up at the oculus window. Jason is examining the walls below, taking shots on his own phone, close-up details of the remains of the old plaster on the lowest ledge of the window.

The photo was taken in front of *Fernvilla,* outside New Ross. The limestone walls, the white-painted windows, and the curved gravel paths beside the lawn are all recognisable. They are standing jauntily, carefree and young, Paddy's arm draped casually over Elma's shoulder and falling down to catch her left hand, which is enclosed in his. Her right hip presses against his and her legs are crossed slightly, one stilettoed foot in front of the other as she smiles. She is wearing the latest Dior styled New Look suit, with nipped-in waist, the skirt following the line of her slim body to mid-shin level. They are both smiling, grossly happy by the look of it. For the first time I realise that I am actually jealous of my parents, or perhaps envious of what they had, something I in all my years have never had. I've never experienced such a feeling before. Whatever has made them so happy it certainly is neither me nor Tess, since we weren't yet born. I have no recollection of either parent displaying such grace and ease together during our actual childhood, although both frequently showed it together in the company of others, or at the house parties they used to host. I note my feelings now, and yes, an unexpected, green-tinged monster lurks there. Paddy and Elma, at some point, had that special bond of being madly in love, madly amused by one another, madly physical with one another too. Even though the photograph is taken outside Paddy's parents' house, I'm certain they had lounged lustfully in those over-soft beds Elma so often complained about.

'Makes you think, doesn't it?' Tess says eventually, rubbing her finger lightly over the photograph, then handing it back to me.

I stare at it again. Elma is one of those women who might have been completely fulfilled without children. It's possible, that like me, she had no need of them. But perhaps Christoph and I needed children, and I denied myself — denied us — out of fear. Fear of repeating the past, fear of having learned Elma's habits. But it's too late for that regret. Christoph and I are fine, will be fine. We have a life that adds up to the best we could do. And that's enough.

'That must be before either of us came on the scene,' I remark laconically.

'Yeah,' Tess agrees, 'The *enfants terribles,* eh?'

'No,' I insist, 'we were *enfants innocents*. Plain and simple.'

'That your parents?' Jason has crept over and as he nestles in, a pall of dust rises and congealed dead leaves and slow cobwebs drift from the rafters above him. I discreetly inhale the lovely, light sweat that emanates from him, that emanated from him the previous night when we lay so close together. It brings me back into myself, eases my fear off and my sense of the house being disturbed. At the other end of the attic, Elma is talking to herself. She no longer seems to require our company as she stares up through the long panes at the sky.

'Cool pic,' he says, 'they look adorable. But I'm not surprised. I mean to say, anyone can see that Elma was *fun*. She *is* a lot of fun. What a girl she must have been! Hey Mrs. Esmond, have you seen this photo?'

Before we can stop him he grabs the album and slides his way across to where she sits, slowly rocking herself. He places it gently on her knee, and points. She bends and squints, uncertain which image he means. Tess and I follow over.

'This one,' I say, pressing it with my finger. 'Here, you and Paddy. In Wexford.'

For a moment she does not speak. Her eyebrows dip as she scrutinises the image with her good eye. She takes her time, gripping it by the edges with both hands, pulling it closer to her face. Her middle finger is now tapping the photo, and she smiles up at me.

'I remember that morning.'

'You do?'

'I'd just made a little discovery. I was very happy. I wanted to get back home to tell my mother and your aunt Elizabeth.'

'You sure do look happy,' Tess says absently. On some level she is now quite detached, as if this is of only academic interest.

Elma grips my wrist. Her grip is surprisingly firm. 'I'd just discovered. . .at least I'd just guessed. . .that I was. . .' Her voice weakens. 'I was expecting you.'

'Me?'

'*You*! It was all we ever wanted. Two or three children. And later. . .when none came, we wanted another girl. For you. A sister.' Her face shivers, as if she might weep. But she doesn't cry. She holds her tears in. A family habit. 'We were so happy that morning, you have no idea. . .'

I glance at Tess. Her face is enigmatic. I say nothing and squeeze Elma's shoulder. I can well imagine that she wanted another girl, a companion for me. I doubt that she wanted another baby and surmise that if Elma could have skipped the first four years and attached a fully-fledged, walking, talking, smiling, second girl to our lives that might have suited her better.

None of us speaks. There's this huge gap between what Paddy and Elma wanted and how their lives together unfolded. Jason has discreetly looked away into the distance and tries to busy himself arranging books. I leave Elma to pore over the photograph and I gather a few more albums and hand them to Tess, who accepts them a little too briskly and then drops them unceremoniously near the attic door. It's not my fault, I feel like saying, that that I arrived first or that life then took a different turn, down a rockier path. I return to the boxes and open a few more, breaking the sticking tape with which Paddy had sealed them. Paddy the chronicler, Paddy the belt-and-braces man. Disappointingly, the boxes reveal ornaments. A broken mantle clock. A pewter rider and horse. Two glass turquoise and black striped vases.

'I remember those. Nana gave them to Elma after they got married.'

'I know the ones you mean. I *loathed* them!' Elma chuckles.

I turn to Tess. 'I like them,' I say, 'I think I'll take them, unless you want one?'

'I loathe them too. I've enough crap in Bleecker Street.'

In this moment, inexplicably, I feel nothing but release from the witnessed past in which I grew. I smile and it isn't phoney or strained. Already, I'm wondering how long Tess will remain in Ireland, or when international air travel will resume, and whether we'll have time to do something bizarre and adventurous together. It has to be something bizarre, though quite what I haven't yet imagined. Ride bareback up in Bragan? Or we could check out a summer rock concert, the Electric Picnic if it ever happens again! I dare to dream that Tess might come home. Finally, I could be her sister.

We move to the window space and look out. Already, the sky is full of stars, the cosmos never clearer in recent decades than now. People in China will have seen it eight hours earlier, and now sleep through a blacker, deeper night, beneath a caul of starlight unseen for a generation. Fish are rushing up-river and up-canal in places hitherto muddied and silted; the muck and mire, the slime, have sunk undisturbed. Life is flowing as we grapple with the question of how to spend our more private-than-ever moments at home. Some will pray in the old fashioned way. Others, in an act of un-prayer, will beat one another black and blue from the frustration of having their faces shoved together twenty-four hours a day. Yet others will kill themselves, lone farmers, overtaken by the desolation of this pause on time's line, smothered by silence. And others, like me, simply look out, ready to sit it out for as long as needed. Tess has come home and will leave again, though not quite yet. She might stay for months. Jason will wait until the time is right for everything. His book. His future. He and I may hatch plans for how we may or may not meet again. I expect the occasional coffee or beer in Dublin, and nothing more. A discreet acknowledgement in the final pages of his book when it's published.

I can't imagine a life without Christoph. Already, I'm dreaming up other maps, our own kind of cartography re-drawn by ourselves, as people eventually must. There's nothing geographical about what spreads within, growing vaster and vaster, a bit like the legend of St Bridget's cloak, which expanded to defy the limitations of an old king. Its terrain can never be trodden on or shaped by others. Already, everything that has captured me for so long, has grown weak, will have no dominion over me.

Down below I see the dark shape of the cat Jimmy prowling through the grass cautiously, tiger-style, one leg raised and frozen, then dropping silently as he stalks. Lottie barks at the sky, letting the world know she is here on her territory. Then, Elma's tired and slightly querulous voice calling at me from the chair, *Frankie, have you let that dog out again? Let her in, please. And will somebody please bring me down to my bed again?* But Elma can wait a few minutes. I sense that she doesn't really believe in heaven, so much as hope for it, which is part of the reason she lives on. Because life is sweet, no matter its pain and inconvenience.

I am the last to leave the attic. I pull the stiff red door shut and follow the others slowly down the steps. Elma moaning softly as Jason bears her weight. She is very tired. The air has cleared and is sweet and fresh. No strange scents of the Orient remain. My bedroom door lies wide open and I hurry to check the room. One of the pink velvet drapes slumps, shredded, from a single, straining curtain hook, viciously ripped down, while in the middle of the floor lies what looks like a gigantic piece of bird-shit, as if something had flown briefly in the open window and deposited its vexation right in my room. *Hello Roddy*, I whisper, forcing myself to breathe slowly and calmly, *everything is alright, you know. No need to make a fuss. You're fine. We're fine. No worries now.* Can the spirit of a house attempt to hold on to someone who loves it so? Have I been more beloved to this house than I ever imagined? Beloved, even, to its ghost? Gently, I shut the door and turn to find Elma in her wheelchair again. She is tugging awkwardly at the knot in her dressing gown, as if she cannot wait to be rid of it and to rest again beneath her green bed-spread.

Jason, tired now, touches my arm, then leans over and places a kiss on my left cheek. He turns to Tess and does the same. 'Goodnight,' he says gently and turns to the door of his own room. Neither Tess nor I speak as he enters, turns once to glance back at us, and clicks the doorknob shut.

Tess turns to me abruptly. 'You know something? I'm not sure this is working for me.'

'What do you mean?' For the first time in my life, I have ceased to care. Our brief touching in the attic has meant nothing to Tess. I was, as ever, mistaken.

'Stella said she'd come and collect me any time I need.'

'Did she?'

'So I was thinking I might hit the road in a day or two?'

'Fine. Do that. I suppose the gardai will let you through.'

Back in bed, Elma lies on her side and looks up at me. 'You're a good girl Frankie, a good girl. Thank you for bringing me up beyond. I never liked that place on my own, you know.

'I know you didn't.'

'It reminded me too much of the room I slept in with granny when I was a child. Your demented and illiterate great grandmother.'

'You shouldn't ever have had to sleep with her,' I say.

'Devil the bit of harm it did me,' she whispers. 'You know something? I cried my heart out when she died. I missed her. I didn't like being alone. But they're all gone now, every last one of my family. You imagine you won't miss the ones you didn't get along with, but in the end you do. I'm the last. Isn't that awful?' Her voice is wobbling, her pale face begins to crumple.

'It's awful,' I agree, and stroke her forehead gently, pushing back a few strands of white hair that have escaped from beneath her wig. I wipe her tears away with my thumb, and she lets me.

She coughs, then her voice steadies again. 'But I'd never have seen that photo if we hadn't gone up there. I'd never have seen that photo of my darling Paddy, my one and only. And that's all thanks to you.'

She closes her eyes and dozes off almost immediately. I move her bedside clock so that she can see it should she awaken, place a half glass of water beside it, and leave.

An hour later, I check on her. Her mouth is slightly open. I gently remove her wig, but she doesn't stir. Her forehead is hot. Her silver white hair now trails the floral pillow-case. I curl a piece of it around one finger. It's so soft. Gently, I spread her hair around her on the pillow, drawing it out to its full length. She gives a low snore. Then she opens her eyes, one wider than the other. The gaze of the open eye locates me staring at her. She murmurs, but I can't make sense of it. Her words emerge in a long, slow emission of *ghraaahbhuff* and *ca-ca-cant-dhghaah*. Her timbre is quite unlike itself, her articulation has broken its syntactic framework and is flowing in a way I can't grasp.

'What's that Mum? Have you a sore throat?' My voice is low, and I am meditating on Elma as if on a religious icon, one hand at my chin as I regard the lopsided head, the pillows which bear its weight, the new fall of the face. My eye wanders the room, following wallpaper patterning, the curve of the brass light fitting in the centre, then the pale shimmer of the yellow drapes which should be drawn. As I wait, Elma breathes on shallowly, her chest rising and falling. Then, her words come back to themselves, slowly, peacefully, in the fullness of meaning. 'Not. . .gone. . .yet. . .'

'I know you're not gone. But maybe a couple of paracetamol might be an idea? You seem a little warm.'

'If you say so,' she manages to whisper.

'They'll bring your temperature down,' I say, breaking the foil on the packet and half filling a glass from the water-jug.

I put my arm around her shoulders and draw her towards me. Slowly, she sips a mouthful from the glass and allows me to slip both tablets into her mouth. Another sip, longer this time, and she swallows, water dribbling down her chin. I mop it with a tissue.

'Thank you Frankie.' Her eyes close and I know she'll sleep.

As I pull the door over without shutting it, my mother's throat emits a soft, phlegmy rattle. I pat my cheeks and eyes with a tissue as I cross the landing and cast one final glance up the attic stairway. An old-fashioned prayer drifts through my head. For my mother's rest tonight. That it will be sweet, that she may be greeted by all the good beings she has ever believed in, from the

Virgin Mary to her demented grandmother, that she may get to sweep the cobwebs off the sky after meeting the old woman with the broom.

*

In Kilnavarn House, there were once three of us. Before Tess. Once again, there are three. After Paddy, after anger, after exile, after adultery, after blame, after secrets, after silence. In this after, between night and morning, I head to the kitchen to wait the hours with my sister, to wait for dawn and a time when there will be none.

Acknowledements

Thank you to my agent Marianne Gunn O'Connor and to editor Alison Walsh for their belief and vision. Warm thanks also to my tireless editor Sean Campbell and Mel, Louise and Beth, the meticulous team at époque press. Damien Donnelly of The Storms Journal published an early excerpt, and both novelist Mary Hosty and the late Eibhear Walshe of UCC read the full manuscript and provided feedback. Some friends blew sparks which kept me going, among them June Caldwell, Mary Costello, and Patrick Holloway. Finally, love and thanks to Martin and Anna, with me from the first spring when the early chapters were set down.

Also by Mary O'Donnell

Novels

The Light Makers (1992 & 1993)
Virgin and the Boy (1996)
The Elysium Testament (1999)
Where They Lie (2014)
Sister Caravaggio, collaboration with Peter Cunningham *(2014)*

Short Stories

Strong Pagans (1991)
Storm over Belfast (2008)
Empire (2018)
Walking Ghosts (2025)
Nomadás Spanish trans. Graciela Eliggi/ Jaime de Pablos *(2026)*

Poetry

Reading the Sunflowers in September (1990)
Spiderwoman's Third Avenue Rhapsody (1993)
Unlegendary Heroes (1998)
September Elegies (2003)
The Place of Miracles, New & Selected Poems (2005)
To the Winds our Sails ed. Mary O'Donnell/Manuela Palacios *(2010)*
Çsodák Fjölde Hungarian trans. Kabdebo Tamas *(2011)*
The Ark Builders (2009)
April Fevers (2015)
Massacre of the Birds (2020)
Onde Estão Os Pássaros Portuguese trans. Luci Collin *(2023)*
Outsiders, Always (2023)
Tenderness (2026)